The Fall of Martin Orchard

Martin Lundqvist

Published by Martin Lundqvist, 2020.

THE FALL OF MARTIN ORCHARD

First edition. March 27, 2020.

Written by Martin Lundqvist.

Also by Martin Lundqvist

Divine Space Gods
Divine Space Gods: Abraham's Follies
Divine Space Gods II: Revolution for Dummies
Divine Space Gods III: Rangda's Shenanigans

Sabina Saves the Future
Sabina's Pursuit of The Holy Grail
Sabina's Quest to Open the Portal in the Sun Pyramid
Sabina's Expedition to Stop the Apocalypse

The Divine Zetan Trilogy
The Divine Dissimulation
The Divine Sedition
The Divine Finalisation

Standalone
Matt's Amazing Week
James Locker The Duality of Fate
The Portal in the Pyramid
Money Laundering in the Laundromat
Pyramidportalen

Matts Fantastiska Vecka
Divine Space Gods Trilogy
Sabina Saves the Future: Complete Trilogy
Diez Historias Aleatorias y Muy Cortas
Ten Random and Very Short Stories
Dieci Storie Casuali e Molto Brevi
Dix Histoires Aléatoires et Très Courtes
Zehn Zufällige und Sehr Kurze Geschichten
Cinco Historias Aleatorias y Muy Cortas
Five Random and Very Short Stories
The Fall of Martin Orchard

Watch for more at martinlundqvist.com.

Chapter 0: Prologue: The Portal in the Pyramid, Egypt: January 2019

I was recovering from a long bilious flight, and I checked in to a cheap and dingy 3-star hotel. The hotel was located on a small block nestled into the busy and crowded city of Cairo. The noise from the heavy traffic, combined with the non-stop humming from the old and dirty air-condition stopped me from sleeping. This destroyed any chance of me recovering from my 17-hour flight from Sydney. The night was young, so I decided that I should explore this magical city of Cairo on my own. My guided tours were due to begin tomorrow morning and I had no plans for the rest of the day. I am a firm believer in exploring cities on my own. I like to stir myself away from the typical tourist traps. This way, I can experience the everyday life of a city's inhabitants and the beauty of their culture.

I switched off the old wooden-framed vintage television. I was about to leave the dilapidated hotel room, when I felt a rush of hesitation and anxiety overwhelm me. Humans tend to overestimate certain dangers. I am, for instance, often afraid of shark attacks when I am swimming in Australian waters, although shark attacks are scarce. As excited as I was, being in Cairo, I feared getting targeted in a terrorist attack. Such things occur often in Egypt, according to the media that continuously influence the unknowing population.

My fear was amplified by the fact that my loving partner of many years, sweet and gentle Elaine, had refused to travel with me to Cairo. Elaine had cited the risk of a terrorist attack as her main reason for not going. Eventually, I brushed off my negative thoughts and calmed myself down. I reminded myself that my daily actions, such as my diet and my exercise, have a larger impact on my life expectancy than terrorist attacks will ever have.

I walked around in Cairo, absorbing everything the magical and lustrous city had to offer. I enjoyed smelling the fragrances and photographing the historic buildings. After walking for hours, I came across a sizeable Egyptian Bazaar. I am not a big fan of shopping, but I remembered that Elaine had asked for a tin of Egyptian perfume. I also wanted to eat something, and the food there smelled delightful.

AFTER EATING AN AUTHENTIC Egyptian meal, I felt a bit fazed by the noise and the massive commotion at the bazaar. Whenever I travel overseas, I always stand out as an obvious tourist, as I am very tall, and I look very North European. This is because I am 190 centimetres tall with North European features. My looks attracted a myriad of salesmen, and they were all trying to peddle me different trinkets. I felt stressed and uncomfortable, as I dislike crowds and people pushing things upon me. After rejecting dozens of street peddlers, I came across something I wanted. It was a shimmering blue crystal, sold from a healing crystal shop, located at the far end of the dingy market.

I studied the mysterious blue crystal for a while. I tried to contact the presumed seller, an old Egyptian woman, who was squatting behind an old wooden table. She smirked and showed off her yellow teeth.

But, why did I want a crystal? I pondered the question, and I couldn't come up with any sensible explanation. I have never had any interest in gemstones or healing crystals. But this enchanting crystal was shining with a bright and wondrous blue light. It was so beautiful that it looked as if the crystal was talking to me. This was something that I hadn't experienced since I ingested LSD and magic mushrooms during my rebellious youth. I picked up the crystal, and I stared at it for a long time. I felt mesmerised by its beauty, for what felt like an eternity.

"Can I help you, Good Sir?"

A young Egyptian man that appeared from the back of the squalid shop.

I came back to my senses when the store clerk approached me. How long had it been? The other street peddlers had swarmed me like bees, but this Egyptian man had taken his time and given me the chance to study his products first. I examined the man, he looked different. While the others wore typical Middle-Eastern garments, this Egyptian man looked like a mysterious time traveller. Or at least, he dressed like he was participating in some sort of Renaissance fair.

"How much is this crystal…?", I stuttered with a confused voice.

"For you sir, this beautiful Zeto crystal is only 1500 pounds!" Said the salesman confidently.

1500 Egyptian pounds. How much was that in Australian Dollars? I calculated the figures in my head and I figured out the answer; it was over 100 Australian Dollars. I hesitated, and I studied the Egyptian salesman and the enchanting crystal for a while. I must have misheard the price of the item.

"Excuse me, did you say 1500 Egyptian Pounds for this piece of glass?" I asked.

"I did, but the price has just gone up. It is now 2,000 Egyptian Pounds!" answered the angry and impatient peddler.

The salesman's answer bewildered me. Street peddlers always lowered their prices at any sign of haggling, but this Egyptian man had increased the price instead. How could this be? I was going to put the crystal away, but I couldn't, I felt compelled to buy it.

"Okay, 2000 Egyptian pounds. That's a deal." I said, as I paid for the strange and glowing blue crystal, and I put it in my pocket. After paying for the enchanting crystal, I took a cab back to my dingy hotel room. My brain was not working, and I desperately needed a good night's sleep.

THE FOLLOWING DAY, I woke up feeling a stabbing pain in my stomach. My food choice the previous day hadn't been a smart one, and I had spent the entire night throwing up in the bathroom. I was considering not showing up for the bus ride to the pyramids, but I decided against it and got myself ready to go. I was only spending a few days in Cairo, before flying back to Sweden to see my dear old parents. Spending my time being sick and indulging in self-pity in this cheap hotel room, was not my version of an ideal holiday.

I passed up on the hotel breakfast. Instead, I bought some refreshing mints and other snacks in the corner shop outside of the hotel. I did this to cover up the stench of my spew from the night before. I didn't want to risk throwing up on the bus, but bringing some mints and a bag of nuts would be handy if I got hungry later. I got on the tour bus. The guide was chirping and sharing some interesting facts about Cairo. At least I believe he did, but my mind was foggy after having a rough night. I slipped into a dreamy abyss and I fell asleep on the bus.

As we reached the pyramids, and I woke up from my nap and I felt a bit better.

A PROBLEM THAT I HAVE, is that the actual world is usually less grand and majestic than I hope it to be. The pyramids are the best example of this. In the idea world, the pyramids are magnificent. They were built by thousands of workers over many years. These ancient artefacts were built following astronomical calculations with almost better accuracy than what we can do with our modern technology.

But in reality, I was standing in the middle of a hot rocky desert watching a pile of crumbled fallen rocks. They looked so unlike the picture-perfect pyramids that you often see in post cards. What an irony.

The smiling tour guide approached me and tapped me on my shoulder. For an optional fee of 1,000 Egyptian pounds, I could follow a guided tour inside one of the pyramids. Otherwise, I could sit at the coffee shop and enjoy the scenery for the next few hours while waiting for the tour guide to take other tourists inside. Paying extra money to crouch around in a dark and cramped tunnel didn't sound fun. But I was already here, and perhaps the pyramid would look better on the inside. I paid the hefty fee, aware that I could be disappointed of the outcome. The tour guide smiled, showing off his sarcastic grin, and stuffed the money in his pocket. He seemed anxious that people could see him take the money, indicating that this was not an official part of the tour. I felt anxious and I didn't want to go with the sly guide.

I wanted to stay outside, but I had already paid for the tour, and I could not get my money back.

A SHORT WHILE LATER, I entered the pyramid together with the tour guide and a few other tour participants. As expected, I didn't enjoy being inside the pyramid. It was dark, filled with stale and damp air, and it was too cramped for a big guy like me to walk around in. Besides, the food poisoning hadn't prepared me for this fantastic adventure that I was about to encounter.

I felt like I was going to throw up again. Being the last person in the group, I snuck off into an empty side passageway to avoid embarrassment. After vomiting, I was ready to get back to the group when out of the blue, I sensed a glowing blue light shining through my khaki pants. The blue crystal, which I had forgotten to take out of my pocket, felt really hot. It shone with a sparkling blue light. It was shining so bright so that it lit up the entire room and hurt my eyes. I picked up the crystal from my pocket and I studied it.

Suddenly, a trap door opened below me, and I slid down a secret passage. I was sliding down for several seconds until I hit the floor with a high speed. I heard a loud cracking noise, and I felt a surge of pain throughout my body. I had landed badly on my right foot, and I had broken it. I looked around and I felt panic take its hold over my body. I was hurt and alone in a very dark tunnel, with no way to get up. I was about to scream for help when something caught my eyes: The blue crystal. In this dark tunnel, it shone stronger than ever before. I crawled to the glowing crystal on the floor and I picked it up.

ONCE I PICKED UP THE glimmering crystal, I heard a strange alien-like beeping and rotating noise. The whole wall had lit up, and it was full of illuminated lines of alien hieroglyphs that I couldn't comprehend. The hieroglyphs struck me with feelings of awe and surprise. I noticed that there was a slot in the wall where my blue crystal would fit perfectly. I made my way to the slot, and I inserted the crystal into it. This caused the entire wall to make a loud screaking noise and the wall shifted in anti-clockwise motion. The wall blocks began to rotate, and they filled up empty wall crevices with more blocks that appeared from inside the wall, like an amazing game of Jenga. This happened for a few minutes, until the rotation stopped, and revealed a giant crevice with mysterious blue light. I tried to feel the back of the wall, and I touched the light. It seemed like it didn't have a surface as my hand sunk straight through it. I pulled out my hand from the blue light, and it was still okay. I felt compelled to know what was on the other side of the shining blue crevice. Relying on my good leg, I decided to jump into the wall crevice and find out what would happen next.

I saw a bright flash, and my body drifted through space, travelling faster than the speed of light. I landed on a soft pillowy pile of dewy leaves. I had ended up in a beautiful courtyard, that looked both ancient and futuristic at the same time. I have never seen anything so beautiful in my whole life, but at the same time, I felt scared. Where was I, and was this the afterlife?

I SAW A GROUP OF STRANGE humanoid creatures approaching me. One of them spoke to me.

"Greetings human. I am Ra, and the Zetans next to me are Zeus, Brahma, and Odin. "

"I don't understand... Am I dead?" I stammered

"Certainly not, as a matter of fact, you'll never be more alive than today," Zeus answered.

"Enough of the pleasantries. Did you bring us any offerings?" Odin scoffed

The request surprised me, but I didn't dare to argue with the strange godlike creatures. I remembered that I had some mints and nuts in my pockets, so I took them out and handed them to Odin. He tasted the food, and he gave me a disapproving look. "What kind of food are humans eating these days?! This food is full of chemicals and rubbish!" Odin sneered.

"I am sorry. I didn't expect to meet deities today, and I didn't bring any offerings," I replied. "Is that so? Then how come all the ancient scriptures mention sacrifices to the gods?" Zeus asked.

Zeus' question confused me, but fortunately, Brahma came to my aid. "Don't be too harsh on the human. How could he foresee that he would stumble upon an interdimensional portal? Humans don't have foresight like we do."

Brahma turned towards me and spoke. "Thank you for your offerings today, please tell me your name, human."

"I am Martin Orchard. You can call me Martin." I answered.

"Nice to meet you, Martin. Unfortunately, your time here today will be short, so please ask anything you'd like to know before you have to go back to your human world." Brahma said

"Can you heal my broken leg? It's so painful." I moaned.

"You are in luck, we still have healing supplies", Brahma answered. He turned to Ra and spoke "Ra, can you please inoculate our guest with a Zetan Healing Serum into his right calf?"

Ra approached me, and he injected the serum. At first, it caused unbearable pain, but it receded quickly. In no time the pain was completely gone, and the leg seemed to be healed.

"What happened? this is a miracle!" I stated

"The serum that we gave you, accelerated your body's healing factor by the equivalent of a month's healing time. Hence you feel the initial immense pain, and then quick healing proceeds." Ra replied.

"So, you healed me with an advanced medical technology?" I asked.

"Yes, Advanced science too complicated for you to understand, so we just call them miracles", Ra replied.

"We have healed people who were blind, make the lame walk again, healed people that suffered from leprosy, it is all written in your bible. We have made you believe that our Zetan race is a one all-knowing God." Ra stated

BRAHMA LOOKED AT ME and spoke, "Our time is short but let me show you around". I got up on my feet, and to my great relief, I could walk, albeit with a bit of a limp. I followed Brahma to a beautiful pond, located next

to a blooming magical Lotus Tree. In the pond, I could see a lot of things happening on Earth.

"Master Brahma. How can you see all these things that are happening on Earth?" I asked.

"When we first came across Earth on our travel across the Milky Way Galaxy, we sent billions of nanotechnology drones. These drones are invisible to human eyes. We did this so that we could see everything on the planet. These drones were powered with advanced Zetan technology and have almost unlimited battery time. Thus, some of these drones are still sending images to us through this lotus pond." Brahma replied.

"Wow! That's amazing!", I replied in awe.

"Yes, when we told your human ancestors that God is all-seeing, we were not lying. We were explaining facts towards your level of intelligence," Brahma said.

"So, are you our Gods and did you create mankind?" I asked.

"No. We didn't create mankind; we gave you our version of intelligence and made you what you are. The True Maker is the true creator of the Universe, she made our race and yours too. We are a more ancient race and more intelligent that you humans. When we came across homo-sapiens some 70,000 years ago, your species were low-tier animals, close to extinction. Your looks resembled apes rather than humans. My Zetan ancestors, altered your genome, and raised your intelligence level and looks, to be more like us. We made you what you have become since then and we have monitored your performances from our world." Brahma replied.

"So, because the Zetans are so much more advanced than humans, you become our God?" I asked.

"Yes. The divine creator, The True Maker, works on a cosmological scale. She doesn't involve herself in our daily lives. For such an omnipotent being, the daily prayers and actions of individuals become insignificant." Brahma replied.

Brahma looked at his wristwatch and seemed keen to move on. "Come, there are more things that I have to show you before you go back, and time is short".

Brahma hurried ahead and opened a door. We entered a bright room that had extremely advanced computerised archives. It was full of lifelike hologram generators and other amazing outer world technologies. "This is the Zetan archives, if you choose to stay here you can have access to all the knowledge and science of the Universe," Brahma said.

"Even the age-old question of the true meaning of life?" I asked.

"Good one, but no. You see, there is no universal answer to that question. The individual has to make up their own answer." Brahma replied.

I studied the room and all the amazing objects in there. Eventually, my eyes fell back onto Brahma. Brahma seemed restless and a bit reluctant, but eventually, he spoke. "So, Martin, it is now time for you to make a choice."

"What choice?" I replied.

"Well, you can either stay here, spend time with us Zetans, and learn everything about the universe. Or, you can go back to humanity on Earth and live in ignorance." Brahma said.

"But why can't I have both?" I asked.

"Because the portal will be closing soon, and once it's closed, we have no means of opening it from here. If you choose to stay, you will have God-like knowledge, but you'll also suffer from eternal physical hunger and loneliness. You'll see everyone you care about dying from age, one by one, through this magical pond."

I PONDERED THE OPTIONS for a while. I realised that the choices didn't only have consequences for me but for everyone else. If I disappeared without a trace, the people I cared about would never get closure. They would always wonder what happened to me. I told Brahma about my decision.

He sighed and replied, "I see. You have chosen the path of ignorance."

"No, I choose to do what is best for the people that I love. Forsaking everyone that cares about me in the pursuit of knowledge is selfish and cruel!", I replied.

Zeus entered the room and spoke: "What did the human choose?" Zeus asked.

"Ignorance," Brahma replied.

"They all do. Only one more thing to do." Zeus said.

After saying this, Zeus pulled me towards him, while Brahma branded my right arm with a luminous tattoo. Zeus then injected me with Zetan Healing Serum while Brahma carried me back towards the portal. The last thing I remember was Brahma repeatedly shouting. *"Find Keila Eisenstein, show her the tattoo on your arm, warn her about Rangda the Deceiver!"*

I fell into the abyss and I blacked out.

I WOKE UP A FEW DAYS later in an Egyptian hospital. My doctor told me that I had a psychotic outbreak caused by a rare form of a food-borne parasite.

"Okay, but can you explain how my broken leg and this freshly inked tattoo on my arm healed so quickly?" I asked.

"Your wound on your leg and the tattoo on your arm are fully healed. It must have happened over a month ago." The doctor answered plainly and then he left the room.

I decided to keep quiet and not say anything. There was nothing to gain from trying to convince these people of an extra-terrestrial encounter. If I tried, they might admit me to a psychiatric ward. Besides, I wasn't too sure myself what had happened, and I thought that perhaps I had just dreamt the whole thing.

As I am lying here in my hospital bed in Egypt in only have two questions:

What happened to me, and how did I get this strange blue coloured tattoo that glows in the dark, with lines of unexplainable hieroglyphs and strange alien symbols?

And most importantly, who the hell is Keila Eisenstein...??!

Chapter 1: Egypt, February 2019

I pulled myself together and got up to a sitting position in my hospital bed. The exertion made my head spin, but I had made up my mind. I couldn't stay in this filthy hospital any longer. It was the 3rd of February, and I had already been here for three days since my ill-fated excursion to the Cheops Pyramid. The two first days in the hospital had been alright. During those days, I was in and out of a coma, and thus unaware of my surroundings. But on the third day, I woke up, and I had realised what a filthy and depressing place that I was in. I needed to get out. I needed to walk in a park and inhale some fresh air. It was a nice warm winter day in Egypt, and a great day to leave this filthy hospital.

As I got up, Dr Abdulrami, the same doctor who had dismissed my story the day before, approached me. "Mr Orchard. Why are you getting up?"

"I need to get out of here, this place is making me feel sick!" I replied.

"But you shouldn't leave the hospital yet. You were unconscious for two days." Dr Abdulrami objected.

"That might be the case, but staying in this filthy hospital won't do wonders for my health either. I will seek further medical attention when I reach Sweden. My flight departs tomorrow." I said and held back some sick feeling that was lurking in my gut.

"Very well, Mr Orchard. I cannot hold you here against your will. Make sure to settle your bill before you leave the hospital." Dr Abdulrami replied unapprovingly, and he walked away.

I walked up to the counter, and I settled my hospital bill. It was a substantial bill, but fortunately, I had travel insurance, courtesy of Elaine's anxiety. Speaking of the devil, she must be worried sick about me. Except for a short email that I had written to her on my first night, I hadn't spoken to her in four days.

I turned on my phone, and as it turned out, I had 32 missed calls and 57 messages from Elaine. While I was happy that she worried about me, it was also a bit draining. I was weak from my ordeal, and the last thing that I wanted, was to spend my mental energy reassuring Elaine that everything was okay. I checked Google Maps for a beautiful park in the neighbourhood, and I settled for the short walk to the Al-Azhar park, to get my mind right.

AN HOUR LATER, I WAS drinking plenty of water while enjoying the cool breeze of Egyptian winter, in the shade under a palm tree. The view was beautiful, and I felt a deep sense of relief from not being in that filthy hospital any longer. I stared at the tattoo on my arm. It was full of alien symbols that made up a three-dimensional holographic map floating over my arm. I couldn't understand why no-one else seemed to notice the wondrous designs and shapes of my other-worldly tattoo.

I realised that my mind was playing tricks on me. I had experienced seeing three-dimensional holograms emerging from two-dimensional patterns in the past. This was when I ingested magic mushrooms and other psychoactive substances almost a decade earlier. But this time, things looked different. Everything looked normal, and it was only my tattoo that stood out.

I woke up from my thoughts, when the phone rang. It was Elaine:

"Martin? Is that you?" Elaine said anxiously.

"Yes, my love." I replied.

"Why haven't you picked up your phone? Your parents and I have been worried sick about you!" Elaine exclaimed.

"I got severe food poisoning, and I ended up in a hospital. But I feel better now, and I will travel to Sweden tomorrow as planned." I replied.

"Don't lie to me, Martin! Tell me what actually happened!" Elaine replied.

I felt stressed, but I decided to defuse the situation. "Login to my internet bank account and check my credit card statement." I replied with a tired voice.

"Okay, I will do that." Elaine replied, and some silence occurred. Eventually, she spoke again. "A AUD 12,000 hospital bill! What happened to you? Did you have an accident?!"

"I had food poisoning the night before I went on a tour to Cheops Pyramid. I fell unconscious, and I broke my leg while walking inside the pyramid. I had to have surgery. Luckily, I got travel insurance otherwise it would have cost us more." I replied.

"I told you Egypt was a bad place to go!" Elaine exclaimed.

"Well, I guess you were right this time. But I got to go, I am starving, and this time I will go to a five-star restaurant to be safe." I said.

"Okay. Take care, Martin. I love you." Elaine said.

"I love you too, my princess." I said and hung up the phone.

I looked at the phone and reflected on our conversation. I hadn't told Elaine the truth. I hadn't told her how I had travelled to another dimension and ended up having a lengthy discussion with extra-terrestrial deities. Or perhaps, the reality was that I had a severe case of food poisoning which sent me hallucinating, and I had imagined everything that happened in the pyramid? I wasn't sure what was real anymore. I checked my phone for nearby five-star hotels to choose my dinner place. Eventually I settled for Four Seasons hotel.

AN HOUR LATER, I WAS sitting at the fabulous restaurant in the Four Seasons Hotel. Usually, I was too frugal to frequent places like this, but I was celebrating that my travel insurance was going to cover most of my hospital bill. At least my finances wouldn't suffer as much as my mind and body did from this holiday. You got to celebrate the small wins in life.

As I was trying to enjoy the Egyptian tasting platter, claimed to be the best in Cairo, I noticed something interesting. A beautiful and sexy blonde woman walked in to the hotel's restaurant, accompanied by a plain-looking balding Jewish man. The entire time they were eating at their table, she looked like she was trying to hook-up with another man sitting at the next table, who happened to also be there with his wife. Both their partners seemed oblivious to what was going on.

Was the Four Seasons hotel in Cairo a swingers' venue, or was it my head that was not right? No matter what, I felt compelled to know how this would turn out, thinking this could be a good story plot for my next book. The sexy blonde woman got up, and she made her way to the toilet. Shortly afterwards her fling also got up, and he was also heading the same way. This was it! I got up, and I observed the man. As I had anticipated, the two lovebirds met up outside the toilets. They looked around cautiously, before the two of them entered the men's room.

But I wanted more evidence. Perhaps the couple were international spies exchanging top-secret information, or perhaps they were having a random hook-up? I headed to the neighbouring toilet, and I leaned my ear to the wall. From the noises, I could confirm that the two of them participated in a session of banging 101. I smiled. This would be a great scenario for my next book.

I got back to my table, paid my bill, and I headed for my room. One more night in Cairo before I travelled to Sweden to visit my dear old parents.

THE NEXT DAY, I WAS sitting at a bar at Cairo International Airport. My plane wasn't due in several hours, and I reckoned that I might as well taste the two local Egyptian beer varieties, Stella and Saqqara. They tasted like any other beer, but at least I got the social media posts of me drinking the local beer varieties. This would be the highlight of this Egyptian holiday.

A few beers in, I saw a familiar face. The beautiful blonde woman that I had seen at Four Seasons Hotel. This time, she was by herself. She looked at me and smiled seductively towards me. Ouch, this was awkward. I panicked with a mix of excitement and anticipation as she approached me. Without even knowing her name, I desired to touch her more than I had ever wanted anyone, not even my sweet and gentle Elaine.

"Why are you here by yourself, wouldn't you be lonely?" The blonde woman said as she approached me and got seated right in front of me.

"I was, but not anymore since you have chosen to accompany me," I replied and tried to stop myself from blushing. I felt like I was close to getting a stroke, my blood pressure had risen to an extreme level around this blonde bombshell. I felt the urge to relieve the stress by fucking her brains out!

"Do you believe in destiny?" the woman asked.

"I am not sure, but perhaps I do." I replied.

"I do. Destiny made us meet here. We are two wayward souls, whose paths crossed briefly never to meet again." The woman said seductively.

"So, what is happening next?" I asked.

The woman turned her eyes to the cleaner's closet and whispered into my ear. "I want you to fuck me. Hard, raw and furiously."

I thought of objecting. This was madness. Who was this woman who I had heard fucking another man yesterday behind her cuckolded husband's back? I didn't even know her name, and god knows what diseases she might be carrying. I thought of Elaine, she was a good woman, I shouldn't do this towards her. A shock of electricity struck my head, and I heard a faint dark growling voice surging in my deepest thoughts.

"You need to release, or you'll die. Copulate with her." The voice in my head was encouraging me to fuck this woman while the pain throbbing in my head felt unbearable. I needed medical attention, not sex, yet I couldn't withhold my desire anymore.

I followed the mysterious and beautiful blonde woman to the closet. Inside the closet, we had a short stint of the most amazing furious sex I have ever experienced. As I came, the immense pressure inside my head miraculously disappeared, and I felt normal again.

"Well, that was fun!" The woman said and smirked at me.

I didn't have the energy to reply, as the sex had drained me. I nodded and let out a pleasurable sigh.

"Last call for Mr John Hines and Mrs Ellen Hines to Cape Town. Please proceed to gate 18, immediately!" I heard the PA system announce.

"Well, that's my flight. Thanks for the amazing sex. What's your name?" Ellen said.

"Orchard, Martin Orchard. You can call me Martin." I replied, uncertain of why I used that old James Bond cliché.

"Very well, Marvin, have a good flight," Ellen said, smiled and rushed off.

I got out of the closet, and I looked at Ellen from a distance. She met her husband outside gate 18, and they had a brief argument as she went missing for 20 minutes, before they rushed onto their flight.

A FEW HOURS LATER, I was sitting on a flight to Sweden to meet my parents. What an incredible holiday this had been. First travelling to another dimension and meeting up with ancient deities, telling me to find someone by the name of Keila Eisenstein. And then waking up in a hospital bed with a blue, glowing holographic tattoo? And finally, I had finished off the holiday by having a brief impromptu affair with this blonde lady by the name of Ellen Hines. How was it all connected?

Ellen's pretty face and our short tryst were etched into the back of my head during the entire flight to Sweden. I decided that I would keep quiet about this encounter. After all, how would my life turn out if I admitted cheating on my wife and if I brought up my meeting with the gods? I could see the scenario in my mind. I would end up being homeless and alone, screaming incoherent nonsense to people passing by, like the homeless and mentally-ill beggars that I had seen on the streets of Cairo.

I convinced myself that the events in Egypt were caused by severe food poisoning that caused hallucinations. I had tripped over and broken my leg in the pyramid, which caused me to be hospitalised for few days. I had not met up with any strange deities, and I hadn't had sex with anyone at all. I was just imagining Ellen. Surely, life would be better if that was the truth? I leaned back into my seat and fell asleep, after sipping a few glasses of in-flight vodka.

Chapter 2: Nepal, May 2020

After enduring severe turbulence in an arboreous 12-hour flight from Sydney, I felt a profound sense of relief when our flight finally landed at Kathmandu International Airport in Nepal. Elaine released her grip of my hand, which had turned my hand nearly blue. She smiled and looked relieved. "God saved us and kept us safe." She said with a massive sigh.

"God would be pretty damn busy, if his intervention is needed to land every single god-damn plane!" I said sarcastically but smiled and then quickly added in, "But nevertheless, I am happy that we landed unharmed. I was a little afraid as well, to be honest. This was the worst flight that I have been on. The turbulences were pretty nerve-wracking."

"Well, I need to believe that someone is looking after me. I feel a little better when I know that God is there to protect us in times of need." Elaine replied.

"Well, good on you. Let's get our stuff and get out of this plane as fast as possible. I can't wait to get some fresh air." I said, and we made our way out of the plane.

A FEW HOURS LATER, we were in Kathmandu, and I wondered what I had gotten myself into. The weather was hazy, and the city was full of smog. Pollution in Kathmandu was terrible, due to the city being in a valley, preventing the winds from clearing the pollutants. I had experienced a few days like this in Sydney during the massive bushfires of 2019, but most days the air quality of Sydney was rather good.

"Hunny, let's take some selfies over there, at the Hanuman Dhoka Palace," Elaine chirped. I obliged. Although it felt a bit uneventful to cover two-thirds of the beautiful sceneries with our silly faces, it is what people are doing these days. After taking many pictures to make sure that we captured decent images of ourselves, I snapped some photos of the buildings and sceneries by themselves. They were, after all, one of the reasons for us to come here.

After doing sightseeing for a couple of hours, we decided to have a traditional Nepalese dinner. We ended up having Dhal Bhat Tarkari, mostly because it was the national dish of Nepal. The flavour was delicious and exquisite.

It felt strange and a bit underwhelming to finally be in Nepal. I had wanted to walk in the Himalayas, the roof of the world, for many years. But Kathmandu reminded me of any city in a 3rd world country. It was crowded, noisy and polluted. Oh well, a couple of days here and then we would find an enjoyable hiking tour and celebrate Elaine's birthday by hiking in the mountains.

I wondered what had made Elaine want to come here. I had wanted to go for the last few years, but she had refused it at first as she thought it was too dangerous. I decided to bring up the topic.

"Hey, lovey. How come you changed your mind about hiking in the Himalayas?" I said.

"Well, I wanted to give you something that we've always wanted for my 35th birthday," Elaine replied sweetly.

"Thanks, that's sweet, but you thought it was too dangerous when I suggested it earlier years?" I asked.

"I still think it's too dangerous. But I don't want to lose you like I almost did when you travelled to Egypt on your own. At least now we are facing danger together." Elaine replied.

"Thank you, babe. Let's get back to the hotel and rest. We can look for a proper tour company tomorrow." I replied.

Having said this, we paid our bill and headed back to the hotel for a good night's sleep.

THE FOLLOWING DAY, we headed out to find a suitable tour company for our hiking tour. When we were looking for a tour agent, Elaine spotted a jewellery shop, exclaimed "I'll check out that shop!" and then she ran off to the gem shop.

I exhaled and felt obliged to go inside the shop. If Elaine had shown that much enthusiasm when we were playing sports together, our mixed Futsal team would have had a lot more success in winning the games! I caught up with her inside the shop. "What are you looking for, Elaine?" I said.

"I am looking for some unique Nepalese jewellery to add to my jewellery collection." Elaine twittered. "Okay, but I am not paying for any overly expensive jewellery!" I replied dismissively.

"Don't worry. I didn't expect you to. There must be cobweb covering your wallet considering how rarely you open it." Elaine smirked.

I was about to say something, when I checked my wallet and there indeed was cobweb! Fair call, Elaine!

"Oh, I love this one!" Elaine said joyfully and pointed at a blue gemstone.

I stared at the gemstone in disbelief. Could it be? Yes, it must be the same type of gemstone that I had bought at a market in Egypt, which activated an interdimensional portal.

I felt numbness in my arm, and as I looked at my tattoo, the flat image became a vibrating three-dimensional blue hologram. The tattoo was glowing in blue light. What was going on, and why was I the only one who was able to see this?

I was brought back to reality when the shop attendant approached us. It was the same mysterious man that I had met in Egypt the previous year, although this time, he wore a traditional Nepalese outfit.

"How can I help you, miss?" the man said to Elaine.

"Oh, I love this blue crystal. How much is it?" Elaine asked excitedly.

"For you, my lovely lady, the price is 10,000 Nepalese Rupees!" The man said with a broad grin.

"Okay, hold on." Elaine replied. She turned towards me and spoke: "How much is that, Martin?"

"Uhm, around 120 Australian Dollars," I replied distantly.

"Oh. Okay" Elaine turned towards the vendor and spoke, "I'll give you 7000 rupees for the clear bluestone."

The man shook his head and replied. "The price just went up; the price is now 15,000 rupees!"

The man's response gave me a déjà vu. This was definitely the same guy that I had met the previous year. No other seller increased the price like that when a customer tried to haggle!

"What? No, I don't want it anymore!" Elaine replied

I realised that I had to get that crystal. It was the key to finding out what really happened to me last year, and perhaps to meet Ellen again.

"I'll take it. Here are 15,000 rupees." I shouted and took out the money from my wallet.

"I said 50 thousand, not 15 thousand" the man replied snidely.

"Whatever, mate. Here is the 50,000. I need that crystal." I urged as I put the wad of cash on the counter.

"Excellent! It is all yours." The man chirped.

"Not so fast. Martin, what the hell are you doing? Why are you paying a fortune for that blue crystal, which I no longer want?" Elaine asked.

The salesman who seemed keen to get the sale added in. "Don't worry, miss! Because you are such a lovely couple, I'll throw in two free hiking tour tickets in the price."

Hearing this, Elaine nodded in agreement, but she didn't say anything, and we left the small shop with a blue crystal and two tour tickets, AUD 600 poorer.

The rest of our day in Kathmandu consisted of Elaine being unhappy about my hurried purchase, which she repeatedly made very clear towards me that it was way too expensive. Oh, my poor ears.

THE FOLLOWING MORNING, we met up outside a tour agency. We had booked a small hiking group tour. We were going to Nagarkot where we would do our mountain hiking with a few other tourists. We travelled on a minibus, which drove up to the mountainous site. During the trip, I decided to get to know all the participants. Accompanying us on the hiking tour were the following people:

- Rajesh, our bubbly Nepalese tour guide and driver.
- Ben and Szymon Yehuda, two Israeli brothers who were on a break from their compulsory military service.
- Pierre Beaumont, a Swiss banker who was passionate about mountain hiking.
- Jorge Santiago and his young daughter Sandra from Mexico, who didn't speak much English.
- Josefina Fiero, a Brazilian femme fatale whose exceptionally sexy body I had to avoid staring at in Elaine's presence.
- James Winter, an American army guy.
- Vladimir Kravchenko, a Russian man of few words, whose presence gave me the creeps.

I was having an exciting time, until an avalanche struck our minibus, causing the minibus to drive off a cliff. After free-falling for a couple of seconds, everything turned black.

I WOKE UP IN A STRANGE undescriptive realm. It reminded me of my visit to the Divine Dimension the previous year, but things were different. Instead of feeling like I was in the future, I felt like I was stuck in the past. I saw a lot of haunting spirits passing by, but they didn't seem to notice me. Was this the afterlife? It seemed likely. Our tour bus had fallen off a cliff, and I had been standing in the middle aisle of the bus when it happened. So, my odds for survival didn't seem that great. "Oh well, we all got to go some time," I said to myself to avoid panicking.

"Martin. Martin. Martin. Wake up! Please!" I heard echoing, over and over. The world around me faded away. I woke up with a terrible headache and my body covered in blood. Elaine was kneeling next to me, and she stared at me in exasperation when I opened my eyes.

"Martin! You are alive. It's a miracle." Elaine exclaimed while sobbing.

I got up on my knees, and I realised that I had been lying in a puddle of blood, my own blood, which had melted the snow around me. How had I survived that? I checked in my pocket, and I took out the blue sapphire crystal that I had bought the previous day. It was dull now, not the lustrous gemstone it had been the day before. Had the crystal saved my life? The idea was far-fetched, but what better explanation was there? It must have contained some healing energy that kept my body warm and alive.

"Oh, you are alive?!" I heard an Israeli voice exclaiming in wonder. It was Ben Yehuda's voice.

"Yes, the afterlife can wait for a bit longer!" I replied.

"Not much longer unless we do something!" Ben Yehuda replied gravely.

"Why is that?" I asked.

"Because we've travelled with an unlicensed tour group and the agency did not inform us that severe weather was on the way. No-one knows that we are here. We need to find shelter, or we'll freeze to death." Ben stated.

"Ping, Ping, Ping" something inside my head was pinging like a radar, and it was indicating where I was meant to go. I got up on my feet and shouted out, "Follow me! I know the way to a nearby cave, where we can sit out the storm!"

Everyone stared at me in awe. Apparently, my return to the living was the miracle of the day. But they all followed me, probably due to lack of other options. Meanwhile, our tour guide was nowhere to be found.

The freezing blizzard got stronger, and it chilled me to the bone. We hadn't prepared for anything like this. Nepal was usually warm in May, even in the mountains, so we must have gotten caught up in extreme weather. *"Keep going, or you'll die."* I heard my inner dark voice say repeatedly.

"Keep going, leave no-one behind!" I shouted, and I got back to Elaine who was struggling behind to make sure that she kept up with the group.

The pinging in my brain got increasingly more intense until it was too much for me, and I collapsed to the ground. As I fell to the ground, I grabbed a stone, which turned out to be the lever to open a hidden path. We stared in amazement as a stairway appeared from nowhere.

Wearing thin jackets in a freezing cold blizzard, we didn't ponder for long, and we all rushed down to the caverns below.

"WE MADE IT!" PIERRE Beaumont exclaimed.

"Is everybody here?" Ben Yehuda wondered.

"My daddy is missing!" Sandra Santiago whimpered.

I looked around. It seemed like Sandra was correct. Her father Jorge, and our tour guide Rajesh were both missing. Out of the two, Jorge was the most important person. We had a seven-year-old girl desperate for her father, who was in grave danger in the terrible conditions outside. We needed to act, but I was powerless to do anything. The adrenaline rush had receded from my body and my injuries were taking their toll on me. I needed to rest, but I feared that I would not wake up if I fell asleep.

"I'll go look for them!" Vladimir Kravchenko said.

"In these conditions? Are you insane?" Pierre Beaumont objected.

"I am not some wimpy Swiss banker. I am a survivor. The things that I had to do to survive in Siberia!" Vladimir yelled.

The room went silent. After a few seconds, Vladimir grabbed his bag, and he went upstairs into the raging blizzard to look for the others.

I looked around. Elaine and Josefina were trying to comfort the inconsolable Sandra. But I had my own fears. "Elaine, come here!" I croaked. Elaine directed her attention towards me, rushed over and looked concerned. "Martin, you're so pale!" Elaine sobbed.

"Yes, I must sleep. But I am afraid that I won't get up. I need you to look after me, to make sure that I don't die in my sleep." I wheezed.

"Okay, I'll watch over you. I'll pray for you!" Elaine sobbed with a brave but solemn voice.

"Okay, baby. I love you." I said, and I let go, falling into unconsciousness.

"YOU CANNOT DIE. YOU need to serve me. This will be the beginning of your new life!" I heard a terrifying female voice saying.

I opened my eyes, and I was in the cave that I had fallen asleep in hours earlier. But the cave was empty. "What is going on? Where is everyone?!" I shouted.

"Mwa-haha. You're asking the wrong question. The question you should ask is, where are you?" The menacing voice replied.

"So, where am I?" I replied.

"You're between the afterlife and the realm of the living. You are in another dimension. This dimension is an exact copy of your world, but it's devoid of all life, except for me and you." The dark voice replied.

"And who are you?" I shouted.

A mirage appeared in the room. It was a terrifying slender creature. The creature stood at around two metres tall, equipped with sharp dinosaur-like claws, sharp fangs, a ripped muscular physique, flaming red hair and glowing purple irises.

"I am Rangda Kaliankan. I have arrived to bring a new era of greatness to humanity. And you'll be my envoy." Rangda replied.

"Rangda? The Zetans warned me about you!" I replied.

"Oh, really? Did they?" Rangda chuckled and then continued with an aggressive hateful tone. *"Where are the Zetans, now that you are hanging on the thread to your life? Who is here to protect you from the dark void of death? I am! You'll either serve me, or you'll die!"*

The fear of my own mortality gripped me and made me succumb to Rangda's command. "I'll serve you if you can save my life. Please help me!" I whimpered.

Hearing this, Rangda's face lit up with a malicious evil grin, and her purple irises sparkled with excitement. *"Excellent. Remember the sequence that I am about to show you. Behind these walls there are nine ancient artefacts. One for each of you, as fate has made it. Take one each, and your minds will expand, and you'll find the way to true greatness."*

I WOKE UP TO THE SOUND of James Winter and Vladimir Kravchenko arguing. As my mind cleared, I could hear what they were saying.

"That is Rajesh's jacket! Where is he?" James shouted.

"I don't know. I only found a jacket." Vladimir hissed.

"Bullshit! Rajesh wouldn't lose his jacket. He wouldn't live long without a jacket in the cold outside." James replied.

"What are you insinuating and what are you going to do about it?" Vladimir threatened and chested up against James.

"Ping, Ping, Ping" my brain echoed. I got up, and Elaine approached me.

"You finally woke up, Martin. I am so afraid. I believe that Vladimir killed our guide," Elaine whispered. "I need to... I need to open the hidden door and find the alien artefacts..." I mumbled while trying to get up.

"Martin, are you sure you can get up?" Elaine whimpered.

"Don't stop me!" I roared, and I shoved Elaine to the ground. The next 20 seconds, I was in a trance, but when I got back to reality, everyone was staring at me. A secret doorway had opened behind one of the walls.

"Wow! What's going on?" Szymon Yehuda exclaimed.

"Our path to greatness lies behind that door. We must follow it, or we will perish." I said.

"Who are you?" Szymon asked in amazement.

"I am just the messenger!" I replied.

A few seconds later, the cave we were in started to collapse. "Follow me!" I shouted as we all rushed into the secret inner sanctum of this mysterious ancient temple.

AS I GOT INTO THE INNER sanctum of the temple, I was amazed by what I saw. The temple was full of golden statues laden with magnificent rare gemstones and massive amounts of gold. The statuettes depicted various ancient deities, and the walls were filled with several types of ancient scriptures. From ancient Egyptian to Chinese, Japanese, French, German, to Nepalese. In the centre of the room there was a large chandelier that emitted a tranquil bluish light.

I recognised the light. It was the same light that I had seen when I entered the portal to the Divine Dimension in Egypt the previous year. We were in a hidden Zetan temple!

Right under the chandelier, there was a pedestal, and on top of the pedestal there were nine futuristic-looking monocles. I raised my hand to signal the others to stop, and I walked up to the stand. As I turned around the others stared at me in awe. After a few seconds I began to speak.

"Welcome to the hidden Zetan Temple. This is a momentous day. There are nine alien artefacts on this pillar. There are nine of us in the room. Together we shall use these artefacts to create a new dawn for humankind. Vladimir, thank you for murdering Rajesh and Jorge to make the numbers right." I proclaimed.

"What is going on? Did you and Vladimir conspire to kill us all?" Josefina exclaimed.

"No. I do not have any association with Vladimir. But his violent nature and insatiable bloodlust, made things go the way they were destined to go." I replied.

"You are insane!" James shouted.

"Sanity is a limitation when it comes to achieving true greatness," I replied.

Having said this, I picked up one of the monocles from the altar and put it over my right eye. I felt an initial fear as the monocle activated, and a small needle attached it to my optical nerve. I shook in pain for a couple of seconds, but when the pain had ended, I felt like a new man. My mind had elevated to a much higher level, I was now a super human!

The group stared at me in awe, and Elaine shouted, "Martin! Your right eye is glowing purple."

"My eye is purple because of my connection to Empress Rangda Kaliankan. She saved me from certain death, and she tasked us with saving humanity's future." I stated.

"This is madness. You must have injured your brain in the crash." James replied.

I heard Rangda voice hissing in the back of my head. *"The participation of these individuals is essential to my plan. Make them cooperate! Subdue them, but don't kill them!"* Rangda instructed.

"Yes, Empress Rangda!" I replied.

I stared at James and said chillingly. "You are going to participate in our plan, whether you want to or not. Bow to our empress or suffer!"

"Fuck you, creep! I am a Navy Seals operative. I won't bow to you." James replied.

"So be it!" I replied.

I had a moment of hesitation. How would I take on a well-trained killer in combat? Although I had the size-advantage, I wouldn't stand a chance against an elite soldier, especially not after sustaining injuries. I heard Rangda's voice, *"Set your monocle to non-lethal combat. Make sure to keep him alive. We will need him."*

I did as Rangda instructed. I felt an incredible surge of adrenaline and how the time slowed down around me. The user interface on the monocle gave me detailed information about the people around me and predicted their next move.

I approached James. I dodged his punches twice, blocked his third strike and broke his nose with a left hook. Unfortunately, James was a fighter, so the broken nose didn't stop him from fighting. Instead, it fuelled him and gave him a adrenaline-rush. He attacked me furiously with a multitude of kicks and punches. Although I could block or dodge James' attacks due to my elevated mind, my body was still taking damage. I needed to knock James unconscious. I saw an opening and jabbed James on the throat, stunning him. I followed up with a massive uppercut on his chin that sent him flying backwards.

Time slowed down to a standstill, and the monocle started beeping. I had mishit James, and the back of his head was on a lethal collision course with a rock on the ground. Fucking hell! I jumped after James, grabbed him, and shielded the back of his head with my left hand. Time resumed, and I felt a sharp pain in my left hand as that hand took the impact from the collision, saving James' life.

I gave out a sharp shriek of pain, and I hoped that this would be it. As it turned out, I was mistaken and instead the Yehuda Brothers had turned hostile. From the ashes to the fire. They ran towards me from different directions. In the exact right moment, I dropped to the ground, causing them to run into each other. I sprung up to the ground, and I noticed that Szymon was still dizzy from the collision, with his head leaning forward. I jump-kicked him in the face knocking him out.

Ben Yehuda charged at me, quicker than I had anticipated. He jumped me, and we both crashed to the ground. Ben came on top of me and was choking me. "Critical Danger!" was flashing on my monocle in red letters.

"No shit." I thought, but my body was drained, and without the assistance of the monocle I was powerless against the very fit Ben Yehuda.

I was close to passing out from asphyxiation when Ben fell unconscious and released his grip around my neck. I looked up. Elaine had saved me by hitting Ben Yehuda in the back of the head with a golden statuette.

I got up. There was one more thing that I needed to do before I could have a well-needed rest from my fight. I hurried over to Vladimir, and I knocked him out with a heavy haymaker punch before he had the chance to turn hostile. Seeing this, Pierre panicked, slipped, and hit his head, which knocked him unconscious.

I dropped exhausted to the ground, and Elaine rushed to my side. "Are you okay, Martin? Why did you start this fight?" Elaine said.

"The World is going to end. The people in this room are the only ones that can save humankind. Admittedly, I could have resolved the issue better." I replied.

"What are you talking about? You are crazy!" Elaine exclaimed.

"Go over there and put on one of the monocles. If I am crazy, nothing will happen. But If I am telling the truth, your mind will expand, and you will understand that I am telling the truth." I said.

Elaine looked hesitant. My monocle described her emotional state as terrified. But I hoped that she would do as I said, so this didn't need to lead to more violence. After a long pause, Elaine walked towards the altar. She picked up a monocle and studied it for a long time. Eventually, Elaine put the Zetan monocle towards her eye. She screamed in pain as the monocle attached to her optical nerve, but after a while, she calmed down, and she looked at me blissfully. "You were right. These monocles are divine in origin, and we have been given an otherworldly mission," Elaine said.

I nodded and turned towards Josefina Fiero who were shielding Sandra Santiago with her body. They were hiding in a corner, terrified of what would happen. "My ladies, I hope that you realise that cooperation is our best option," I said. Josefina and Sandra looked down, and they didn't dare to respond.

I got up and turned towards Elaine. "Elaine, get two of those monocles. It is time to recruit two more members to our cause." Elaine did as I instructed, and we walked towards Josefina and Sandra, who was shivering in terror.

"Okay ladies. I would prefer to avoid violence, so I'd much rather you join me willingly." I said.

"Or else, you'll kill us as you did to the others'?" Josefina backchatted.

I shook my head and replied, "I haven't killed anyone. They are still breathing. But I prefer if I can convince you to join us."

"Okay. Please don't hurt the girl or me." Josefina pleaded.

"I promise to not hurt either of you," I replied and handed Josefina the monocle.

She stared at it in horror, but eventually she gave in and attached the Zetan monocle to her eye. She screamed in pain, which terrified Sandra.

"You promised that you wouldn't hurt us." Sandra sobbed.

"We won't hurt you," Elaine reassured, and she hugged Sandra. When Sandra had calmed down, Elaine attached the monocle to her eye.

After a while, Josefina and Sandra calmed down. They now looked like serene intelligent superhumans.

"This is amazing. What do we do now?" Josefina said.

"We connect the others to the technology. There are nine of us in the room, and there are nine monocles. This is not a coincidence. This is destiny. Once we have connected everyone, Mistress Rangda will give us instructions." I replied.

Josefina and Elaine did as I instructed. Half an hour later, everyone in the room was connected, conscious, and sitting in a semi-circle. It was time for Rangda to give us instructions.

Rangda appeared as a mirage in the centre of the room. She gave everyone a loud screech and spoke, *"Greetings. I am Empress Rangda Kaliankan, the saviour of humankind. Earth is dying, and the nine of you are the only ones who can secure the future of humanity. In 111 years from now, a massive Gamma Ray burst will hit Earth, and cause the extinction of humanity. This event will kill everyone on the planet. The only future for your species is to develop your technology so you can spread around the galaxy. But your leaders are weak, and your compassion is holding you back. You need to focus your efforts on developing as a space-faring race. You need to stop wasting resources looking after the sick or preserving inferior species. Every species that goes extinct because of humanity, are weak and deserve to go extinct. Such is the law of nature.*

In the past, I have led my Xenos troops to greatness. But those treacherous Zetans fought us and destroyed all our progress. That is why the Milky Way Galaxy is a mostly lifeless galaxy. But I have returned, and together we will lead humanity to a new golden age.

The nine of you in this room are Rangda's Chosen Ones. Together you'll elevate humanity to greatness. Humanity will become an unrelenting force that will conquer the vastness of space. I'll give you instructions as time passes. For now, you must all put your hands on the blue sphere next to that door. That will open an escape tunnel back to the surface. Farewell until we meet again, My Chosen Ones."

Having finished her speech, Rangda disappeared out into thin air, and we stared at each other in awe and amazement. We had a new purpose in life, which was both terrifying and inspiring.

"SO, WHAT DO WE DO NOW?" Pierre asked.

"We will do what we Rangda told us to do," I replied.

Pierre gave me a puzzled look, but I assumed that he was still dizzy from the concussion, so I continued speaking. "Okay, everyone. Let's activate that blue sphere through all of us laying our hands on it at the same time."

The others did as I instructed, and a passageway opened. We followed the passage to the surface where the blizzard had ended, and it was a lovely sunny day. My phone buzzed, and I picked it up. To my amazement two days had passed. I called an ambulance flight to pick us up, as we were too wounded to make our way back on our own.

WE FLEW BACK TO SYDNEY the following day. We hadn't told the ambulance staff about the deaths of Rajesh and Jorge. But their bodies would be found soon. I was more nervous about my headaches than I was about their unfortunate deaths. While I had covered up that Vladimir had killed them, that was also my only crime. This was something that would be hard for the authorities to prove. But my headaches... How severe were my injuries? I had been comatose between life and death when Rangda brought me back to life to serve her. Why had she saved me? If she needed to make sure that she had nine people to serve her, it would make more sense to let me die and save Rajesh or Jorge?

I leaned back and decided to not think about it. I had never been religious before, but now I had a higher purpose. The apocalypse was coming. The Gamma-Ray Blast would hit Earth on the 20th October 2131, and I needed to make sure that humanity survived the apocalypse.

Exhausted from the ordeal, I leaned back in my seat and slept the entire long flight back to Sydney.

Chapter 3: Sydney, June 2020

I was in the bathroom of the Prince of Wales Hospital, and I stared into my reflection. My eyes looked normal, alas not the same nuance of blue as before. One of the first things I had done when I returned to Sydney was to get tinted lenses. While the monocle expanded my mind, it was exhausting to always be so aware of my surroundings, so I needed to switch off every now and then.

Since the incident in the hidden Zetan Temple in Nepal, the colour of my right eye had changed irrevocably. My right eye was now luminescent purple. While the monocle could hide my eye colour, this wasn't the case when I took it off.

I had settled for using tinted blue lenses. While the lenses made my eye look like I had glaucoma, they didn't impede my vision. Appearing to have glaucoma was also less noticeable than having a shiny purple iris.

I was due to meet my neurologist. I felt trepidatious and anxious. I had visited last week, and I had received a call-back urging me to return as quick as possible. My panic attack caused my vision to blur, and I ended up purging into the toilet bowl.

I pulled myself together. There was nothing for me to fear. I had returned from the dead. What was the worst that could happen? That the CT scan indicated my imminent death? Hah, been there done that. I splashed some water on my face to freshen up. I exited the toilet, and I approached the doctor's reception with my head held high.

"MR ORCHARD. I HAVE some unwelcome news." Dr Ramsay said and wrinkled her forehead.

"I figured as much when I got the urgent call-back," I replied.

"Your CT scans show a massive amount of scarring on your brain. It's a miracle that you are still alive." Dr Ramsay explained.

"I thought this was a hospital. What can you do for me?" I replied.

"Not much, I am afraid. But I would appreciate if you'd volunteer for medical studies. You are unique as far as I know." Dr Ramsay said.

"I am sorry, but spending my remaining years being a human guinea pig is not on the top of my priorities." I replied dismissively.

"I understand. But please tell me. What symptoms do you experience? Seizures? Hallucinations? Migraines?" Dr Ramsay asked.

"All of them. But, since you're unable to assist me, I'd rather spend my time somewhere else. Goodbye, Dr Ramsay!" I replied. After that I got up, opened the door, and slammed it behind me. This caused everyone in the reception area to stare at me as I took off.

"SO, WHAT DID THEY SAY at the hospital?" Elaine wondered when I got home.

"They said that my survival was a miracle, and they wanted to use me as a human guinea pig!" I yelled.

"Perhaps you'll be happier if you appreciate that miracle then?" Elaine replied.

"So, what do you suggest that I do?" I asked.

"Wear the monocle. It helps your brain to function." Elaine suggested.

"I'll think about it. I need to have a rest now." I said, and I walked to the bedroom.

Lying in bed, I pondered on Elaine's suggestion. While the monocle had helped my brain function and sped up my mind, it came with an adverse side effect. I was contactable by Rangda. The last thing that I wanted in life was to be contacted by that malicious creature. Rangda had claimed that she wanted to help humanity survive the future apocalypse, but I didn't believe her. Yet, what were my other options?

I plugged in the monocle, and there she was, Rangda, appearing right in front of my eyes.

"*Tsk, tsk, tsk. Look who is back.*" Rangda smirked

"I don't have much choice, do I? My brain is beyond repair, and I can't function without the monocle." I sighed.

"*The Chosen One usually doesn't have a choice. That's why it's called the Chosen One. I chose you, not the other way around.*" Rangda replied.

"And why did you choose me?" I asked.

Rangda stayed silent for a while, and she seemed to be looking for a good explanation.

"*A lot of fortunate coincidences. I could track you because of your Zetan tattoo, which acts as a tracking device. When you got to Nepal, I was fortunate that you came across a replicated Zeto Crystal.*" Rangda explained.

"A replicated Zeto Crystal? What is that?" I interrupted.

"*My enemies, the Zetans, were the most advanced species ever to roam the Milky Way. Aeons ago, they found a way to make replicas of the primordial Zeto Crystals.*"

"So, what is a primordial Zeto Crystal?" I asked.

"*A primordial Zeto Crystal contains the soul of the True Maker. They are incredibly powerful, and they can create almost unlimited energy. There is one primordial Zeto Crystal hidden somewhere on Earth, and one day you shall help me find it. The replicated Zeto Crystals, on the other hand, are one-time usage fuel cells. Non-rechargeable batteries if you will.*" Rangda explained.

"So, was it the replicated Zeto Crystals that opened the portal in Egypt and saved me from certain death during the accident in Nepal? "I asked.

"*Yes, but the real prize is the primordial Zeto Crystal. Possessing that artefact, you can heal your brain damage, and you can save the future of humanity.*" Rangda said.

"So, how do I find the Zeto Crystal?" I asked.

Rangda grinned and spoke, "*I love your enthusiasm. Self-interest is the most potent force of the universe. To find the primordial Zeto Crystal, you'll need to find Pachamama's Veil, hidden somewhere in the Andes. Once it's found. we will have more clues to continue our search.*"

"But how can I afford that? I don't have enough money to travel the world for years, looking for alien artefacts." I replied.

Rangda gave me a disapproving look and shook her head. *"Tsk, Tsk. Money! This fictional concept that governs your species and is holding you back from achieving true greatness!"* Rangda exclaimed.

"Well it's still the reality on Earth regardless of what you think of it," I objected.

Rangda gave me a hateful look and shrieked. *"Do not disrespect me, human! Eeeeeeerrrkkk!"*

Rangda's shrieking was too much for me. I collapsed to the floor with a terrible migraine, and my vision was flickering. "I am. I am sorry. Please spare me." I whimpered

"You forgot to address me as Empress Rangda! Very well. I'll give you money. Will USD 1 billion suffice?" Rangda said

"That's an absolute fortune." I replied.

"I thought so. Make your way to New York. You'll need to play the winning Powerball numbers." Rangda said.

"That's easier said than done." I replied.

"You are forgetting who is helping you. Predicting the outcome of human lotteries is easy for me with my premonitions. But to get the money you must promise to serve me!" Rangda said.

"Didn't I promise that already?" I asked.

"Bah. A promise given out of desperation to save your life. Not worth much, and besides I cannot enforce it. Go to New York. Once you are there, you'll renew your promise, and I'll satisfy your lust for money!" Rangda said.

After saying this, Rangda disappeared into thin air, and I was alone to deal with my terrible headache. I disconnected the monocle and collapsed on the bed, falling into a deep dreamless sleep.

"I AM COMING WITH YOU!" Elaine said in determination.

The room was still spinning. Elaine had woken me up after I collapsed on the bed.

"But we don't know if she is telling the truth?" I objected.

"After the miracles that we witnessed in Nepal, I am ready to give it a shot. Besides..." Elaine stopped mid-sentence and burst out into tears.

"What is it, honey?" I asked.

"I went to your neurologist after our conversation earlier today. She didn't want to disclose much, but she confirmed that you were severely wounded and hanging in the balance. You risk dying at any moment. I want to be by your side. If you believe that things can get better from visiting New York, then what else can we do?" Elaine sighed.

I got up to a seated position and hugged Elaine tightly. "Thank you, Elaine. We'll get through this together." I whispered.

After that, we sat in silence for a long time before we finally fell asleep.

Chapter 4: New York, July 2020

We landed in New York a couple of weeks later. Long-haul flights had never been a favourite of mine. But we had lightened the burden through having stopovers in Hawaii and California. Elaine had suggested that we would explore America while we were going on the trip. I couldn't argue against it. It was insane travelling all the way to New York, hoping for an extra-terrestrial demi-god to give me a lot of money. But going on a USA holiday made a lot of sense.

We had a lot of fun during our trip. We had hiked around the Hawaiian national parks and volcanoes. We had Scuba-dived in Hawaiian lagoons. We had visited Hollywood. We had fired guns and gambled in Las Vegas. While in Rome, do what the Romans do, so to speak. While we hadn't gained 20 kilos yet, it was a work in progress. The only drawback was that my migraine and flickering vision had impaired my senses. But since the medical professionals couldn't help me, I had decided that I should enjoy life as much as I could, while I still could.

As we reached our hotel, I realised that I needed to contact Rangda about my mission. Without her, I would soon run out of money. I went to bed and connected my Zetan Monocle.

"YOU BLOODY FOOL! HOW could it take you two weeks to travel to New York?" Rangda roared.

"Well, Elaine suggested that we saw some other destinations on the way here. Besides, you never gave me a timeline?" I replied.

"Do I have to spell everything out to you? When I give an instruction, I expect priority. Your interpersonal relationship will have to come in second place." Rangda replied.

"Apologies, Empress Rangda. So, what do we do now?"

"Well, because of your oversight, you lost the opportunity to become a billionaire. Someone else already won it." Rangda sniped.

"But I could have bought that ticket from anywhere. Why did I need to come to New York in the first place?" I argued.

Rangda shook her head and ground her teeth in disapproval. *"Eeeeeeeerrrkk!!"* She shrieked, and the terrible noise hit me like a sledgehammer right in the face. *"Stop arguing, Human. I am your Empress, and you must obey me."*

"Yes, Empress. Forgive me." I gasped.

"I don't believe in forgiveness. But you are not useful to me dead. There is a $300 million jackpot on tomorrow night. But to get it, you need to do something for me first." Rangda said.

"What do you command, Empress?" I replied.

Rangda smiled maliciously and replied in a condescending tone. *"Aaaarrh! Look at you. You're learning fast. I reckon you can become a good pet!"*

I didn't reply. There was no point in arguing with Rangda. Besides, I suspected that her terrible shrieking could kill me if she intended to. I nodded, and I went down to the floor, bowing to her.

"Excellent! There is a Zetan artefact in New York that I need you to get for me. It's small and not particularly valuable, yet I need you to get it to prove your loyalty. Get the artefact, and I'll make you wealthy and powerful." Rangda instructed.

"Understood. What do I need to do?" I replied.

"The American rapper Fay Zhed owns a Zetan Angel chip. He has made a custom-made earring using the Zetan microchip. I need you to get it and insert the chip into your brain. Once you have inserted the chip, I will give you the winning lottery numbers." Rangda instructed.

"So, you want me to steal the earring? Where is he located?" I asked.

"You can rob him, steal it covertly, blackmail him, buy it, or receive it as a gift. There are many scenarios where you get the Zetan artefact. I leave it to your creativity to determine how." Rangda replied.

"Okay. How do I find Fay Zhed?" I asked.

Rangda shook her head and replied. *"So much for using your creativity, eh? He'll be in his room in The Marriott Hotel for another half an hour. Room 907. I'll talk to you later."*

After saying this, Rangda disappeared from my vision. I got up to my feet and ran towards the window. My memory served me right. The Marriott Hotel was just across the street. The Angel Zetan chip and my salvation were so close, and I had to pursue it now. I left my phone on the bed and ran towards the door.

"Where are you going?" Elaine shouted. I didn't respond. There was no time to lose, and besides, I didn't want her to know about my mission!

I WAS AT THE NINTH level of the Marriott Hotel Downtown, courtesy of the key card that I had pickpocketed from one of the hotel cleaners. I looked at the corridor ahead of me. There was a security guard stationed outside one of the rooms. This was no doubt to make sure that no crazy fans disturbed Fay Zhed before his performance this evening.

I had my course of action clear in my head. When Fay Zhed would walk past me, I'd fake a trip and pull his earring with me in the fall. It wasn't the best idea, and I hated Rangda for telling me to use my creativity. I wasn't a bloody thief, what would I know about stealing things?

As I was spying on the guard from behind the corner, I noticed that he received a phone call and walked away from the door. New plan! I would use my stolen key card and get into Fay Zhed's room as a hotel housekeeper, and steal the earring while the guard was away.

I went to the housekeeper's room, knocked the housekeeper unconscious, and dressed up as a housekeeper. I walked briskly towards Fay's room, and I used the key card to get in. As I entered the room, I felt the thick smoke of marijuana and Fay Zhed lying unconscious on the bed. Next to him, there was some paraphernalia made of glass, half-full of a substance that I assumed to be heroin. 'I am in luck' I thought, as I detached the earring which contained the Zetan angel chip from Fay's right ear.

Suddenly, the door opened behind me, and time seemed to slow down. "Hey, who are you?"

I heard the guard shout.

'Combat mode: Non-lethal options unavailable. Please authorise lethal force.' My monocle showed. Oh shit! I had to kill to get out of this mess. I authorised lethal force. With the help of the monocle, I found a hidden gun located on the bedside table. I jumped towards the gun, grabbed it, and turned around to shoot the guard. My shot missed.

How could this be, what was going on? The guard fired at me and missed. The monocle showed me the situation in slow motion. It predicted the guard's movements, and I hit him right between the eyes with my second shot, but not before the guard had fired a second shot. I got up and looked at Fay Zhed. The guard had accidentally hit Fay in the throat, and he was bleeding out. Oh shit! Fucking hell. What would I do now?

I THREW THE EARRING to the floor, and I stomped on it. The Earring shattered and revealed the Zetan angel chip. I inserted the Zetan angel chip into my head, it merged with the skin and was absorbed into the brain. I heard Rangda's voice.

"Interesting approached. A bit crude and not highly creative!" Rangda mocked

"So what do I do now? I asked in desperation.

"The monocle can't get you out of this mess, but I can. Relinquish control over your body to me for the next ten minutes."

"Relinquish control? This is insane!" I growled.

"Okay, so I assume you'd rather die in a shootout with the cops? Such a shame. We could have achieved so much together!" Rangda sneered.

"Sorry, Empress. I will do as you say." I whimpered.

Having said this, I opened the settings for the technology. Inside the settings, I surrendered control over my body for the next ten minutes.

After releasing control, everything became like a movie. I was a passive spectator witnessing my own actions. I placed my pistol in the dying Fay Zhed's hand and squeezed his hand to make sure that his fingerprints covered up mine. After that, I ran out of the room. I ran towards the fire stairs and followed them all the way down to the basement.

Once I was in the basement, I activated the fire alarm. I hid in the toilet while everyone was evacuating the building. A few minutes later, I entered the security office. Inside the office I typed in the password, and I deleted all the security footage of the building. After that, I picked up a chef's jacket and left the building via the delivery entrance. As I got out, I dumped the chef's coat in a dumpster. I got back to the main road, crossed the street, and walked back to my hotel.

"MARTIN, YOU'RE BLEEDING!" Elaine said as I returned to our hotel room. Rangda released control over my body, and I got back to my senses. Ouch, my neck stung a lot. I put my hand on the wound, and it got soaked by blood. I realised that the cut wasn't deep enough to bleed me out, but there was another terrible implication. Had I left my blood at the crime scene? I recalled how the bodyguard's shot had grazed my neck before it had killed Fay Zhed. My blood was at the crime scene, and I was in trouble! I thought of jumping out of the window to end it all, but I controlled myself. Why would I let my paranoia cause my downfall?

"Martin, you need to go to the hospital!" Elaine nagged.

But I wouldn't go to a hospital. Having my blood sampled by the American authorities? What an idiotic idea. "No! I cannot go to the hospital. You worked as a nurse back in the days, go to the pharmacy and get some threads and needles. You need to stitch me up!" I replied.

"I hate your stubbornness!" Elaine exclaimed.

"That might be, but you'll do as I say, or we'll both go to jail. I reckon you'd rather share the 300 million US dollars." I replied coldly.

Elaine said nothing. Instead, she left the hotel room to collect the necessary supplies. 30 minutes later, she returned. Elaine stitched me up without uttering a word.

"3, 22, 23, 32, 37, 58. Powerball 2."

Rangda whispered as I was filling in my Powerball lottery ticket at a lottery agent in Manhattan. I hadn't been out all day, but I needed to hand in that winning lottery ticket. I had watched the morning news on the TV. The official broadcast was that Fay Zhed had a drug-induced psychotic breakdown. He had started shooting at his bodyguard who had returned fire, and both men had died in the altercation.

It amazed me that the police had made such a sloppy investigation, but I felt relieved at the same time. Perhaps, that was the reason I missed the first shot that I fired? If the monocle had enabled me to kill the guard with the first shot, Fay would still be alive, and I'd be a fugitive. The idea startled me. Who was in control of my life?

I knew the answer. It was the same entity who was now giving me the winning Powerball numbers. I thought for a second to throw away the ticket, but I stopped myself. Regardless of what I did, I was now a murderer. For all intents and purposes, it was better to be a wealthy murderer than a raving lunatic locked away at an institution.

"COME ON, GUYS. SMILE a bit more!" The photographer said with a pretended cheerfulness. I am sure that Elaine and I were the first couple ever to win the Powerball, who wasn't smiling to the camera. I didn't want to have my picture taken. I'd rather be wealthy without having my picture all over the news, but apparently the lottery had to disclose the winners.

"Please smile so that we can get out of here," I whispered to Elaine.

I felt an epileptic shock when the photography flash struck my eyes. As I got back to my senses, I heard the photographer's cheerful tone. "That's a great picture. Let's wrap this up."

As I left the Powerball office, I felt strange. Like most people, I had sometimes dreamt about winning the lottery. But now that I had all the money in the world, or close to it at least, I felt like a prisoner, crushed under the responsibility bestowed upon me. I had sworn to aid Rangda, and while I had been able to disconnect her before, I was now bound to serve her. The Angel chip, which had merged with my brain, made it impossible for me to ignore her. And the bloody thing was irremovable, at least that's what Rangda want-ed me to believe.

Thinking of Rangda, I heard her chilling voice. *"There is a jewellery store over there. They have a replicated Zeto Crystal in stock. Enough to keep you alive for a bit longer."* I thought of asking for more details, but not now. For now, I'd buy the crystal with my newfound riches.

A while later, I bought the crystal, pressed it against my skull, where the migraine was tremoring. The relief was immediate, and I felt like a new man. I looked at the crystal. It was dull again, just a useless blue rock. I dropped it in a beggar's cup and continued walking when Elaine ran up to me.

"Why did you give the beggar the sapphire?" Elaine asked.

"Because it's useless now. I used up its power to heal my wounds." I replied.

"How can you be so stupid? I love sapphires, and what good are they to the beggar? Give me some money!" Elaine commanded.

"Sure, here you go!" I replied and handed her a wad of cash.

Elaine ran back to the beggar, and a minute later she came back. "This stone is beautiful. I will have it cut in half and use it for our wedding bands!" Elaine chirped.

THE FOLLOWING DAY, we were at JFK airport. We were heading for Li-ma in Peru. Rangda had commanded me to find Pachamama's Veil. The Veil was apparently a crucial artefact to re-energise the Primordial Zeto Crystal once.

Elaine was acquiring a new wardrobe from our ill-gotten gains while I was drinking a beer at the airport bar. While I wouldn't mind some new clothes, there was little use for fashion brands on our upcoming expedition. But money was plentiful, and if she wanted to go shopping to clear her mind, who was I to object?

As I was drinking my third beer, James Winter approached me. He was also wearing his monocle. "Martin Orchard. We meet again." James grunted. Clearly, he hadn't gotten over our last encounter in Nepal. I had beaten him senseless and then attached the monocle to his eye, forever changing his outlook on life.

"James. It's been a while. How are things?" I said with fake enthusiasm. I felt terrified. James Winter was younger and a lot fitter than me. During our last encounter, I had worn the monocle, and he hadn't. This had enabled me to knock him out. If we both had elevated minds, however, I stood no chance against the trained military officer opposite me.

"Don't worry, Martin. I came to thank you for taking out Fay Zhed for us." James said

"Us?" I asked.

"I am with the CIA now. But I have been talking to Pierre, Ben and Szymon. We have bigger plans for the World." James revealed.

"So, why did you want him dead?" I asked.

"Why do you ask? You killed him, what was in it for you." James smirked

"It was an accident. I needed something of his." I replied.

"Very well. Your motives don't concern me." James replied.

"We wanted Fay Zhed dead because he was a Muslim hip-hopper who propagated Jihadism and religious terror. We can't have that. Your pathetic attempts at concealing your crimes didn't trick me. But I got your back this time." James scorned.

"So, why are you helping me?" I asked.

"It's not about helping you. This is an excellent opportunity to frame Iranian intelligence operatives for the murder. We wouldn't want a sad stagnating world, would we?" James asked rhetorically.

"Well, thanks for helping me. Good luck," I replied.

James got up and spoke: "It looks like your wife is back. Enjoy your Lottery winnings and your Peruvian holiday. We will keep in touch."

I didn't reply. I looked at James as he approached Elaine. James greeted her briefly and then disappeared into the crowd. Elaine approached me with a worried expression on her face. "James knows what you did!" Elaine shuddered.

"Yes, but let's get out of here before he decides to use that knowledge against us," I urged.

After that, we hurried to our plane that would take us to Lima, the Peruvian capital.

Chapter 5: Peru, October 2020

I was squatting the flies around me while sweating and panting profusely. I struggled to breathe in the filthy hotel room with my sweet Elaine by my side. We had been to Peru for three months and we had not had any success in our search for Pachamama's Veil. Instead, my guilt and paranoia over what happened in New York had driven me to opioid addiction. It had happened since I had almost unlimited money in a country where drugs were plentiful. I tried to get up, but I fell backwards, hit my head on the bed frame and fell unconscious.

I was floating in space. I recognised the feeling from my interdimensional travel and my near-death experience in Nepal. Was I dying again? Today's date was surrounding me. 20th October 2020. In exactly 111 years from now, a Gamma Ray Burst would hit Earth and destroy humanity. What was it to me, anyway? No matter what I did, I would be long gone by then.

"Individuals are expendable. It's the collective that matters!" Rangda chanted.

Her statement angered me. Rangda was all about herself! Rangda had started a galactical war between the Xenos and Zetans alien species, to avenge her mother. Aeons ago, her mother Kalianka was abandoned and left for dead by Zetani scientists. If it wasn't for the Xenos who found her mother and took her in, Rangda would never have borne so much hatred and jealousy. So much pain and suffering took place because Rangda wanted to get her revenge. While I knew that Rangda was a divine being that was to be feared and obeyed, I had to do what my heart wanted to do, to save the world from apocalypse.

"War is the epitome of progress and development. It rids the universe of the weak lifeforms so that the strong ones may live on." I heard Rangda's voice echo in my head.

"Well, perhaps I am weak, and it's time for me to make room for the strong?" I suggested.

"Maybe. But a Gamma Ray Burst won't benefit the sake of humanity, although the strongest species may still survive." Rangda replied.

"Why is that?" I wondered.

"Because the strongest of species are single-cell organisms. They can survive anything. Although humanity has been constantly making medications and antibiotics to kill these micro-organisms, they still thrive. A gamma-ray burst would kill all humans and animals. Strong and weak alike. Thus, it wouldn't separate the weak from the strong." Rangda ranted.

"Why did you choose me?" I shouted.

"I didn't. Destiny made our paths cross, and now it's up to you to save humankind. The only way you can do that is to do my bidding." Rangda replied.

"But what if I don't want to save humanity?" I asked.

"Your preferences on this matter is of no concern to me. Now get up and get to work. You are not meant to die here!" Rangda said and disconnected from my mind. Once Rangda had disconnected, I fell into deep dreamless sleep.

SPLASH! I WOKE UP WITH a twitch as the icy water brought me back to my senses. "Get up! I found a lead. It's time to get to work!" Elaine commanded.

"What happened?" I wondered.

"That happened," Elaine replied and pointed to the stash of opioids and various pills.

"You left me unconscious to continue on our mission," I complained.

"I'm sorry. The mission is crucial for the future. Not even your life matters that much." Elaine lamented.

"I am sorry, Elaine," I replied and looked away. Elaine hugged me and said nothing.

After a period of silence, Elaine spoke. "So, why do you keep doing this shit? Humanity's future is at stake, and you're busy overdosing on recreational drugs!"

"I am acting this way because of the immense pressure of my mission. Also, I killed two men, remember!" I replied.

"Fay Zhed was a scumbag paedophile rapist, and his bodyguard was complicit. You made the world better by killing those men!" Elaine stated.

"That was CIA propaganda" I remarked.

"Yes. But we are better off if you believe it, so we can get on with the mission!" Elaine replied.

"You are right," I sighed, and I got up from the floor.

HALF AN HOUR LATER, we were having breakfast in the hotel restaurant. I felt sick, but I knew that I needed to sustain myself if I wanted to carry on with the mission. As I had my second cup of coffee, Elaine spoke. "I have located an artefact that is crucial for our mission."

"That's great news. Where is it?" I asked.

Elaine handed me a tablet with a picture of a silver statuette and spoke. "Well, you see that's the problem. It's located at the National Museum here in Lima."

"So, what do you suggest? That we buy it? Or that we steal it?" I asked.

"I'd suggest neither of those. I already spoke to the museum manager. He won't sell their national treasures to some cashed-up gringos. And stealing it? Well that plan didn't work out too well in New York, did it?" Elaine challenged.

I sighed. The headache and nausea were too much for me, and I couldn't think straight. "So, what do you suggest?" I asked.

"Well. I have realised that the museum manager, Alejandro Orihuela, is a very traditional family man with strong hidden desires. He is secretly into men." Elaine smirked

"Why do I give a shit?" I asked.

"Well, blackmailing is the way to convince Alejandro to steal the statuette for us. Being the museum manager, he can delete the record of the statuette so that no-one knows that it was ever there." Elaine revealed.

"I still don't know what you're suggesting." I yawned

"We need to make sure that Alejandro has sex with a man, and film it. Then we threaten to reveal the images. That will force him to help us." Elaine explained.

"No fucking way. I am not having sex with a man!" I exclaimed, a bit too loud, so people at the neighbouring tables stared at us.

"Tsk, tsk, tsk. Don't think too highly of yourself. You're not that irresistible. I have hired an accomplice who is willing to play on with our plan. Miguel will do the seducing part." Elaine jeered.

As Elaine mentioned his name, Miguel strutted in with his hands on his slender hip, cat walking to our table and delivered a kiss. He was a femininely handsome Latin American man in his twenties, and I was confident that he would do an excellent job at seducing Alejandro. But at the same time, I felt jealous. If Elaine had hired this man, what had stopped her from utilising his services herself? He might as well be bisexual, and open to any sexual requests. I sought eye-contact with Elaine, who was staring at Miguel's bum and abs.

"Ah, fuck it!" I thought as I zoned out while Elaine explained the details of her blackmailing plan.

A FEW HOURS LATER, we were sitting in a windowless van, following Miguel's advancements with Alejandro. I didn't know why we had to do things this way, but I didn't want to argue. I hadn't found a lead for months, due to my failed self-medication against my anxiety and guilt. I felt like a paparazzi, the worst kind of bottom feeder with no life on my own. This feeling was amplified by sitting in a hot car with no air-conditioning.

"Don't be a sourpuss, our plan is working," Elaine said, and she was correct. The video images revealed that Miguel and Alejandro were getting undressed in a hotel room, which we had rented for the setup. "Do I need to watch this shit!" I fumed.

"Yes. Please do. Miguel is a professional. You might learn a thing or two." Elaine smirked.

"Did you learn a thing or two from him?" I lashed back.

"Ha-ha-ha. As tempting as it would be if he weren't a gay prostitute, but well he is a gay prostitute. So, no I didn't." Elaine replied.

"Whatever. Are we done here?" I replied.

"I'd say so. We are not posting the video on Pornhub, after all." Elaine teased.

"Okay, I am out of here, I need some fresh air," I groused.

"Very well. I'll see you back at the hotel. After all, I have saved the day." Elaine teased as I left the van.

A COUPLE OF DAYS LATER, we were in the mountains close to Lake Titicaca. I held the Pachamama silver statuette in my hand, feeling both relief and anger. Relief that we had the first clue in the pursuit of the Primordial Zeto Crystal. Anger over how Elaine had acquired it. She had blackmailed Alejandro Orihuela into stealing the statuette for us. Elaine did this through threatening to reveal the video of Alejandro's homosexual encounter to his family members. Alejandro had obliged, and we had the figurine, but it was an immoral way of conducting business.

I snapped out of my moralising. Elaine had done what she had to do to retrieve the statuette, and at least no-one had died this time. The figurine was crucial to finding the Incan deity, Pachamama's tomb, where her legendary veil was located. Rangda couldn't tell us anything about the tomb. But she claimed that Pachamama's veil was crucial for re-energising the primordial Zeto Crystal. It was clear that we needed to find it and secure more clues.

"Hmm. Eee Mook Chiearei Taww Roookmwino. Google Translate says it means - Open your heart from the mouth of the lake." Elaine read from the inscription on the statuette written in the ancient Incan language.

"Are you sure that is the correct translation?" I asked.

"No. Why don't you try?" Elaine snapped. I sighed and looked at the figurine. While the monocle heightened my senses and intelligence, it didn't make me an expert at every single language on Earth.

"I am sorry, babe. My Zetan monocle read the same translation." I said.

"So, what does it mean?" Elaine pondered.

"Hmm the mouth of a lake, I guess it would be where the water flows into the lake. Open your heart might mean to keep an open mind. Many ancient civilisations thought that the mind was in the heart." I replied.

"So, open your mind?" Elaine pondered.

"Exactly. The safest place to hide something would at the bottom of the lake. There is an underwater temple built by the Tiwanaku people. That would be our best bet." I replied.

"Well, let's go. But we better get some dive instructors with us. We only got basic certifications in diving." Elaine suggested.

"No, we better not involve others if we can avoid it. Let's go and get some equipment." I replied and rushed ahead.

I WAS STUDYING THE majestic view where the Ramis River connected to Lake Titicaca. My head was pinging, and I could sense that a Zeto Crystal was near. It was probably a replicated one, but I needed to find out. I couldn't leave any stones unturned. We had encountered a practical problem that we should have foreseen. There were no dive shops close to the lake, and when I dipped my toe in the water, I realised why. The water was freezing and not suitable for a recreational dive.

'Ping, ping, ping' kept humming in the back of my head. A Zeto Crystal of some sort was nearby. Severe paranoia gripped me. It would take days to get the required scuba equipment to this location. What if someone else was going to find the crystal in that time? I knew that my thought made no sense, but when fear and paranoia strike you, logic stops working!

Against better judgement, I got undressed, ran towards the lake, dived down, and looked for the crystal without equipment. I didn't get far as the icy water shocked my body and made me come back up as quickly as I went in!

"You'll enjoy swimming more at Mancora Beach," A female voice said. I froze and slowly turned around. There she was, Josefina Fiero, the Latin American femme fatale I hadn't seen since Nepal, five months earlier.

At first, I felt like an idiot, shivering in my wet swimwear. This was particularly embarrassing since the freezing water had shrunk certain body parts. But then, paranoia struck me. Why was Josefina here, and how did she find us?

"Josefina, what brings me the pleasure?" I said, faking enthusiasm.

"I am bringing news about the guy that you blackmailed, Alejandro. Despite your well-meaning attempts at improving his sex life, he ended up committing suicide. What a tragedy!" Josefina jested.

Hearing this, I realised that Josefina had us under surveillance, and I freaked out. The monocle must have acted as some kind of telepathic device, and I quickly activated the combat mode on my monocle to identify any threats in the surroundings.

"I wouldn't try that. I tested out the technology, and I concluded that it couldn't identify threats more than a kilometre away on the standard-setting. And I have snipers outside of that range." Josefina stated.

"You are lying!" I exclaimed.

"Perhaps, but are you willing to take that risk to fight a woman who came in peace?" Josefina asked.

I sighed, tapped the top of my monocle, and removed it, revealing my purple iris. Josefina followed suit and removed her monocle as well. After that, she handed me a towel, and we walked towards a picnic table and got seated.

"So, Martin. Tell me why you're here." Josefina wondered.

"Can't a couple visit this beautiful location without an ulterior motive?" I argued.

"Tourists don't blackmail museum managers into handing out priceless artefacts!" Josefina replied.

"So, you have been spying on me for a while?" I replied.

"Well, not personally but my associates have. I have got a successful business to run." Josefina replied.

"A lot more successful due to a certain artefact, I'd assume?" I replied.

Josefina smiled seductively at me and replied: "Yes, and that's why I have come to help you. I need to know what your goals are, and my organisation can help you reach them."

I hesitated for a moment, and then I gave in to Josefina's suggestion. There was no way I could say no to a smile like hers, and besides she had come in peace.

"We are looking for an alien artefact. The Veil of Pachamama. A Zetan alien who posed as an Incan goddess." I revealed.

"Oh, a treasure hunt. How exciting!" Josefina enthused.

"Well, I hope it can save me. Since the incident in Nepal, I have been living on borrowed time. I have severe brain injuries that should have killed me." I replied.

Josefina's smile disappeared, and she gave me a concerned look. "I am so sorry to hear that. You're the reason I am still alive, with a heightened awareness. If there is anything that I could do for you, just say the word!" Josefina consoled.

Josefina's kind word moved me, and I was close to breaking down. But I kept my composure and replied. "Thank you, Josefina. If you could organise for express delivery of Scuba gear and a dry suit, that would help."

"Of course. I'll tell my helicopter pilot to bring the supplies here after dropping me off at the airport. I'll need to go back to Brazil now. Let's keep in touch." Josefina said, hugged me and rushed off towards an approaching helicopter. As she got on it, I saw several men with sniper rifles. I was grateful that I hadn't tested Josefina's claim about her men surrounding the location.

I WOKE UP AS THE FROST was chilling into my bones. Despite being close to the equator, the high altitude caused the region to be barren and cold. I hated the thought of getting into the lake's chilly water, and I hoped that the dry suit would work.

I nudged Elaine to wake her up. She looked at me with worried eyes. "Martin, I don't like this. Why did Josefina come here?" Elaine shivered.

"I don't know. Considering that Josefina brought several snipers to the meeting, that means she doesn't trust us either. But she did deliver scuba gear, and we need to get going." I replied.

"I guess you're correct. If she wanted us dead, we'd already been dead, right?" Elaine pondered. "Correct. Josefina got the resources to kill us. Let's go." I said

I got up, left the tent, and watched the magnificent sunrise over the picturesque lake.

I WAS PLEASANTLY SURPRISED when I entered the water with the scuba gear that Josefina had provided. She hadn't spared any expense, and the dry suit kept me warm and comfortable in the freezing water. I had opted to have a full-face mask instead of a typical scuba mask. I needed to be able to communicate with Elaine who was on a boat at the surface looking out for dangers.

"Your video link is up and running," Elaine said via the radio.

"Copy that. I am moving towards the ping of the Zeto Crystal. Martin out" I replied and disregarded Elaine's follow-up messages.

The water in the lake was blurry and not ideal for diving. This was because I was at the lake's inlet where a river brought freshwater and sediment to the lake. But I was where I needed to be. The inscription had mentioned the mouth of the river, and I could feel the Zeto Crystal acting like a beacon. The pinging in my brain was becoming louder as I approached the crystal in the depths.

I checked the depth gauge. I was below 30 metres depths, way deeper than I had ever been before, and the visibility was poor. I felt like death surrounded me, and I struggled to keep calm. I took a deep breath to calm down, and I saw a rock formation that looked like an old temple carved into the mountainside.

'Ping, ping, ping'. The Zeto Crystal was near. I closed my eyes to visualise, and I noticed a hidden compartment of the wall. I swam towards it, but it couldn't nudge the door. Fuck! If I had only worn the monocle when diving. Then I would know what to do. Unfortunately, I had to take it off to fit my full-face diving mask.

I realised that Rangda might know how to open the doorway. I contacted her via the Zetan Angel Chip. "Empress Rangda. I am lost. I know there is a Zeto Crystal behind this hidden wall, but I don't know how to open it."

"Bloody fool. Haven't you expanded your mind from using the Zetan Monocle?" Rangda hissed.

"I had to take it off to fit on my scuba mask. Sorry, Empress Rangda." I replied.

"Very well. Look around in every direction. Move your head slowly. I'll access your vision, and I'll let you know if I see anything." Rangda replied.

I started looking around, hoping for Rangda's enhanced awareness to detect something that I was missing. After a few minutes I heard Rangda screeching: *"Look, over there. A hidden lever masked as a broken-off twig!"*

"What? That looks like a normal piece of debris." I objected

"You fool! That twig is from a non-native tree. How do you think it got there?" Rangda hissed.

"I am sorry, Empress Rangda," I replied.

"So, so. Apologies won't get us closer to finding the Zeto Crystal. Swim over there and pull the secret lever!" Rangda commanded.

I did as Rangda instructed, and I made my way to the secret lever. I tried moving the lever, but it seemed to be stuck. What should I do? I didn't want to ask Rangda and have her taunt me again, so I looked around for a suitable tool.

I saw a medium-sized stone a few metres away from me. I tried to lift it, but I couldn't. I thought about it for a few seconds and then I got an idea. I inflated my diving vest a bit while holding the stone. This gave me enough buoyancy to lift the rock off the bottom of the lake. I swam towards the lever with the stone clutched to my chest.

As I reached the lever, I grabbed the stone with both hands and slammed the lever. I heard a noise, the bar moved, and a secret passageway opened in the cave.

I swam towards the passageway when I heard a terrifying loud alarm go off. 'Beep, beep, beep!'. I froze as several squid-like robots approached me.

"Rangda. Help!" I shuddered.

"Hmm. I should have known that the hidden temple had defences in place. Be completely still and don't resist. Most Zetan defensive measures are set to be non-lethal by default. I'll try to come up with something." Rangda said.

"Yes, Empress!" I replied.

I stared in horror as the horrible robots approached me. They looked like they came straight from a nightmare, and my heart told me to get the fuck out of there. The quickest way was up. If I inflated my vest and dropped my weights, I could reach the surface and the boat quickly. But I'd never survive the decompression sickness. I was 40 metres below the surface, and unless I got rid of excess gas in my bloodstream through following diving protocols, I was a goner.

One of the squid-like robots wrapped my leg with its metal tentacles, and all I wanted was to wake up from the nightmare. But I wasn't sleeping, and I was gasping for air as it squeezed my body. As the metal tentacles slithered over my body, the robot disconnected the regulator hose to my compressed air tank. Shit! I was going to die! I wriggled to get out of the robot's grip but to no avail, and things faded to black.

'Gulp!' I woke up in shock as I ingested a mouthful of water. I had lost my scuba mask. On the flip side, the robots seemed to be deactivated. My vision was blurry, but I saw my salvation. The iridescent blue light of a Zeto Crystal in front of my arms. I grabbed the crystal, dropped my weight belt and inflated my diving vest. I could no longer worry about decompression sickness, I needed to get up.

A few seconds later, I reached the surface, and Elaine dragged me unto the boat. Then everything turned black.

"BARRRRRFFFF!"

I woke up vomiting up water. Elaine was wearing scuba gear, and she was doing chest compressions on me. I realised that I needed to get to a decompression chamber quickly. But how would I get to one on time?

"Get me to the hospital!" I wheezed.

"Oh, thank god! You're alive! What were those horrible things?" Elaine asked.

"Zetan sentry robots. The inscription on the statuette lured us into a clever trap." I replied.

"Yes. I saw the video link. I panicked when I saw those squid-like robots coming after you. I wonder why the robots suddenly turned still?" Elaine wondered.

"They were probably running out of battery. I must have died and returned. I almost passed out when one of those squid-like robots had its tentacles wrapping my leg, and in just a brink of the time I saw the Zeto Crystal, grabbed it and squeezed it to save my dear life. After that, everything went black." I reiterated.

"Yes, I saw it all on the video screen. The Zeto crystal caused an underwater explosion that destroyed the squid-like robots around you. Your body went into shock and you passed out. You were lifeless for over a minute. I got into my scuba gear hoping to save you, but then you floated up to the surface." Elaine revealed.

"Well. Let's hope that I won't get decompression sickness after all that has happened." I sighed and closed my eyes in calmed perseverance.

"Yes. I'll call an ambulance helicopter, and I'll pray for you." Elaine replied.

I fell asleep and started dreaming. I dreamt about my visit to the Divine Dimension the previous year and my conversation with Brahma. He had warned me about Rangda the Deceiver, but here I was, serving her. Then again, Brahma and the Zetans had asked me to warn Keila Eisenstein of Rangda the Deceiver, but did not mention about me not being able to follow her commands. The Zetans had abandoned me, while Rangda had saved my life and made me wealthy. So, who was good and who was bad?

'Wake up!' I heard echoing in the back of my head, and as I opened my eyes, a helicopter was approaching.

"WE ARE SAFE. HELP HAS arrived!" Elaine beamed when we looked at the incoming helicopter. I wanted to share Elaine's positive affirmation, but something was gnawing in my head. How had the helicopter arrived so quickly?

I looked at my broken diving equipment, and I saw something. Hidden inside a ripped seam were a camera and a GPS tracker. Josefina Fiero must have decided to spy on us when she gave us the equipment. This helicopter was likely to be piloted by her men in disguise. In that case we would better run off and hide.

I grabbed the replicated Zeto Crystal and directed its energy to heal my damaged lungs. Then I sprung to my feet and yelled: "Elaine, grab your stuff. We must run and hide."

"Martin, what's wrong?" Elaine asked.

"Josefina was spying on us. The helicopter crew must be her men. We need to get out of here." I urged.

Elaine believed me, and we grabbed our bags and made a run for it before the helicopter had landed. We ran until we had made our way to a small cave. Once we were out of sight, we collapsed to the ground.

"WHAT HAPPENED BACK there?" Elaine asked.

"I realised that Josefina had rigged our equipment with spy cameras and GPS trackers. I also found it strange that the ambulance helicopter came so fast!" I replied.

"Do you think Josefina wants to hurt us?" Elaine asked.

"I am not sure. But I don't trust someone who rigs my equipment with tracking devices and spy cameras." I replied.

"So, what do we do?" Elaine asked.

"We need to find Pachamama's temple, steal the veil and get away from Peru as quickly as possible," I replied.

Elaine looked at her tablet. "Hmm, I saw a map on the wall when you were unconscious in the underwater temple," Elaine said.

"Let me have a look," I replied.

"Sure, I took a screenshot of the map," Elaine replied and handed me the tablet.

I grabbed the tablet and looked at the map. It resembled the Titicaca region, but it was different. Did the area look like this, several centuries ago?

I studied the map together with Elaine. "What do you think about this?" I asked.

"I don't know. Maybe we should plug in our monocles?" Elaine suggested.

"I would rather not. That will alert Josefina about our position." I replied.

"42! 42 is the answer." I heard a faint whisper.

"Rangda?" I asked, but there was no response.

I looked at the map again. 42 degrees northeast of us there was a location marked in the Incan language. I didn't want to use the monocle to confirm my theory, but staying here didn't seem like a smart idea either. I made up my mind. We would move to the cave, which was located a few kilometres away from us. We would move at nightfall when it was harder for Josefina's men to spot us.

I told Elaine about the idea, and while she wasn't enthusiastic, she didn't argue against it. We were in a tight spot, and we had to act.

A FEW HOURS LATER, we were outside an ancient temple, dug out into the mountain. I felt a deep sense of relief. My intuition had led me in the right direction.

I picked up the shiny, silver Pachamama statuette that I had packed down in my scratched and weather-worn backpack. I looked at Elaine, and she nodded. This was it. This was the sacred tomb of Pachamama, the Incan goddess of Earth, a Zetan alien who had taken a divine form to gain human followers.

I compared the tomb with the map on my tablet. This was indeed the location from the map in the underwater temple. We had the key to get into to this hidden temple, which was the statuette that we stole from the museum.

I looked at the wall. There was an empty opening area, shaped like our Pachamama statuette. I was about to insert the figurine into the hollowed compartment when I heard Elaine's softly spoken voice, "Martin, I'm feeling nervous. Are we really meant to see a dead deity? What if she isn't dead?"

"Don't worry, Elaine. The Zetans are not real gods. If Pachamama was locked up here centuries ago, she would have perished by now." I replied confidently, although I felt that my partner's unease was influencing my sense of reassurance.

I pushed away my fears. I was here on a mission, and I would complete that mission. I inserted the figurine in the tiny opening area, and I waited for something to happen. Suddenly, the wall made a really loud cracking noise, shifted in a 270-degree rotation and revealed a massive tunnel. I heard a loud and shrill piercing voice, hissing nonsensical chants in an alien language coming from the end of the tunnel.

"What's that noise??" Elaine squealed.

"It's just a recording. Pachamama used that to keep the locals away back in the day," I lied "Anyway, we have a mission, and I am going in!" I asserted.

"I am not going in there!!" Elaine insisted.

"Okay, then I'll go myself," I seethed, and I walked into the tunnel.

As I entered into the inner sanctum of the Pachamama temple, an extremely sweet and off-pungent herby smell overwhelmed my nostrils. Where did the overwhelming stench come from? I found the source of the distinct smell in the centre of the room, where the body of Pachamama was lying on an altar.

Elaine changed her mind and ran to me. "Did you find the veil?" She asked.

"So, it would seem, but there is only one way to find out," I replied.

"But why would a corpse smell like that?" Elaine asked.

"It is probably because of a Zetan preservation technology." I replied as I walked up to Pachamama and touched her ancient garment. The body was slender and pale, her face had kept the appearance of a beautiful but sickly Mother queen and she appeared to be sleeping peacefully. Her face and body were turquoise, her garment was ridden with exotic gems and she was holding a white veil on her pale ample bosom. The perfectly preserved dead deity filled me disgust, but at the same time I was in awe with what was displayed right in front of my eyes.

"What do I do now?" I asked Rangda.

"Your mission here is to get Pachamama's Veil. Burn the body, humanity is not ready to find out the truth." Rangda replied.

"Elaine, we better take the veil and burn this body so that no one will ever know it existed," I replied and took the veil.

Elaine quietly agreed. After taking the majestic white veil from Pachamama's preserved body, we burnt the dead body and walked out of the secret ancient tunnel. We closed the wall by taking the statuette away, and we left the temple without uttering a word. Our real mission was still ahead of us!

Chapter 6: Sydney, February 2021

I ran for the tennis ball gravitating into the sky while gasping for air. I missed hitting it and collapsed to the ground, feeling exhausted after a friendly tennis match. It wasn't shocking or unexpected. I had busted my lungs from the fast ascent back to the lake surface when I was diving in Lake Titicaca, and it was a miracle that I was still alive. I knew that I shouldn't push myself physically with my current lung condition, but I didn't worry too much. It wouldn't kill me anyway.

I had survived severe brain damage in Nepal, a shootout in New York, a drug overdose in Lima and a diving accident in Lake Titicaca. The divine plan wanted to keep me alive and save humankind from the oncoming apocalypse in the form of a gamma-ray burst, which would happen on the 20th October 2131. If the divine plan intended for me to survive all this to die during a tennis match, then so be it. I smiled at the thought, it would indeed be an ironic ending to me.

My tennis partner, Sebastian Santiago, ran up to me. "Are you okay?" Sebastian smiled and lent me a hand to get up. I grabbed his hand and got up to standing, still feeling exhausted.

"I have been better. I guess I'll have to give you this match. I'll beat you next time." I replied.

"That will have to be in Colombia. I am moving back home tomorrow. Remember?" Sebastian replied.

I had forgotten about it. My mind was all over the place, and it didn't help being technically braindead. But I didn't want to share this, so instead, I replied. "Oh yeah, I had hoped that I wouldn't have to go all the way to Colombia to set things right. But I'll find a proper coach, and I will swing by and beat you."

"Ha-ha. I'll take that as a promise. Are you still coming by next year?" Sebastian asked.

"Yes, there is a cultural event celebrating the Guane people next February. I have a keen interest in attending that event." I replied.

"Ha-ha. Your main concern is probably acquiring high-grade marching powder. But all good, tell Elaine the Guane story." Sebastian chortled.

"I definitely will. See you next year. Say hi to La Patrona from me." I said.

"Sure thing. See you next year." Sebastian replied.

As Sebastian walked off, I made a mental note to find myself a tennis coach so that I could keep playing. It wouldn't be the same, but I would rather have a friend I paid to play with than not playing. And in the grand scheme of things, what better use did I have for my wealth?

"SO HOW WAS TENNIS TODAY?" Elaine asked.

"It was alright until my lungs gave in. A pity I couldn't send Sebastian back home as a loser!" I sighed.

Elaine gave me a worried look and spoke: "How are you feeling? You shouldn't push yourself too hard!"

Elaine's concern annoyed me. I should be dead, but I wasn't. So why should I let my impending death affect my everyday life? "I'll do what I want. Playing tennis and writing books are among the things that take my mind off what has happened in the last few years." I lashed out.

"Don't be angry at me. I am concerned about you." Elaine replied.

"Yeah, whatever. I am going for a walk. I'll see you later" I said and took off.

AN HOUR LATER, MY WALK had taken me to Bondi Junction when some familiar faces approached me. It was the Yehuda Brothers, Ben & Szymon Yehuda. They were participating in a funeral procession when they broke out from the group to speak to me.

"Martin Orchard, we meet again," Ben Yehuda said.

"Yes. What brings you to Sydney?" I asked.

"You would have known if you had worn the monocle. Such ingratitude refusing to wear the God-given artefact that allows the great Yahweh to communicate with us!" Szymon Yehuda stated.

Szymon's statement confused me. It wasn't Yahweh who communicated via the monocle. Or was it? How could I tell for sure, whether it was them, or I that was being duped? Perhaps the voice in my head was Rangda, but to them it was Yahweh? I didn't want to discuss the matter with the Yehuda Brothers, so instead, I replied: "I hope Yahweh forgives me. I am too weak to carry out his divine will."

Ben studied me for a while and spoke: "Yes, you are weak. But you were the one who showed us our purpose: To make sure that our Jewish people will rule the planet for the sake of our great God, Yahweh. If you are looking for a purpose, you are welcome to join us."

"But, I am not Jewish. Are you sure that I am good enough to join?" I sniggered.

Szymon ignored my sarcastic tone and replied: "Yes. You are not Jewish, Mr Orchard. But you can still serve our great lord. My brother and I are planning to reignite an ancient order tasked with enforcing the divine will upon the world."

"Which order would that be?" I asked.

"The Knights Templar." Szymon proclaimed.

"They are Christian, not Jewish," I remarked.

"Yes. But through pretending to be Christian Knights we can seize and influence the minds of the naïve society and usurp power." Szymon replied.

"Is that what you're doing here? Setting up the Knights Templar home base?" I asked.

Ben shook his head and gave me a disapproving look. "No. We are here for the funeral procession of Josef Silverstein. A local Rabbi who advocated for peace and tolerance. He might or might not have been killed by a radical Muslim." Ben said and twirled his moustache.

I nodded. Szymon tapped my shoulder and spoke. "I am sorry, but we have to get back to our funeral procession now. It was a pleasure seeing you. Please consider our offer."

"Yes, don't squander your gift on nothing. Yahweh would punish you for that in the afterlife." Ben added in.

"I'll consider it," I replied.

As I watched Ben and Szymon re-join with the procession, I felt perplexed. Had Rangda told us different things, or were Rangda and Yahweh both aliases for something else? Or perhaps, this was all a work of the Annunaki? I was sure about one thing, though. I would not get myself involved in the age-old conflict between Judaism and Islam, Christianity, nor any other religions. Life was too short for that, for we will never be able to find out the real certainty of origins of life!

I WAS LYING IN BED, drenched in sweat and unable to move. The afterlife was approaching me, and in a way, I felt relieved. Soon my headaches, my guilt, and my physical ailments would be gone. Yes, the end could be a clean start. I smiled at the thought, and I closed my eyes, waiting for the inevitable.

I felt a powerful surge of energy striking through my body, bringing me back to life. As I opened my eyes, I saw Elaine and Pierre Beaumont looking at me. How long had I been gone?

"Welcome back, Martin!" Pierre greeted and smiled slyly.

"What are you doing here, Pierre?" I asked.

"Just helping a friend out. When Elaine asked me to come to Australia and bring a special type of blue sapphire, I felt perplexed. But we came to a mutually beneficial deal, your wife and I." Pierre replied.

"Let me hear it!" I sighed.

Pierre licked his lips and tasted the words for a few seconds before he replied. "I would like to become the CEO of the World Bank. And I would like the two of you to help me."

"Why do you want us to help you?" I asked.

"Well, Mr Orchard. I am not a man of violence. I am a man of finance." Pierre replied.

"That doesn't reveal what you want us to do." I snarled back.

"Correct. You asked me why, and I answered that question. Cause and ef-fect, Martin. Don't ask a question if you want to know something else." Pierre remarked.

"So, what do you want us to do?" I sighed.

Pierre took out a photo from his wallet and handed it to me. I studied the picture. It was of a South-Eastern Indian man in business attire who I had never seen before. "Who is this?" I asked.

"That is Chakri Apinya. The current CEO of the World Bank. A useless idealist who is risking the future of the bank and in extension, the future of humankind. I want to take his place. I want him dead."

"I am not a paid assassin. There is nothing that you can offer me, which would change my mind." I snorted.

"Yes, there is. Actually, there are two things." Pierre smirked

Having said this, Pierre handed me a photo of me leaving Fay Zhed's ho-tel room.

"Alright, you are blackmailing me into committing another murder, so I can cover up my first murder? Why would I accept this threat? It'd make more sense to kill you." I hissed.

"Such ingratitude after saving your life," Pierre mocked, paused and then changed his tone. "I wasn't going to blackmail you. I believe in the whip and the prize, and I haven't shown you the golden gem yet."

"So, what's the reward?" I sighed.

"The blue crystal that saved your life. If you help me become the CEO of the World Bank, I'll direct some of the bank's vast resources to find more crystals for you." Pierre promised.

Inner conflict filled my mind. I didn't want to murder people for Pierre, but on the other hand, I knew that Pierre could help our future. Humanity needed greed and power if we were to develop as a space-faring species. Cre-ating colonies on other planets was the only way to ensure the future sur-vival of our species. Empress Rangda had shown me as much. "One moment, Pierre," I said and zoned out. A few seconds later, I had established a connec-tion with Rangda.

"Pierre is correct. Humanity is better off with Chakri resting 6 feet below the ground. I want Pierre to run the World Bank." Rangda revealed and then disconnected from my mind.

"Okay. I will help you, Pierre." I whispered.

"I knew you would. It's for a great cause. Chakri Apinya will be in Geneva for the World Economic Forum in a couple of weeks. The Buddhist leader Arhat Somchai will also attend. This is the perfect opportunity to kill two birds with one stone." Pierre said and rubbed his hands.

"How many are on that hit list exactly?" I moaned.

"There is only Chakri. But someone must take the blame for the murder, and Arhat is the perfect candidate." Pierre replied.

"So, we are not targeting the Muslims anymore?" I jeered.

"I was never going to. Religion is just opium for the masses. The real god is money." Pierre said.

I didn't reply, and Pierre spoke again. "I need to leave now, Martin. I will give you all the instructions on my private jet back to Switzerland."

'KLONK!'

The glass that was once filled with red wine shattered against the wall, leaving a dirty stain.

"What is wrong with you! Why did you throw that glass to the wall!" Elaine chastised.

"Why did you ask Pierre to come here?" I exploded.

"I had to. You were in a coma, and I didn't know how to find those alien crystals that saved you. Pierre had a theory, and he found us a suitable stone." Elaine replied.

I calmed down. I couldn't blame Elaine for my decisions. Although she was the one who had invited Pierre, I was the one who had agreed to his terms. If anyone was at fault, it was me. "I am sorry. What was Pierre's hypothesis?" I asked.

"He guessed that the crystal you needed would be radioactive and detectable in other wavelengths than visible light. He was correct, and here you are." Elaine revealed.

"Okay. So, what do we do now?" I asked

"Well, you'd better clean up this mess right now!" Elaine stated and handed me a mop.

Fair call, Elaine!

Chapter 7: Switzerland, March 2021

I took a deep breath of the cold Swiss mountain air, and I felt Zen. The air was refreshing, and the view from Mont Salève overlooking the Geneva region was breathtaking. I sighed. I had told Elaine that I wanted to be alone to prepare for tonight's mission. The last year's events burdened me. I had killed some people in New York, due to spur of the moment mistakes during a botched robbery. But today, I was not going to create a big mess and take Elaine with me in my awkward demeanour. My mission was to break into a man's house and murder him in cold blood, leaving no evidence behind.

The current CEO of the World Bank, Chakri Apinya, was my next target. He was against Pierre Beaumont's attempts at financing a large mining complex in the Daen Lao region of Thailand. I sympathised with Chakri as natural preservation was important. However, Pierre's suggested mines were crucial for our survival as a species. Under the Daen Lao mountain range, lay a unique range of rare earth minerals. These minerals were pivotal for our technological advancement as a species. Chakri's unwillingness to mine them would slow down our technological progress. The clock was ticking, only 110 years left until the gamma-ray-burst would hit Earth.

Pierre would frame the famous Buddhist leader Arhat Somchai for the murders. Pierre hadn't revealed how, but it was of no concern to me. Framing Somchai made a lot of sense. Arhat Somchai was a leader of a Buddhist order who considered the Daen Lao mountain range sacred. But if Pierre framed Arhat for Chakri's murder, that would bring Arhat's movement into disrepute. After that, they wouldn't be able to stand against Pierre's ambitions.

I laid calmly in a sunbed, sipping a warm cup of coffee. Despite being in a snowy mountain, the sun warmed my face and soothed my nerves. I wrapped a blanket around my body, and I fell asleep.

ELAINE AND I WERE SITTING in a windowless van with fake plates. We were close to Chakri's rented mansion. Pierre had promised that there would be a change of guards at midnight, and that was the time to strike. I looked at my watch, it was five to midnight.

"How are you feeling?" Elaine asked.

"Not too flashy. I wonder if it would be better if I were to die. What's the point of killing people to stay alive?" I pondered.

"I understand where you are coming from, but this is bigger than any of us. The future of humanity is at stake." Elaine urged.

"But, what if it's all a lie?" I asked.

Elaine looked away, and I could hear her sobbing. I touched her gently on the shoulder. She turned around with teary eyes and spoke.

"I used to believe that there was no God, even though I had been drilled with stories of The Bible since I was very young. Now that I have witnessed true miracles, how can I not believe in the divine will and our purpose. Finding the monocles were our evidence of a true calling." Elaine proselytized.

I didn't have the time to respond, as it was midnight and my screen showed that Chakri's bodyguards were leaving the house.

"I got to go now, I will speak to you again later," I said, pointed at the screen and grabbed my silenced pistol.

I WAS AT THE FRONT gate of Chakri's mansion. I used the access card that Pierre had given me, and the door opened. I walked across the courtyard and entered the pin number at the front door. I pressed '5432', and the door opened. It was almost too easy, as if everything had been set up by Pierre, who wanted Chakri dead.

I needed to move quickly. Pierre had said that the changing of the guards would only take a couple of minutes, and I didn't want to be in the mansion when the new bodyguards arrived. I rushed towards the master bedroom of the palace, as I assumed that Chakri would sleep there. Pierre had planned for Chakri's wife to attend a late fundraising party, so that I wouldn't have to deal with her.

I sneaked into Chakri's bedroom, but to my dismay, he was wide awake.

"Hey, who are you?!" Chakri shuddered.

I had no intention of answering that question, and I aimed my pistol at Chakri. I was about to shoot when a voice startled me.

"Daddy, I can't sleep!"

I turned around and in a flash of a second, I accidentally pulled my trigger towards the voice. I realised to my shock and terror that I had shot Chakri's toddler, who was now bleeding and laying on the floor. Chakri fell down to his knees, looking aghast and petrified. Hurting a toddler put me in a state of shock, and I froze for several seconds. I came back to my senses, when my monocle flashed, 'Danger, dodge NOW!'. I managed to dodge the bedside lamp that Chakri swung aggressively towards me, while he was screaming madly in Hindi. I turned my pistol towards him and shot Chakri from a kneeling position, hitting him with several bullets, his blood splashing all over me.

I got up and were about to leave the room when I heard Rangda's voice. *"You cannot leave a witness!"* She said. I froze for a second while I was looking at Chakri's wounded boy. The monocle revealed that my bullet had ruptured the boy's spine. If I spared him, he would grow up as a cripple, who had witnessed the murder of his father. The merciful thing to do would be to kill him. I shot the boy between the eyes and I ran away from the scene.

A minute later, I got back into the van. Elaine stared at my blood-soaked clothes and said: "What happened to your clothes? I hope you didn't mess up again!"

"I'll tell you later, just drive!" I shouted.

Elaine smirked, did as I instructed, and we left the scene.

I WAS SITTING IN PIERRE'S office, at the Switzerland branch of the World Bank. My head was spinning from exhaustion and shock. I hadn't slept for three days, and everything seemed unreal, almost like this was all a nightmare that I desperately wanted to wake up from.

"I would prefer to praise your work, but you fucked up, didn't you?" Pierre scoffed

"You didn't tell me about the child! This is your fault!" I lashed out.

"Bah! Don't blame me for your lack of research. How could I get the child out of Chakri's house at night? And besides, it shouldn't have been an issue for an assassin like you." Pierre replied.

"I had no intention to kill a child, how else was I supposed to kill Chakri and leave no trace?" I asked.

"All you needed to do was to shoot Chakri first, and then knock the toddler out. A child that young can't testify in court. He could have lived. Instead, you were terrified at his sudden appearance and pulled the trigger at him, froze up, and then got into a fight with Chakri instead of shooting him immediately. You have created a mess instead of a clean crime scene." Pierre replied.

"How do you know this?" I shouted.

"Have a look!" Pierre said and handed me a tablet.

I checked the tablet. It was the security footage from Chakri's mansion. Pierre had recorded my every move. Seeing this, I sunk down into my chair, filled with despair.

"Don't worry too much, Martin. I am looking out for you. Look what I have organised." Pierre said, smiled cunningly, and handed me another tablet. On the tablet, there was an edited video where I had been digitally replaced with Arhat Somchai. I kept watching and the next video clips showed how a group of police had arrested the Buddhist monk, torturing and made him confessed to the murder that he didn't commit. Arhat declared his manifesto while in jail, praised Buddha and finally slit his own throat.

"How did you do this?" I asked in amazement.

"I told you already. The monocle gives me many great manipulating talents. Vladimir was a significant help. Thank you, Vladimir." Pierre said and gestured to someone behind me.

I looked around and there he was, Vladimir Kravchenko. The full-blown psychopath who had killed Rajesh and Jorge Santiago during our ordeal in Nepal the previous year.

"I can smell fear," Vladimir threatened.

"So, so, Vladimir. Act civilised. You're working for the police, remember?" Pierre said.

"Yes, Pierre," Vladimir said, and got seated next to me.

"Vladimir is incredibly talented. While you were messing up your hit on Chakri, Vladimir drugged and kidnapped Arhat Somchai. Vladimir did so well with Arhat's videos so that he covered all your actions. His video editing skills were the work of a true professional." Pierre revealed

"So, why did you need my help in the first place? You could have asked Vladimir to kill Chakri!" I lashed out.

"Because I was testing you. And now I own you." Pierre stated.

"No, you don't!" I shouted. I got up, and I was ready to punch Pierre.

"Vladimir, subdue him!" Pierre commanded. A second later, everything turned black.

I WOKE UP IN A BEAUTIFUL room, overlooking the Geneva city surrounded by The Alps and the Jura mountains. Spring had come and melted away the last remains of snow. Beautiful flowers filled the entire valley, and there was a sweet smell of tulip in the air. Elaine smiled at me.

"Welcome back, Martin," Elaine greeted.

"What happened?" I mumbled.

"Pierre threatened to expose your murders, and he asked me to heal you. He sent his agents to find another crystal for his next mission." Elaine replied.

"And he found another crystal I presume?" I asked.

"Yes. Pierre is no longer at the World Bank Tower. He needed to leave to supervise the new mining project in the Daen Lao mountains in Thailand. The initial reports indicate that the mountains are incredibly rich in rare earth minerals. These minerals are crucial for development of our future. We have to kill and destroy to create a better future. Such is our fates." Elaine said.

I pondered whether I should tell Elaine the truth. That I had murdered Chakri's toddler and how Pierre had played me around. I decided against it. It wouldn't make us happier, and besides, everything was turning out good in the end. At least I hoped that it would. Instead, I asked: "So, what are we going to do now?"

Elaine looked out through the window and replied. "I want us to stay here for a while. This is such a beautiful region, and I want to paint the landscape. You need the rest, and these beautiful mountains can give you inspiration for the book you're writing."

I considered Elaine's suggestion, and I decided to follow it. This was a beautiful location and perhaps some meditation and solace could bring me peace. Besides, I didn't have anywhere I needed to go until my mission in Colombia the following year.

"You're right, love. Let's stay here for a while and focus on our creativity and our arts." I said.

Elaine smiled seductively at me and spoke. "Perhaps, we can focus on something else for the next twenty minutes, since there are no one else in the room?"

"Sure, why not!" I purred and smiled sweetly at her.

Chapter 8: Colombia, February 2022

"Senor, please come with me."

I sighed in silence when the Colombian customs officer called me over. We had landed at El Dorado International Airport in Bogota, and I'd rather not have this headache. Strictly speaking, I didn't carry any illegal goods. Although I'd prefer if some random border official did not examine my alien artefacts!

"Senor, times are tough in Colombia. Perhaps we can help each other out." The border official insinuated. I studied his name tag. It read 'Miguel Santos'.

I hated corrupt officials. It was always a tricky balancing act when asked for bribes in countries like these. If I was too keen to pay, they would see me as weak and press me for more money. But if I was too obstinate, they might detain me for hours. In the worst-case scenario, they could plant confiscated drugs in my bags to make my life difficult.

"Miguel, I don't find you helpful at this stage. I have a hotel to get to after a long flight." I argued.

"Well, Mr Orchard. I am a hard-working official who is only doing my job. My duties include random bag checks, and the process could take several hours if you don't cooperate." Miguel warned.

"And how do you suggest that I cooperate?" I sneered.

"Like I said, times are tough in Colombia for hard-working government officials." Miguel hinted.

Now I was in a dilemma. Flaunt my wealth, and I would have every corrupt official in the country pursuing me for pocket money. While it wouldn't make me bankrupt, it wasn't the kind of attention that I wanted. However, if I were too obstinate, I would also face troubles ahead. I pretended to be an ignorant wealthy tourist, and I handed Miguel a 2000-peso banknote.

Miguel shook his head and replied: "Mr Orchard, that is less than a dollar. It won't feed my starving wife and kids!"

I faked surprise and replied, "Oh, I thought that 2000 pesos was a lot of money. I have never been to Colombia before. How about this one?" I said and handed Miguel a crumbled 50,000-peso note.

Miguel looked at me for a few seconds, and then he took the banknote. "That will do fine. You're clear for entry to Colombia. I hope you'll enjoy our famous Colombian hospitality." Miguel said and brandished a big smile, showcasing a coked-up nostril and several missing teeth.

"Thank you, Miguel. Have a wonderful day." I taunted, grabbed my bag, and walked off.

I made a mental note to make sure to carry enough cash for bribes. While it was irritating that some custom official blackmailed me for $22, I was wealthy and the money didn't matter to me. I was just annoyed that he was taking up my precious time, and I thought it would have helped if he could say the sum he wanted straight away, without all the goddamn guessing games!

"6-0, 6-0. I AM BACK with a vengeance!" I exclaimed, as I ran towards my Colombian tennis buddy.

"Impressive! I didn't think you had it in you. How did you get this good?" Sebastian sneered.

"I spent six months in Switzerland with Elaine, pursuing some creative goals. During that time, I had daily lessons at the tennis academy that taught Roger Federer." I replied.

"Oh, really? I thought that was an academy for gifted youngsters. How did YOU get in?" Sebastian joked.

"Money rules the world, my friend. It wasn't cheap but I did get in. I got flogged by the kids but persevered and now here I am! 6-0, 6-0!" I declared.

"Yeah, I'll play you a few more times. Can't let our tennis skills deteriorate!" Sebastian said.

"Be my guest. I'll stay here in Bogota for another week before I travel around the country. But let's find something to eat. The place across the road looks promising. My shout!" I said, and we headed to the local restaurant across the street.

Once we were inside the restaurant, I ordered one of each dish from the menu. While it was a waste of food, I'd rather support local business owners with my cash than giving it to corrupt officials.

"Did you enjoy the food?" Sebastian asked Elaine.

"Yes, you must send me the recipes later on social media!" she replied excitedly. I smiled. No matter what the mission was, Elaine hadn't lost her love for cooking.

"So how are your books going? Any sales?" Sebastian asked.

"Oh, my latest book, James Locker 3rd sequel, had a million downloads. I don't charge money for my books. It's my gift to humanity, I just like to share my brilliant ideas." I said and winked.

"Any new fans?" Sebastian teased.

"Well, it's probably a good thing that I use my pen name Martin Lundqvist on the books, instead of Martin Orchard." I said and pointed my tongue out cheekily.

"Your books are not that bad. I've read several of them." Sebastian replied.

"That's because I paid you to narrate the Spanish translations," I remarked.

"The payments certainly helped to keep me interested," Sebastian admitted and laughed.

A waiter came in with dessert, and I realised that I wouldn't get fitter today either, when I saw the selection of desserts. After finishing everyone's desserts, Sebastian unbuckled his belt and spoke, "Peew! That was a lot to eat! so, where are you guys visiting in Colombia? I am happy to take you around. I offer mate's rates!"

"Cool. I am open to suggestions; we want to visit many places but we need to be in Valle de Los Muertos by next Thursday." I replied.

Hearing this, Sebastian's playful attitude disappeared, and he looked at me with a worried face. "Valle de Los Muertos? Why on Earth would you want to go there?"

"Oh. I thought that I told you. I came to Colombia to look for the alien artefact that can be found on leap years in the Guane people's territory." I replied.

"Well, I am happy to show you other parts of Colombia, but I cannot take you there," Sebastian said.

"Why is that? Do you have an angry ex-girlfriend living there?" I teased.

"A cartel led by the infamous Andres Juarez controls that region. He is the most brutal drug lord ever to torment my beautiful country. You'd be crazy to go there." Sebastian warned.

"Alright. Let's catch up tomorrow, and you can direct us to some better destinations." I replied as I didn't want to discuss the matter closer.

"Very well. I'll see you guys tomorrow." Sebastian said as we paid and left the restaurant.

"WHAT SHALL WE DO?" Elaine fretted.

"We'll have to proceed as planned. The temple is only visible once every four years. Neither Rangda nor I can accept a four-year-delay in our mission because of some drug lord's dominance." I replied.

"Is that you or Rangda speaking? She has never spoken to me; I only hear about her from you." Elaine stated.

"The two of us are in agreement on this matter," I stated.

Elaine seemed nervous, and she paced over to the kettle in our hotel room. "Would you like some hot cuppa?" Elaine asked.

I looked at her sceptically and replied. "Yes, but let's not change the topic."

"Okay, so you insist on going? Then we should get some help at least." Elaine urged.

"What do you suggest?" I asked.

"Well, Josefina Fiero is running one of the largest companies in South America. Perhaps she can send some people to help us." Elaine suggested.

I considered Elaine's idea. I hadn't heard from Josefina since our meeting in Peru the previous year. She had helped me back then, but she had also planted secret cameras in the equipment that she had given us. And what about the helicopter she had sent looking for us? In my paranoid state after the Zetans drone attack, I had assumed that she had sent men to kill us. But if that had been the case, she would have tried again at some stage. Nonetheless, I didn't trust Josefina, and I didn't want to involve her in my current mission.

"No. I don't trust Josefina. Besides, we are better off visiting Valle de Los Muertos on our own. Bringing armed guards will only get us more public attention." I said.

"You are right, we get enough attention as it is. We don't blend in here in South America, you being so blonde and Scandinavian and me being Asian." Elaine replied.

"Ah-huh. We better get some guns for our own protection. Let's organise this trip tomorrow." I said and drank my sweet tea.

"Yes, let's rest. We have busy days ahead of us." Elaine replied and we went to bed snugged together.

WE WERE HAVING LUNCH at a local restaurant in the jungle of Valle de Los Muertos. It was a rainy season, so the jungle was humid and hot, and it was not a great time for sightseeing. But we were here on a mission. To-morrow, the secret door to the lost Guane temple would open. It was a door carved into one of the mountains that surrounded the valley, hidden right behind leafy green grass and rocky walls, deep inside woodland of chestnut trees.

We had just finished our meals when trouble entered in the form of two local enforcers for the Juarez cartel. I looked down at my food, hoping that they wouldn't notice me. As it turned out, my hopes were in vain, and a bearded man wielding a machete approached me.

The man stopped uncomfortably close to me and spoke. "Hey, Gringo! Who gave you permission to visit this region?"

The man's breath stank of booze, he had scars and tattoos all over his face, and his gold teeth and muscular body made his clenched jaws extra fearsome.

"We are here as tourists. We just want to visit this beautiful place and hike around. I can show you my passport and the stamp from immigration." I replied.

"Bullshit! No tourists ever come here. You are CIA dogs. I know it!" The man roared.

"Look. If this is about money... I am willing to pay you." I replied.

The gangster's response came in the form of a fist to my face that knocked me to the floor.

"Money? Do you think this is about money? Fucking white dog! Andres Juarez has more money than he can spend. This is about protecting our turf. You were pissing on us when you entered our territory without our permission!" The gangster shouted.

I tried to get up, but I collapsed in a heap when the other gangster ran up to me and kicked me in the chest.

'Danger, danger' The Zetan Monocle displayed. 'No shit!' I thought.

'Authorise lethal force.' I sent to the monocle, and the combat mode opened, which slowed down my perception of time. I rolled around, and I grabbed the small revolver, which I had holstered at my ankle, snuggly hidden behind my ankle high boots.

The targeting indicators showed that I would aim for the head of my enemies. I was angry, and I wanted them to suffer. I shot the testicles of the man who had kicked me and then swiftly did the same thing to the gangster with the machete.

I got up on my feet, and I shot both my adversaries in the kneecaps. Then I picked up the machete and slammed it into the shoulder of the machete-wielding man, pinning him to the floor.

"Let's go!" I shouted to Elaine.

"What were you doing? You didn't need to kill them." Elaine shouted back.

"Those assholes didn't deserve living!" I roared.

"But what if the police come?" Elaine asked.

"I'd worry more about the cartel! Let's hurry to the Guane Temple. We need to grab the artefact and get the hell out of here!" I urged.

Elaine didn't argue. We ran to our rented jeep and left the scene.

"WHY ISN'T ANYTHING happening?" Elaine asked in disappointment.

I stared at the empty cave wall looking for an answer. We were in the right place, and from the inscriptions in Pachamama's white veil, a secret Zetan temple would reveal at this location. Of course, the temple wouldn't reveal itself, lest it wouldn't be a hidden temple, but there would be a way to find it.

We had deciphered the code to open the door in the time that had passed since our Peruvian expedition. At least we thought that we had. Since there was no Rosetta stone for the Zetan language, all our speculations were guesswork, and I hated to think that we might be wrong.

I reassured myself. Even if Elaine and I had not understood the Zetan language, there would be one that knew, Rangda. I contacted her to find out why the Zetan text wasn't visible.

"Rangda. I am certain that we are in the right spot. Why isn't the Zetan symbols visible?" I asked. *"You bloody fool. You should wait until midnight."* Rangda hissed.

"What are you talking about? It's ten minutes past midnight?" I replied.

"The Zetan temple is aligned to solar midnight. Humans are using time zones, giving a large area of the Earth the same time. But that is incorrect. Your area will have astronomical midnight in ten minutes." Rangda revealed and disconnected from my mind.

"It's okay, Elaine. I spoke to Rangda. The Zetan code will show in ten minutes." I reassured.

"I hope you're right. I want to get out of this place. We are in serious trouble." Elaine replied.

I nodded but didn't say anything. A few more minutes of waiting and then we'd find the artefact hidden behind that cliffside.

A few minutes later, I felt excited when luminescent Zetan symbols appeared on the cave wall. This was it. Now I needed to decipher the code using the monocle and the hints from the Zetan tattoo on my arm. Then we'd find the passageway to the Zetan temple, which would hopefully contain the primordial Zeto Crystal.

'Danger, danger' my monocle displayed, and I heard a voice. "Hijo de puta! Hey motherfucker!"

I turned around, and I saw a large group of cartel members dressed in combat gear, aiming their assault rifles at us.

'Likelihood of surviving armed encounter is extremely low. You're recommended to surrender.' The monocle displayed. I glanced at Elaine. It seemed that she had received the same recommendation. "We surrender!" I shouted to the armed men, and I raised my arms up in the air. A few of them walked down to subdue us.

"What is that blue text?" One of the men asked.

"It's just blue luminescent paint. We are making phony documentaries for the internet." I replied.

"Whatever, motherfucker. The boss wants to see you, and you won't like it!" The man threatened

After saying this, the man hit me in the back of the head with the stock of his rifle, knocking me unconscious.

I WOKE UP FROM SHOCK when someone poured a bucket of icy water over me. I was in my underwear, tied to a chair. A greasy South American man sweating in his expensive suit smiled menacingly towards me.

"Mr Orchard. I assume you are not feeling so tough now?" The man grunted like a mad pig.

"I have been better. I assume you're the boss around here, Andres Juarez?" I asked.

"Hahaha! Yes. And you must be a CIA agent sent here to cause me trouble. Is that why you have come here, Mr Orchard?" Andres taunted.

I didn't respond. I had no time for this bloody conversation. I needed to open the Zetan temple while it was still the correct date in the Guane people calendar. If I missed this opportunity, I would have to wait for another four years. The last thing that I wanted was a four-year-delay!

"I don't have time for this shit. I have places to be. Let me go now, and nobody will get hurt." I threatened.

As expected, my terrible attempt at diplomacy didn't work out. Although to be fair, I don't think any diplomacy would work when you are the prisoner of a drug lord, especially after killing some of his men. Andres swung at me with a mighty haymaker punch hitting me over the monocle. The force from the blow knocked me to the ground. As I hit the ground, I heard the sound of a crack, indicating that the chair I was bound to had been broken.

As I got back to my senses, I looked up and I noticed that Andres was in pain. He had burned his hand from hitting the invisible forcefield that protected the monocle.

"Puta! What fucking CIA technology is that? I burnt my hand, you motherfucker!" Andres shouted.

"You think this is CIA technology? This is Zetan technology controlled by the Xeno Empress Rangda Kaliankan. You have signed your own death warrant, Andres!" I shouted.

"Shut the fuck up, American dog!" Andres' henchman exclaimed and kicked me in the kidney. Ouch!

"Bring the wife," Andres said to one of his men.

A few minutes later, Andres' henchman dragged Elaine into the room.

"Mr Orchard. You have been misbehaving. I will rape your wife in front of your eyes. Then I'll kill the two of you slowly! This will send a message to the CIA to stop sending people after me!" Andres grunted like a rabies-ridden pig.

I realised that the only way to get out of this was to invoke Rangda.

"Rangda. Please help me. I need you to get me out of this mess. I want you to help me kill them all, kill the whole bloody cartel, and save my dear Elaine" I pleaded.

"So, you are giving in to your rage? Excellent, I will help you. Let me take control of your body." Rangda responded.

After that, I felt how my blood was surging through my veins. I gained an extreme strength and power. I ripped the ropes that bound me, and then I grabbed the closest henchman and used him as a human shield. I grabbed the pistol from his holster and shot Andres between the eyes before he had the time to react. The other henchmen fired at me with their submachine guns, but my human shield took all their bullets.

I shoved the lifeless corpse in front of me and swiftly fired off four head-shots, killing all the coked-up rookies in the room.

"Set your monocle to combat mode, maximum casualties!" I shouted to Elaine.

"But it states excessive collateral damage, I can't turn it to combat mode!" Elaine panicked.

"Don't worry about that. We need to get out of here. We need to fight!" I roared.

Elaine grabbed a submachine gun and some magazines. Then she dodged as more adversaries had reached the scene and bullets were flying around our heads.

"What do we do?" Elaine whimpered.

I slowed down my perception of time using the predictive capabilities of the monocle. If we were to fight our way through, we would minimise collateral damage. But then we would have less than 20% chance of survival. If we took the zipline down to the military attack helicopter in the middle of the compound and fired off all the weapon systems. Then we would face catastrophic civilian casualties, but our survival rate would be 78 %.

I fired back at the closest militiaman and killed him, and then I shouted. "We'll take the zipline route. Get on my back!"

I got up to the window and grabbed hold of the zipline with both my arms. Elaine got on my back, holding on to me with her legs and one arm while firing her submachine gun at our enemies with her other hand. The terrible noise of the submachine gun deafened me and made the whole battlefield seem surreal.

At the end of our zip line ride, we fell to the ground close to the attack helicopter. A militiaman attacked us with a machete. I dodged his strike and slammed him in the head with Elaine's empty gun. Then I ran to the helicopter. I smashed the window with the stock of my rifle, and I got in.

I couldn't control the helicopter as bullets were whizzing around me like angry bumblebees. Instead, I was crawling on the floor of the helicopter. I flipped all the switches, and I fired off all the weapon systems aimlessly.

After a few seconds of cacophony, I looked up, and I saw corpses and fires all over the complex.

"Get in the chopper!" I shouted to Elaine, but she shook her head.

"It's no use. You destroyed the helicopter." Elaine replied.

I realised that she was right.

"Come with me, there is a functional car over there!" Elaine shouted and ran towards the car.

I followed her, and we got to a limousine with many bullet holes and the dead driver sitting in the driver's seat.

"I'll drive!" Elaine shouted, and she threw the dead driver out of the car, while I leaned back in the passenger seat.

Elaine drove the limousine to the main gate of the compound. I witnessed the destruction that the attack helicopter had caused on the nearby village. Stray rockets and missile from the helicopter had caused several buildings to explode. The explosions had caused the cocaine and meth labs to destabilise and blow up as a wildfire spread across the valley.

"Elaine, I don't feel too well!" I wheezed as I noticed the multitude of bullet holes riddling my body.

"Hold on, we are getting out of here!" Elaine shouted as she was driving towards the serpentine road up the mountain, which was the only way out of the valley.

"More trouble!" I wheezed as several cartel members on motorbikes were firing after us with their submachine guns.

Suddenly, time slowed down to an almost standstill. My monocle revealed the hidden pistol in the glovebox compartment of the car. As I picked up the gun, a few tiny targets appeared on top of the hill on my monocle. I fired instinctively without thinking.

As time reverted back to normal, I realised what I had done. My monocle was still set to cause maximum damage. So, instead of shooting the pursuing cartel members, I had destroyed a large fuel cistern causing it to flood down the hill with petrol. The petrol caught fire when it hit the flames below and it engulfed the motorbikes in pursuit of us.

In the last second, I grabbed the steering wheel from Elaine, and I caused our car to drive off a cliff into a small lake to avoid the fire.

The impact from the car crash knocked me unconscious.

"YOU CREATED A MASSIVE mess, Mr Orchard."

I opened my eyes, and I was in a windowless, advanced medical facility. Elaine, James Winter, Josefina Fiero and Pierre Beaumont were in the room.

"What happened, James?" I mumbled.

"You caused a big mess, and you died. You have been dead for days." James replied.

"I don't understand?" I asked.

"Your death is unremarkable. You got hit with many bullets, and your car crashed into a lake. I don't know whether the bullets, the crash, or the drowning caused your demise, but in the big scheme of things, it's irrelevant." James stated.

"But I am not dead?" I remarked.

"Yes, your resurrection is a miracle. Elaine asked us to bring her and your body out of Colombia. You were dead. We put your body on ice, and we were planning to do a thorough autopsy. That's when Pierre called us and said that he wanted to resurrect you with a special type of blue crystal. Somehow, the crystal that did nothing to other corpses, brought you back from the dead." James revealed.

I was silent for a few seconds and took it all in. Eventually, I spoke. "So, what happens now?"

I noticed that tears were running down Elaine's cheeks, and she spoke. "I am leaving you, Martin. I fulfilled my marriage obligation and I stayed with you until death did us apart."

"But, I am not dead now though." I objected.

"I know, and that is what makes this so painful to me. The wildfire, which you started during the battle with Andres Juarez, burned down the entire village. This killed hundreds of innocents. I know that you chose to accept collateral damage during the battle to increase your chance of survival. It wasn't right. I saw the devastation that occurred. Small children were dying from burns and suffocation. All this because you value your life higher than that of your fellow humans." Elaine ranted.

"But I did it to save you as well." I replied.

Elaine wiped her tears and replied. "I know, and I still love you. But I cannot wake up next to the man who will give me constant nightmares about burnt children. Besides, I have some new goals."

I nodded and replied. "I understand. What are your new goals?"

Elaine's face shifted, and she looked proud as she replied. "Well, Pierre and Josefina made me realise my true potential and what I am meant to achieve."

"I see and what is that?" I asked.

"It's time for me to crush my duplicitous uncles. It's time for me to take control over the Harapan Conglomerate and elevate my fellow comrades to glory." Elaine proclaimed.

"Okay. I wish you the best of luck." I replied.

"Thanks. I am leaving now. But I'll always be your friend. Let's keep in touch and let me know if you ever need any help." Elaine said.

After that, Elaine left the room.

"I am leaving as well. As charming as you guys are, I have a business to run, and I am already late for my flight. Can I expect continued support from the CIA and the World Bank?" Josefina asked.

"Yes, for as long as our interests coincide," Pierre assured.

"And they will. I wouldn't fight the mightiest puppet masters on the planet." Josefina heckled, bowed theatrically and left the room.

"So, what about me?" I sighed.

"Well, I hope that our interests will match as well," Pierre said.

"And what are your interests?" I asked.

"Well, your resurrection is a miracle. We need to study you in this secret facility." James replied.

"And I suppose it would be detrimental for me if our interests don't coincide?" I taunted.

"Yes, that would be extremely unwise on your behalf," James replied.

"But don't worry. Your stay here will not be that long. After helping us with our research, you are free to go." Pierre added in.

I sighed. Coming back from the dead to get dumped by my wife and then getting locked up in a medical facility as a guinea pig. What a terrible resurrection experience!

Chapter 9: South Africa, October 2023.

I was sitting in my hotel room, situated on a hill overlooking the magnificent Kruger National Park in South Africa. I had always wanted to see the majestic wildlife of the African savannah. Now when I was finally free from CIA's secret medical facility, it was time to tick this thing off my bucket list.

I closed my eyes, and Ellen Hines was flashing in front of my eyes. How crazy was that? The woman I had a short tryst with almost five years earlier had affected my decision to go to South Africa. My decision to visit the Kruger National Park was my justification for stalking the rendezvous from five years ago. I shook off the thought of seeing her again. I was here because I loved the majestic African wildlife. The possibility to reconnect with the beautiful Ellen after my painful separation with Elaine was just wishful thinking.

I had met up with Elaine in Jakarta before coming here. She had used her uncles' deceit and paranoia to her advantage and manipulated them into eliminating each other. In the end, Elaine had become the only heir to the company. She had achieved this by taking justice with her own hands and brought them to a deserving and humiliating defeat. I had questioned Elaine's morals. To me, it was the same thing whether she had killed them herself, or manipulated her uncles into killing each other, to become the leader of Harapan Conglomerate. Elaine had become furious and told me that her evil uncles had deserved to die, as they had stolen her father's inheritance when he died, two years earlier. I had left Indonesia the following day, when all the legal papers were settled. I realised that Elaine had a fair point, and that I shouldn't have said anything.

Thinking of Elaine, I closed my eyes. I loved her dearly, but the curse that she spoke of affected me as well. Instead of seeing Elaine, I saw the charred remains of dead children and burning villages. With hurt and trauma between us, things could never be okay again.

I poured a large glass of scotch from the mini bar in my hotel room, closed my eyes, and thought of Ellen Hines. When the darkness closed in on me, my mind needed a sanctuary. Ellen was that sanctuary, she provided me with feelings of excitement, passion, and joy. I finished my drink, lay down in my bed, and experienced another night of orgasmic masturbation while thinking of her luscious hair, beautiful face and the faint smell of her body which I never seemed to forget.

"MR ORCHARD. YOU ARE my only customer today." The tour guide, Chim Mwanza, said to me.

"Fair enough, but I didn't book a private tour. Where are the rest of the travellers?" I objected.

"I am sorry, sir. All the tourists have stopped coming. You were the only person keen to come to this place." Chim replied.

I sighed. I had been rushing to get away from my disappointing reunion with Elaine, and I hadn't done my research. South Africa was on the verge of civil war, it was full of terrorists and was in the state of chaos. It was the last place that any sane person would want to go to. Somehow, I had found myself in trouble again.

"Take this, Sir!" Chim said and handed me a hunting rifle.

"I am here to watch the wildlife, not kill them," I argued, while rejecting the weapon.

"This is a dangerous area. We need weapons to be safe. We need to keep ourselves safe from animals and other forms of danger." Chim warned, with his thick African accent.

"I understand. Thank you." I said as I took the rifle from Chim and carefully put it to my side.

'Fucking hell! What have I gotten myself into?' I swore to myself as we got into Chim's Jeep that would take us around the park.

As Chim drove around the park, I noticed the complete lack of wildlife. Well, except for small common critters that you could see anywhere else. Eventually, I had enough of the awkward silence and started speaking.

"What is going on? Where are all the animals that I am here to see?" I complained.

"They are closer to the centre of the park, Sir. I am sure there are more wildlife there. But I'm afraid to go there as that's a very dangerous area." Chim replied.

"How is that? The animals won't get to us in the car. I didn't come here to watch deer, rabbits, and common birds. Drive over to that area!" I urged.

"That area is full of poachers and criminals. It's not safe for us to visit, Sir." Chim replied.

"What about the park rangers, aren't they hired to stop the poachers?" I quipped.

Chim gave me a nervous look and replied. "I think you are not very up to date about South Africa's political condition, Sir Mr Orchard."

"I don't give a shit about your domestic policies. I came to see big animals." I replied.

"Alright. To make you aware of the situation. the World Bank wanted the South African government to give up all of our mines as collateral for their debts. Our government refused, and a few days later the media reported about several alleged human rights violations. This caused international protest and UN sanctions to stop tourism, destroying our economy. Many of the park rangers quit their jobs, and some even joined the poachers. There are no one left to protect the animals in the park, most have been killed off or sold to the Zoos." Chim revealed.

I ground my teeth in frustration. All these needless killings of majestic animals because some rich Chinese prick thought that ground rhino horn could give him an instant boner? Because some other rich cunt felt high and mighty with elephant ivory decorations and lion fur drapery hanging all over his 6-bedroom luxurious townhouse? I couldn't deal with these rich fuckwits, but I could kill some poachers to vent my anger and to teach the others a lesson.

"Hey Chim, do you love the animals of Kruger National Park?" I shouted.

My loud and aggressive stance scared Chim, who stopped the car and got out.

"I can't hear you. Answer my question." I yelled.

"Yes, Sir!" Chim mumbled.

"Speak louder!" I yelled again.

"Yes, I love the wild animals, and I hate the poachers who have betrayed what they once stood for, and they are now killing these animals for money!" Chim exclaimed.

"Good!" I replied.

"So, what do I do now?" Chim asked.

"We'll leave the park to get some equipment. Tonight, we will return to kill these scumbags and show the world that people are willing to stand up for what is right." I preached.

"You are insane, but you are right. Sir. Let's do it your way." Chim said while smiling away showing his perfectly white set of teeth, in contrast with his very dark but glowy skin.

"You'll love it. Let's keep going!" I said and Chim drove towards the dangerous area.

"WHY WOULD I CARE IF poachers are killing the animals for money? It's the natural order that humans kill them and eat them." Rangda ranted, while Chim was busy driving the Jeep further into the dangerous territory.

I waited to contact Rangda again, until we reached a strategic position, close to the dead body of a headless rhino.

"Empress Rangda. These filthy humans are killing these animals and leaving the meat to spoil. It makes me furious that the meat goes to waste. Please give me the strength to kill some of the poachers so that others will fear me." I said to Rangda.

Rangda went silent for a while. Eventually, she replied, *"You are correct. Let us kill these blasphemous and greedy pigs. Let the hunters be the hunted. Let's embrace the bloodlust that you carry deep within yourself. Heeheeeeheeee!"*

"As you wish, Empress. I will contact you when I am outside their camp and need your assistance." I said.

I walked over to Chim, who stared at me in awe. "Who were you whispering to, Sir? You are possessed, aren't you? We believe in the supernatural, and I think you are speaking to a ghost," Chim asked.

"I am speaking to the goddess of vengeance. Let's avenge your wildlife. Let's kill the greedy pigs who have betrayed your values." I stated.

Chim seemed hesitant, but eventually, he spoke. "I'll help you, Sir Martin Orchard. I am a dead man anyway, as I cannot afford to pay my HIV medication since no tourists are coming here anymore. I might as well die knowing that I have helped kill some poachers."

"Excellent. If we get through this alive, I'll pay for your medication. Now let's go!" I urged.

AFTER NIGHTFALL, WE snuck into the poacher's camp. I had attached a night-vision camera to my outfit. I was going to record my killings on video and broadcast it on the internet using an anonymous account. There was no point in killing these poachers if their deaths weren't made public, as it wouldn't scare off other poachers. My identity, however, had to remain hidden, so I covered my face with a mask and I equipped a voice distorter to change my pitch. "Attack from the far end of the camp," I whispered to Chim.

I turned on 'combat mode: stealthy approach' on my monocle, and I snuck up on the closest poacher. I slit his throat with the knife in my right arm, while I covered his mouth with my left hand so that he couldn't scream. After a short struggle, he lay dead on the ground, and I dragged the corpse to the cover of darkness.

Suddenly, I heard loud shouting and gunfire. I realised that Chim had stuffed up and that I needed to change my approach. I adjusted my monocle to 'combat mode, maximum casualties.' I pulled up my two pistols, and I ran towards the campfire in the middle of the camp. I shot the two men near the fireplace in the back as they were facing Chim's direction. After that, I shot a few holes in the camps fuel tank, and picked up a burning ember from the campfire and chucked it at the tank. This caused a massive explosion.

I grimaced in pain, what a stupid idea it was to pick up embers with my bare hand. On the bright side, the explosion had set the camp on fire, and several of the poachers were set ablaze. I picked up an AK47 from a fallen poacher and shot the tents, killing anyone that were inside. Using my monocle, I was truly unbeatable. I ran to Chim, who was on the ground, severely wounded.

"Sir Martin Orchard, please help me. I don't want to die." Chim whimpered.

"I am sorry, Chim," I said and shot him in the head with my pistol, sparing him of his pain.

I studied the scene via my monocle. There were seven dead and fifteen wounded poachers on the ground. I could kill them one by one, but I had a better plan for poetic justice.

I went to the enclosed area where the captured lions were kept, and I opened the gate. That would give the poachers justice, letting the lions eat these people alive. I got back into my jeep. From there, I watched how the lions and hyenas were amassing for a well-deserved meal. After that, I started the vehicle and drove out of the park, returning to my hotel.

OH SHIT! THE VIDEO recording! Fucking hell!!

I had taken the overnight train to Cape Town, and I was now in a predicament. That damn recording was evidence against me. In Chim's recording, he had mentioned my name and I had mentioned his. It wouldn't be hard for the authorities to figure out who I was from the records that Chim was a tour guide and I was one of his customers.

I wrapped the bandage and the soothing lotion around my burned hand. What had I been thinking? Of course, Chim would stuff up the covert attack. He was a regular dude dying from HIV. He wasn't a seasoned killer, aided by alien technology. Why did I even care? I loved eating meat, and I wasn't a fanatical advocate for animal rights.

I realised that I had projected my own pain and aggression towards the poachers. I had murdered them to fill the void within myself. I had acted the way I did because I could behave that way. I had already been dead once, so

I did not experience the fear of dying. This freed up my mind for better or worse, and made me feel justified.

I pondered my options. I realised that I should get out of South Africa as soon as possible. My best option was to hide in a country, which was on bad terms with the South African government, so I wouldn't get extradited.

But I had come here with a mission. I needed to see Ellen Hines, the mysterious and beautiful woman I had a short tryst with. she was the only ray of light in my dark and puzzled mind.

I disconnected my monocle and inserted a blue-tinted lens to cover my purple predator eye. I had caused enough damage. When the police came for me, it was better if I wasn't aided by alien technology.

I walked out of the train station, and I ordered a cab to Ellen's house in the affluent Baileys Muckleneuk suburb.

I WAS SITTING IN THE coffee shop across the road from Ellen's luxurious mansion. My obsession with her had driven me here, but now that I was here, I felt like an idiot. What good would it do, to knock on Ellen's door and introduce myself? Did she even remember me, and if she did, what did I hope to achieve by meeting her?

I realised that if I loved Ellen, or whatever I called my obsession, I should step away and allow her to live a happy life. While I was wealthy, I was also mentally damaged. I was responsible for hundreds of deaths, and possessed by an evil extra-terrestrial deity. This was not the perfect circumstances to become a good partner.

I kept looking at the house, and I saw a man playing with a young blonde girl at the front yard. Could that be Ellen's daughter? Could that be mine? If so, that was another good reason for me to stay.

I was about to leave the coffee shop when a servant from Ellen's luxurious mansion approached the establishment. The maid spoke to the cashier. "I am here to collect the cake for the Hines household, Miss," she said with a thick African accent.

"Of course, It's right here. That will be 300 Rand," the cashier said.

The maid paid for the cake, and as the cashier brought the cake, I quickly glanced at it. The icing on the cake read, '20th October 2023. Happy Fourth Birthday, Sabina My Dear.'

This stunned me. Thinking back, I knew I had a tryst with Ellen in Egypt on the 2nd of February 2019. This date was stuck in my head for years.

Counting from the time that Sabina was born, which would have been 20th October 2019, she could very much be my daughter. The realisation stunned me, and I didn't know how to react.

Loud screaming and sounds of gunfire from the streets brought me back to my senses.

"The SVAPO movement has arrived!! They hate white people! You cannot stay here any longer, you must leave!!" The cashier trembled.

Hearing this, I ran to the backdoor of the cafeteria. I inserted my monocle, set it to 'Avoid Confrontation', and I escaped the scene unharmed.

I WATCHED THE BIG TV screen at Cape Town International Airport. All the regular flights had been cancelled, and people were screaming and yelling. I looked at another screen, which was showing the local news. The terrible images made me freeze. SVAPO rebels had butchered several affluent white families. One of the pictures was of a young blonde girl. Could that be Sabina, my potential daughter? In any case, I needed to get the hell out of here.

Suddenly, I saw a familiar face enter the terminal. It was Ben Yehuda.

I ran towards him and spoke. "Ben Yehuda. What are you doing here?" I wondered.

"The Israeli government have assigned me to rescue our Jewish South African brethren from this chaos. Is this your doing?" Ben Yehuda said and looked at me sternly.

"Of course not. I am just looking to get the hell out of here." I replied.

Ben twirled his moustache and looked cunningly at me. "I'm sceptical, Mr Orchard. Apparently, SVAPO rebels killed those white people as an act of revenge. A white man murdered the SVAPO leader Amadi Aren in Kruger

National Park, just the other day. SVAPO claims that the murderer was a white man and he was accompanied by an African tour guide." Ben revealed.

I froze, and I didn't say anything. My head was spinning, and I had to take it all in. Had my decision to kill the poachers indirectly caused the massacres of these people, and possibly the death of Ellen and her daughter?

Ben spoke again. "Look, I know it was you who killed the leader, Amadi. SVAPO is a terrorist organisation, and their claims have no credibility in the eyes of the law. As soon as you're out of South Africa, you'll be safe. How unfortunate that all those flights are cancelled."

"Ben. Please help me!" I pleaded.

"Oh, so now you want my help? You didn't seem very keen during our last meeting." Ben mocked.

"Circumstances change!" I replied.

"They do. You're in luck. Despite your shortcomings, I still believe you would be a suitable candidate to lead the Knights Templar." Ben replied.

"Thank you, Ben. I owe you big time." I replied.

"More than you can dream of. You'll need a new identity, and I still want you to join our Knight Templars. As a matter of fact, I have already made up a name for you. From now on, you'll go under the name Martin Al-Sham, you will be one of us." Ben replied

"I accept this offer. Thank you, Ben," I replied, not knowing where to go.

Ben didn't have the time to reply as a massive explosion struck the building, and the shockwave knocked us to the ground. Ben pulled me up and shouted. "Get up, Al-Sham. Time to go."

We rushed to a private jet plane that Ben had organised, and from the air we saw the chaos that the fighting between SVAPO and the South African government had caused.

Oh boy, I should have left those poachers alone!

Chapter 10: Rome, March 2025

"Ahh! Yes!!"

I sighed in relief as I ejaculated after my 30-minutes intercourse with the trashy and methed out local whore, Fabiana Diamante.

I sniffed another line of meth that was lying on the table, and rolled over to the side of the bed and stared into the ceiling. It had been a while since I had sex, as my assignment with the Templars had kept me busy. But since today was my 40th birthday, I have decided to treat myself to a 3 hours long whore-fucking session. Five pills of Viagra, 1g of meth and acid, random fucking with three Russian whores, plenty of intoxicating drinks, and playing Russian poker. Things could not have been better for the 40-year old sad and lonely me.

As I looked at the other two Russian whores that were sleeping soundly while laying naked on the bed, I had a moment of realisation and burst of random angst. Didn't the whores look noticeably younger comparing to their profile photos that were posted on the dating app UberFucks? I struggled to keep my eyes open as I had taken a little too much acid and meth.

"Hrmphhhh, Fabiana. How old are you again?" I mumbled.

"I am 22, suga' babe" Fabiana responded with her fake American accent, while smoking a lit-up slim cigarette and crossing her long slender bare legs.

I brushed my suspicions aside. I had enough on my mind to worry about the age of consent and the actual age of these young sex workers. They could very well be only 16, now that realisation surged in after the sensation of orgasmic sex was over, but my mind chose to ignore it. "Can you please bring me a glass of bourbon and coke from the minibar and then give me a massage, sweetie?" I asked and handed Fabiana a stash of 100 Euro banknotes.

"Yes, hunny. I'll be right back." Fabiana replied while jumping skittishly to the mini bar.

I closed my eyes, relaxed, and fell asleep as I felt her tiny little fingers worked through my sore back muscles. The other two slightly older looking prostitutes were still soundly sleeping. There were worse things in life.

WHEN I OPENED MY EYES, I was up for a rude awakening. Instead of seeing the face of the sweet Russian girl, Fabiana, massaging my aching shoulders, I was face-to-face with the Yehuda Brothers. None of the girls were seen in the room. I must have slept for some time. Was there a sleeping pill in that drink that she gave me?

"Hrmmpph!! Cover your fucking cock, Martin!" Szymon Yehuda snarked and threw a towel to cover my crotch.

I gasped, bound the towel around my crotch and got up immediately.

"So, is this how you celebrate your 40th birthday, indulging in cheap whores and recreational drugs!" Ben mocked.

"Gaaah! What would you have me do?" I argued back.

"Well, as a Knight's Templar, I'd prefer if you prayed and sought spiritual enlightenment," Ben replied.

"Very funny. Why did you come to see me?" I asked.

Szymon handed me a tablet and spoke. "There is going to be a terrorist attack against Pope Septimus today. The Salafist leader Salman Bin Saladin is not happy with the Pope's effort to reconcile religious differences between the Muslims and Catholics."

"Why do I give a shit? I don't even like the man." I replied.

"Because this can end in several ways. In the best of worlds, you'll stop the terrorist attack and our Templar Knights movement will gain Papal recognition. But if the attack succeeds, we'll experience international wars and upheavals between these two religions. Whatever the outcome is, we cannot accept that you are here copulating with prostitutes instead of doing your rightful duty. I am sure the Catholic followers wouldn't appreciate if that news spread. Since you are a spy working for us, we cannot have them thinking that you are complicit in the attack." Ben threatened.

"So, what do you want me to do?" I asked.

"The attack will take place today at 6pm during Palm Sunday Mass in the Vatican City. That gives you six hours from now. Find James and Michael and brief them on the situation. They are waiting for you in Santa Maria Church." Szymon replied.

'Sprankkkk!' Our conversation was interrupted when Fabiana appeared from behind the curtains, breaking the drink glasses upon seeing the Yehuda Brothers. Her legs were trembling with fear.

"Oh baby! Who are those scary men?" Fabiana shouted in her broken Russian English.

Szymon looked at Fabiana lustfully and replied, "We are business partners of Martin. Unfortunately, he has some urgent business to attend to, but I am happy to fill his slot. I assume he has already paid your service. Now it's our turn to have fun!" Szymon licked his lips excitedly.

Fabiana looked at me, and she replied to Szymon. "Of course, handsome Sir. I am happy to make more money. Let me have a shower, and I'll tell my colleagues to come out. They are hiding in the bathroom."

I left the brothel feeling very annoyed. It was typical of self-righteous devout Jewish people to first reprimand sinners and then act the same way themselves. Szimon and Ben Yehuda were truly a bunch of hypocrites!

AS I ARRIVED IN VATICAN City, I found Michael and James kneeling in front of a statue of the Virgin Mary. What a waste of time religion was, kneeling in front of a dead statue when there were other better things to do. But I had to play along with the charade. I was the leader of the Knights Templar Order, and as such, I needed to act like an extremely devout Catholic. It didn't matter that the unholy alliance between the World Bank and the Mossad had secretly funded our movement, we still had tasks to do.

"Michael, James. We need to go!" I said.

Michael turned around and spoke. "Greetings, Grandmaster Martin Al-Sham. Where have you been?"

I wasn't about to tell them the truth, so instead I replied, "I have been to a meeting with some Vatican policemen. They received tips from some Jewish spies that there will be an attack against the Pope today. We need to prevent the attack to gain Papal recognition."

James gave me a worried expression and spoke. "Martin, I am worried about you. You are too trusting towards the Jews. We are devout Catholics, serving our Lord through The Knights Templar Order. Do not correlate with the traitors who murdered our Saviour Jesus Christ."

I thought of telling James that I was in reality one of those spies myself, but instead I replied, "Don't blame the Jews for the death of Jesus Christ, our Saviour. His death and resurrection were what proved his divinity to humankind."

"Amen! Glory to Christ, Grandmaster Al-Sham!" James replied.

'Damn, if we could stop wasting time with these empty bullshit sentences.' I thought. But instead, I replied. "Amen! Glory to Our Christ, Brother James!"

To my relief, Michael got to the point. "So, this supposed attack. What do we know about it?"

"According to the Vatican police, terrorists sponsored by Muslim leader Salman Bin Saladin will attack the Pope tonight. The attack will take place during the Palm Sunday Mass at 6pm. The lives of the Pope and hundreds of others are at risk. We need to find and stop the terrorists now!" I stated.

James and Michael looked at each other. They didn't seem surprised over my revelation. Had someone else already briefed them, or did they have other means of finding out? "Martin, I don't think saving the life of Pope Septimus is in the best interest of our order. Leave this to the hands of the Vatican police force," Michael said.

Before I had the time to reply, Rangda spoke inside my head. *"Michael is correct. What good is seeking understanding and Papal reconciliation, what good does it bring to a group of warrior monks such as yourself? Letting him being killed my Muslim terrorists opens more opportunities for you to excel."*

"Stop influencing my mind, goddammit!" I roared.

Michael and James stared at me in disbelief. Damn, I had to stop arguing with Rangda when other people were around. I cleared my throat and spoke. "I have been thinking about inaction. But what you are suggesting is treason, as it is our duty to protect the innocents, and many innocents will die."

to which James responded with, "Yes, but we are not equipped with the right artillery to fight, leave it to the Vatican militia."

I sighed. I wasn't going to argue with my subordinates when they spoke my words. Pope Septimus needed to go, and the collateral damage was a necessary sacrifice. "Okay, Michael. What do you suggest?"

"Cardinal Jose Santamaria won't be attending tonight's mass. We will plant evidence that he was conspiring against the Holy See. That will destroy him and discredit every Catholic who suggests peace with the Muslims." Michael replied.

"I am sure you have something in mind for me to do?" I asked sarcastically.

Michael bent a knee and bowed to me with fake humility. "I would never dream of commanding you, Grandmaster Martin Al-Sham. The only ones who can command you are the Pope and God." Michael said.

I shook my head and struggled to contain my irritation. Bloody sycophants. "Okay, what would you suggest that I ask for God's input on?" I asked.

"I'd suggest that you ask whether you should delay Cardinal Paul Montebianco's attendance from the Palm Sunday Mass so that he doesn't die a martyr's death tonight." Michael replied.

I thought about Michael's suggestion. Cardinal Montebianco was a man with a fervent militant zeal. He would be the perfect chess piece replacement to further the Templars reach and influence in the Catholic world. "God has spoken. He agrees to the wisdom in your words."

"Excellent. Godspeed to you Grandmaster Al-Sham. Towards a better future for the Knights Templar Order. In Omnia Paratus!" Michael said.

"Domine, dirige nos!" I replied and rushed off. I needed to get to Cardinal Montebianco in time.

"WELCOME TO MY HUMBLE abode, Knights Templar Leader, Martin Al-Sham." Cardinal Paul Montebianco greeted me as I entered Palazzo Farnese, a beautiful Vatican palace in the heart of Rome.

The Cardinal had acquired the luxurious Renaissance palace from the French Government a few years earlier. It was anything but humble, he lived in extravagantly wealthy palace. But since religion was big money-making scheme for the naïve and obliging society, it made sense that Cardinal Montebianco was super wealthy and powerful.

"Thank you, Cardinal. I need to discuss something with you in private." I said.

"I am sorry, Martin Al-Sham. I need to attend the Palm Sunday evening mass, and so should you." Paul Montebianco replied.

I froze for a second. I needed to come up with something that would stop Cardinal Montebianco from being at the site where there will be an upcoming terrorist attack. But I couldn't reveal my prior knowledge about the attack. I didn't know whether Paul would be ruthless enough to let the attack take place to elevate his own position.

"The Cardinal is keen on your interest in seeing him. Use that to your advantage." Rangda whispered in the back of my head. This time, I controlled my impulse to argue back with Rangda.

"Please, Cardinal Paul. Hear me out. There is a personal matter that is tormenting me. I feel that you are the only one in the Vatican that would understand what I am going through." I said and stroked the Cardinal gently over his right shoulder.

"Very well. Please come with me for some wine in my private quarters. I hope that the pope won't notice our absence during Mass." Paul replied.

Paul led the way to his private quarters of the residence, and I walked behind him nervously. I needed to find a way to delay his attending the Mass, but I was definitely not going to succumb to satisfying a closeted homosexual man.

Paul closed the door behind him and poured us two glasses of red wine.

"I know why you are here, Martin," Paul said.

"Yes, Cardinal Montebianco. I have a burden that is weakening my spirit. A forbidden carnal desire." I replied.

"Hmmm, I think I know what you are up to!" Paul exclaimed.

"Huh? I don't understand what you are implying," I said.

"You are here to delay my attendance at the Palm Sunday Mass, in the hope that you can blackmail me should I become the new pope. Everyone knows that Pope Septimus' days are numbered, and you are hedging your bets. But let me tell you something. You got nothing on me. Homosexuality and paedophilia are very prevalent among the clergy. Who else would commit to not getting married and not fathering children for the sake of a job?" Paul ranted.

"I didn't come to blackmail you. I came to save you." I replied.

"Save me from what? How could a paid killer save me from my own desires? You are a tool to get rid of undesirables while I focus on higher goals." Paul ranted.

"Very well. If that's how you feel, I guess I'll be leaving." I said and got up.

"Good. For future reference. Don't fuck female prostitutes just hours before you confess your 'homosexuality sins' to your Cardinal. And stop involving yourself with the Mossad. They don't share the goals of the Catholic Church." Paul shouted.

I walked off without saying a word. I realised that I would have to deal with Paul Montebianco at some stage, but it was unwise to act now.

I called James. "James, we have a problem. Cardinal Montebianco is still going to attend the mass."

After a few seconds of silence, James replied. "I see, well it seems we'll have to save the pope, after all. Meet us at St Peters Square."

I LOOKED DOWN TOWARDS St Peters Square from the attic of one of the nearby buildings. I had got to the attic in time and stopped the Middle Eastern sniper who had been overlooking the square. I exhaled. Finding and killing the man had been easy. I had used my Zetan monocle to detect him. Once I knew where he was, it was easy to sneak up on him and slit his throat.

I exhaled. Murdering people was always stressful. At least I could tell myself that it was necessary, and no innocents got harmed this time. I considered whether I should report the occurrence to the police or if should clean up the crime scene and disappear. While I wanted to get the credit for saving the Pope's life, there was a risk that the police would charge me with murder. My role as a Knight's Templar didn't give me the authority to murder people.

I saw the Papal procession walking across the square. Cardinal Montebianco was on the pope's right-hand side. For a second, I thought of picking up the sniper rifle and silence him. I decided against it. It was too conspicuous. Instead, I decided to wipe the crime scene of evidence, get back to my apartment and get dressed for the mass.

I was about to leave when I heard screeching tires from a truck, heading towards the procession. So that was how the Muslim terrorists had planned the attack? Driving a garbage truck against the heavy roadblocks, killing a massive number of pedestrians and the innocent crowds and then shoot the pope during the confusion and chaos that ensues.

The truck drove straight into the roadblock and came to a screeching halt. 'A failed terrorist attack, nothing to write about.' I thought for a second. Then I saw a massive explosion, and despite being on the 12th floor, I had to duck for cover to avoid getting hit by shrapnel. As I got back on my feet, I studied the carnage below. The entire square was full of dead and wounded people. With the help of my Zetan Monocle, I concluded that both Pope Septimus and Cardinal Montebianco were among the fatalities.

I set my monocle to 'avoid confrontation', and I hurried back to my apartment.

"YOU MADE SOME INTERESTING choices!" Ben Yehuda mocked and passed me the tablet with today's news headline. It read: 'Pope Septimus among hundreds of fatalities in a Salafist terrorist attack in Rome.'

"Was there any way I could have stopped this?" I asked.

"Yes. My monocle predicted several outcomes where you would stop the attack and save the day." Ben replied.

"Well, I didn't have the information that you had. If I had known earlier, things could have ended differently." I replied.

"Yes, but to be honest, I am not sure you wanted things to happen in any other way," Ben replied.

"So, what happens now?" I asked.

Szymon sighed. "It's difficult to predict, Martin. In all our simulations, either Pope Septimus or Cardinal Montebianco survived the attack. But no forecast is a 100 per cent accurate. Regardless, we are re-assigning you. We can't see a scenario where the Mossad controls the Catholic Church anymore." Szymon said.

"I see, where would you have me re-assigned to?" I asked.

"I don't give a shit. Just go on a holiday without causing any massacres or chaos. And don't let the booze or hookers kill you. We'll find you when we need you. Can you do that?" Ben scoffed.

I nodded, but I didn't reply. I walked towards the door. Once I had opened the door, I turned around and spoke. "What happened to James and Michael?"

"They are in the hospital. They survived, but not thanks to you. Now get the fuck out of here, Al-Sham!" Ben exclaimed.

I turned around without saying anything. Death and destruction seemed to follow me across the globe. Both my actions and my inactions caused terrible consequences wherever I went. Was I cursed, and what should I do with my life from there on?

Chapter 11: Colombia, February 2026

"You killed me." The echoing voice of a charred haunting girl terrified me into the core of my soul.

"I am sorry." I pleaded.

"You are not sorry. Sorry is just a word. Never say sorry, if you would do it all again." The voice echoed.

"But I had to do it. The fate of humanity is in my hands." I replied.

"If the fate of humanity is in the hands of those that are inhumane, our species are already doomed." The girl said.

The haunting girl gripped me with her arms. In her firm grip, I felt like I was on fire.

"Let me go, you wicked demon! I must live on!" I shouted.

"I will never let go of you." The girl replied and set me on fire.

The girl stared into my eyes. I don't know what caused me to most pain: her dead gaze or the fire. Eventually, maggots came out of the girl's eyes, and I screamed my lungs out.

I OPENED MY EYES, AND Pierre was shaking his head.

"If I had known there would be so much screaming on this trip, I would have brought a soundproof camping van." Pierre mocked.

"This place gives me terrible nightmares!" I replied.

"You did humankind a favour, ridding this place of that human vermin that inhabited the valley. Besides, the fires gave us invaluable insights that will make us billions." Pierre smirked.

"How is that?" I asked.

Pierre sniggered and replied with an arrogant tone. "Technology. Josefina, Sandra, and I have used our heightened intellects to develop new technologies. These technologies will drive humankind forward. One of those technologies can detect the chemical composition of the soil from bushfire smoke. It has proven crucial for our interests." Pierre lectured.

Pierre's answer confused me, and I didn't understand what any of this had to do with me. Besides, the haunting voice of the child from my nightmares kept echoing in the back of my head. Pierre sensed my confusion and clarified what he meant.

"Josefina and I developed a satellite technology that could detect rare earth minerals in bushfire smoke. This technology is suitable with the increased prevalence of blazes due to global warming. The blaze that you and Elaine caused proved that this valley is rich in natural resources. Since you killed off the inhabitants, we bought the land and the mining rights at a low cost from the Colombian government." Pierre revealed.

"So, you profit from human tragedy. How do you sleep at night?" I chastised.

"Well, the tragedy will happen in any case, due to the likes of you. We only choose to profit from the opportunity that people like you create for us. How do you sleep at night?" Pierre taunted back.

"I don't." I sighed.

"Well, as moved as I am by your sleeplessness and guilt, I am a busy man. Have some Valium. We have a busy day tomorrow." Pierre said and handed me some Valium.

I swallowed a pill without a word and went back to bed. There was no point in arguing with Pierre, and we did have a busy day ahead of us.

"DID YOU SLEEP WELL?" I asked and tried to grab Elaine's hand.

"No, I didn't," Elaine replied and pushed my hand away.

"So, so. Don't argue, lovebirds." Josefina said and smiled.

"Imagine that we have all gathered again, after all this time." James Winter said.

"Don't say that Vladimir is coming. That bastard killed my father. If I see him, I'll kill him." Sandra Santiago shouted.

"I'd kill him as well. But I am sure Pierre has more sense than bringing his attack dog?" Josefina added in.

"Vladimir is on a mission for the bank in Eastern Europe. He is sorting out some customer arrears." Pierre said with a distant voice.

A period of silence ensued. We were not particularly close to each other, and we shared both mutual distrust and mutual interdependence. The monocles had expanded our minds and made us unique. For better or worse, we were the only ones of our kind, and at some level, we still confided in each other.

"So, tonight is the night, Martin and Elaine. Can you lead us to the secret Guane temple?", Pierre asked.

"It's not as easy as it sounds. This place looked hugely different before the fires, and we lost all our possessions in the blaze." I replied.

"Fucking hell, Al-Sham. Why didn't you tell us? The lost temple is the only reason for me to come here!" Pierre exclaimed.

"I am sorry, Pierre," I replied.

"Don't worry. I had Martin and Elaine under satellite surveillance back in 2022. I know where the Juarez cartel ambushed them." James Winter revealed.

I felt relieved. My plan had worked. The others didn't know that I still had Pachamama's Veil, and James Winter had revealed his secret knowledge.

"Very well, James. If you can lead the way, that would be helpful." I said.

"Okay. I'll need to organise a perimeter with my CIA associates. I have sent the coordinates to your encrypted phones." James replied.

I opened my phone. The coordinates read '7.1127 south, 75.9458 west'. Perfect. James had given us the correct coordinates. Now we needed to avoid falling into a trap and secure the entrance.

"DID YOU LOSE PACHAMAMA'S Veil?" Elaine said with a worried expression on her face.

"What difference does it make to you?" I replied.

Elaine sighed and shook her head. "It means the world to me. The primordial Zeto Crystal can save the future of our species. But it won't do anything unless we charge it." Elaine said.

"So why do you need the Zeto Crystal, and what would you do with it?" I asked.

"Well, I don't need it for my own sake. The monocle is elevating my mind, and the Harapan Conglomerate is flourishing under my supervision. You should come to visit me in Indonesia someday. It has developed a lot since your last visit in 2023." Elaine enthused.

"I'd love to come with you to Indonesia once we have finished our mission here," I replied.

"Great, I am looking forward to showing you the new city we are building," Elaine said.

I studied Elaine. I trusted her and I believed that she would use the powers of the primordial Zeto Crystal to improve humankind and avert the future apocalypse. Out of the people in our group, Elaine or Josefina would do the most good if they got the crystal. If Pierre got the crystal, he would only use it to accumulate more money for himself. The Yehuda Brothers would use the crystal to start a religious war against anyone who isn't Jewish, which would kill millions.

"You have Pachamama's Veil. I left it for you when I last visited you." I said.

"Is that so? How come I haven't seen it?" Elaine asked.

"I left it where you would never look," I replied.

"And where is that?" Elaine asked.

"At the bottom of your drawer. You always pick the top pair and never look at the bottom of your clothes." I replied.

"Oh, you know me too well," Elaine said and smiled.

"Well, technically our divorce never finalised," I said and winked.

"And yet, we haven't had sex for four years!" Elaine replied and stroke my cheek.

"You drive a tough bargain, but okay," I replied, winked, and closed the trailer door.

IT WAS CLOSE TO MIDNIGHT, and we stood at the same cliffside where the Andres Juarez cartel had ambushed us four years earlier. It felt different this time. The last time I had worried about the cartel coming after me. I had chosen to not involve the others, and my choice had ended in a terrifying tragedy. This time, allies surrounded me. Although with 'friends' like these, I would have preferred solitude.

I got back to my senses when James Winter arrived, carrying a heavy crate together with a CIA operative. "That's it, Adam. Go back to the base camp. I will meet you there later." James said, and the CIA operative left us where we stood without a word.

"What's going on, James? What is in that box?" I asked.

"EMP grenades and EMP rifles." James replied.

"Huh, what is that?" Elaine asked.

"Electromagnetic Pulse weapons. Useful if we face any of the robotic sentries that you encountered at Lake Titicaca." James explained.

"Right. Well-thought. We better arm ourselves." I said and we all armed ourselves with EMP rifles and EMP grenades from the box.

After that, James gave a short presentation on how to operate and use these battery-powered prototype weapons.

20 MINUTES LATER, THE cliffside lit up with alien symbols. I recognised the symbols. They were similar to the symbols I had on my Zetan tattoo. But, no matter how much I studied the tattoo, I couldn't find and decipher the password written on the cliffside.

"It's hopeless. I cannot decipher the code." I sighed.

"Bah, you are a brain-damaged zombie. Let someone intelligent solve this code." Pierre said.

Pierre walked up to me, glanced at my glowing tattoo and then pushed some of the markings on the wall.

A melody played, and a secret passageway opened. "See? Not too hard to decipher for someone who got half a brain!" Pierre taunted, and he entered the tunnel.

The rest of us grabbed our flashlights and weapons, following Pierre into the darkness.

"Looks like you weren't the first to decipher the code on the wall," Josefina snarked, as we stumbled across some decomposed corpses. I recognised them from the insignia on their clothes. They were from the Juarez Cartel and were likely to be some of the men that had captured us four years ago.

"What happened here?" Pierre exclaimed.

"They probably died due to asphyxiation, as someone who isn't worth mentioning, set the whole valley ablaze," James replied.

"We don't have the time for this. Let's keep going." Szymon urged, and we continued our descent.

We reached the inner sanctum of the temple, and there was intense blue light from a crystal in the centre of the room. It was emitting the same blue light like the one we saw in the hidden temple in Nepal.

"Finally. With this priceless artefact in our possession, the bank will be unstoppable." Pierre stated.

"Shut up, you greedy money-worshipping pig. We will use the crystal to rid the Holy Land from the non-Jewish vermin. We need it to restore the Solomon Temple to its former glory." Ben Yehuda shouted.

"This crystal is South American, and I need it to develop the South American continent," Josefina added in.

Everyone started shouting at each other, and their arguing caused my mind to wander. I closed my eyes and heard Rangda's voice. *"They are arguing over nothing. That's a charged replicated Zeto Crystal. While powerful, it's nothing compared to the real prize, the Primordial Zeto Crystal."*

"But, Empress Rangda. This crystal emits a lot more energy than the crystals that saved my life." I replied.

"Yes, those were minor crystals. This is still a powerful one. But you have a more urgent problem at hand." Rangda said and disconnected from my mind.

'Beep, Beep, Beep.' The sound of the screeching alarm put an end to the argument. A wall opened and several hovering sentry robots entered the temple. The robots were like the ones that had attacked me at Lake Titicaca.

"Ua iloa le mea na tupu. Ttafai sa'o po o le alu i le itu i saute." The robot stated.

"What is that thing!" Sandra exclaimed in terror.

"Upu le sao. Faamolemole alu ese mai le itu i saute." The robot replied.

"Fuck this. Shoot those things." James exclaimed and started shooting at the sentry robots with his EMP rifle.

"Bad choice. Those weapons can't do anything against the robots!" Rangda whispered in the back of my head.

"Na mata'ituina galuega fa'afefe. Fa'ase'ene'eina sini." The robot responded. The robot rushed James and slammed him into the wall, knocking him unconscious.

"Fuck this toy gun!" Szymon exclaimed and pulled up his pistol to shoot at the robot. The gun did nothing, and we watched in awe as the bullets stopped mid-air and dropped to the ground, a metre from the robot. More robots entered the room, and they approached the Yehuda Brothers and knocked them unconscious.

'Fighting is futile. The recommended course of action: Say the following phrase to the robots. Matou te tu'uina atu, fa'amolemole aua le fasioti i matou.' Rangda spoke to me.

'Here goes nothing' I thought as I expressed the phrase that Rangda showed me.

'Incorrect pronunciation. Please try again!' The monocle displayed.

'No shit!' I thought to myself.

While my attempt at speaking to the robots in the non-sense language had failed, it had gotten me the robots' attention.

"Hurry up and grab that replicated Zeto Crystal, squeezed it to release a psionic blast. But best of luck with the voice-controlled pronunciation if you prefer that method to disarm the robots." Rangda remarked.

I decided to not give the voice control another attempt. It was hard enough to get my smartphone to understand my heavy Swedish-accented English! I rushed to the crystal, squeezed it, and released a psionic blast that knocked me unconscious.

I WOKE UP A WHILE LATER in a pitch-black room. On the bright side, I knew that I was still alive. I had died here in Colombia, on this day, four years earlier and I had seen no signs of the afterlife, just nothingness like before I was born.

I switched my monocle to display infrared light. To my great relief, I noticed that the others were alive. I rushed over to the closest source of Infrared light. It turned out to be the young Sandra Santiago. I nudged her, and she woke up.

"Uh, don't kill me, please!" Sandra wailed.

"Relax Sandra. The blast deactivated the robots. Switch to infrared on your monocle." I instructed.

Sandra did as I instructed her, and she seemed relieved to see me. "Why is it so dark in here? What do we do?" Sandra asked.

"It's dark because the EMP weapons destroyed all the electronics in here. Do you have a lighter by any chance?" I replied.

"I do. But don't tell my mother that I smoke weed." Sandra replied.

"I don't even know your mother?" I replied in confusion.

"Josefina. She adopted me after my father died. She hates drugs. She claims drugs have destroyed our continent." Sandra revealed.

"I see. Your secret is safe with me. Hand me your lighter and your joint." I replied.

Sandra did as I asked her, and I felt a deep sense of relief as I lit up the joint. More importantly, the monocle amplified the limited light from the joint a thousandfold, so the room became visible. I gathered the others, and we left the temple.

WE HAD GATHERED IN a semi-circle, studying the map of Earth on the temple wall. A few rough days had passed. The EMP weapons that James had brought had turned out to be mega effective on human technology. They were so effective, so the shockwave from the EMP grenades had destroyed our equipment that was outside of the hidden temple. Because of the secrecy of our mission, no-one else had accompanied us. Our only option had been to walk 15 kilometres through the charred landscape to reach the mining camp that the World Bank had set up. Not the easiest of tasks, especially not after almost getting killed by alien sentry robots.

I looked at the world map on the wall. It was an ancient map, different from how the landmasses looked today. I realised that it was from the last ice age when the sea levels were lower. The map showed four pyramids and several smaller temples scattered across the Earth. Of the smaller ones, I had already visited this one, as well as the ones in Nepal and Peru. The main temple marked on the map was in Jerusalem.

Ben Yehuda shone with pride and spoke: "This is the proof, gentlemen. Yahweh is the one true God and Jerusalem is the holy land."

"Not so fast, Ben. This is map resembles Earth before the end of the last ice age. That's 10,000 years ago. That's way before your little religion was even created." Pierre remarked with his Swiss French air of arrogance.

"Bullshit. This map is of Earth before the great flood." Ben argued back.

"Shut up, the two of you. Let's focus on what we can understand of this map." I shouted.

To my great relief, I got the others to shut up, and I spoke again. "So, this map. I have been to several of these smaller temples. I have also been to the Cheops Pyramid, and I have heard about the Sun Pyramid and the Great Pyramid of China. But what about this pyramid in the Pacific Ocean. There are no pyramids in the Pacific Ocean."

"Hold on. We found the monocles that expanded our minds in the Nepalese cave. But there doesn't seem to be any useful artefacts in this temple." Pierre objected.

"Perhaps, the crystal that Martin destroyed to repel the sentries was the valuable artefact in this temple." Josefina speculated.

"Hey, don't blame this on me," I argued.

"I am not blaming you. I am thankful that you saved me. I'd rather be alive than owning another artefact." Josefina replied.

A moment of silence spread over the group. Eventually, I decided to speak: "So, what do we do now?"

"We are going back to Jerusalem. This map proves the importance of the Holy City, and we need to find the hidden artefact." Ben Yehuda said.

"I have some pressing issues to deal with for the bank. This expedition has been a fiasco. Several days delay, almost getting killed and finding no valuable artefacts." Pierre whinged.

"I am going home too. Coming here was the wrong choice. I love you, Martin. But we got nowhere, and we almost died. I need to focus on my company and improving my beloved home country.", Elaine said.

The others gave similar answers, and as I left the cave, I was full of doubts on what my future would hold. I realised that the answer might lie in one of the pyramids.

Chapter 12: Egypt & Kiribati, October 2026

I was back in the hidden room in the Cheops Pyramid, where I had entered an interdimensional portal seven years earlier. The room was dark and uninspiring, not at all like the impressive display of alien technology I had seen on my last visit. The replicated Zeto Crystal, which I had found in a small Zetan sanctuary in the Pyrenees mountain range in Spain, didn't seem to react with the room. I tried slotting the crystal into the opening in the wall, but nothing happened.

"Why is the portal not opening?" I growled.

"Bloody fool. Replicated Zeto Crystals usually don't open interdimensional portals." Rangda screeched in my head.

"But why did it happen in 2019 then?" I asked.

"Due to a rare phenomenon. The distance between the Divine Dimension and the portal in Egypt was at its shortest. So, the limited energy of the replicated Zeto Crystal was enough to open the portal. This will not happen again during your lifetime." Rangda replied.

"So, what do I do then?" I asked.

"You'll need to find and charge the primordial Zeto Crystal. Once it's charged, it's powerful enough to open the portal. Then you can make your way to the Divine Dimension and free me." Rangda stated.

"And if I can't find it?" I asked.

Rangda paused for a bit. She seems like she was putting in some effort to contain one of her rage-induced outbursts for once. After a long pause, she spoke. *"There is another way. The four pyramids are connected and can be powered by the energy from Earth's rotation. Find the switches in the four pyramids and we can take it from there."* Rangda replied and disconnected from my mind.

I figured that there was nothing left to do at the dark tunnel in the Cheops Pyramid. I dislodged the Zeto Crystal from the slot and put it in my pocket. After that, I headed to the airport. I needed to fly to Kiribati and find the sunken pyramid that was there somewhere, deep under the surface of the Pacific Ocean. Once I knew the location of the missing pyramid, I could contact Elaine. Together, we could figure out a way to open the portals and free Empress Rangda, to save the future of humankind.

I WAS SITTING ON A boat in the middle of the Pacific Ocean. I was in the tiny island republic of Kiribati, studying the vastness of the sea. As I sat on the boat, staring at the horizon, I felt like giving it all up, what was the point of my struggle.

A beeping sound from my sonar got me back to my senses. There was something hidden here at a depth of 100 metres. Could it be the pyramid, and how come no one had found it throughout the years?

I realised that the vastness of the ocean meant that it held many secrets. After all, only a small fraction of the oceans had been charted. I needed to get down there and check it out. But how would I do it? I couldn't swim down there. Although it was possible to dive that deep with specific training and gas mixture, I had neither.

I thought of Elaine. The Harapan Conglomerate had grown to be the largest company in Indonesia under her leadership. Would she be willing to help me out?

I decided to call her.

"Hi, Elaine. Can you help me with a mission?" I asked.

"I don't think so. People tend to die during your missions. I'll give this one a pass." Elaine replied.

"Please Elaine, I need your help. I am about to rediscover the Sunken Pyramid of Kiribati. Imagine what wondrous technologies that might lie within." I pleaded.

There was a long silence on the other end. Eventually, Elaine spoke. "Okay, Martin. What do you need?"

"I need you to bring a submarine and some loyal followers. I also need a diversion as I believe that I am under satellite surveillance. I want us to uncover this astonishing discovery together without involving the others." I replied.

"Okay. Meet me at Banaba Island in two days. I have a research team there investigating whether we can extract energy from the volcano. I'll make sure to supply them with a submarine." Elaine said.

"Thank you, Elaine. I'll see you in two days." I replied.

"Yes. One more thing. Try to avoid violence this time." Elaine replied and hung up the phone.

THE SULPHUR SMOKE WAS thick at Banaba Island, and I didn't understand why Elaine wanted to meet at this location. For a second, I feared a trap. I was stuck on an abandoned volcanic island together with my estranged wife and her associates. Hardly a comfortable scenario. I relaxed when Elaine approached me with a friendly body language.

"Welcome to Banaba Island. I hope that my associates were friendly to you?" Elaine asked.

"Well, I didn't speak to them that much, but they weren't causing me any grief," I replied.

"Tolong, tinggalkan kami. Saya akan menghubungi Anda nanti." Elaine said to her bodyguards and they left us alone.

"What did you tell them?" I asked.

"You should know. We were together for over ten years before our separation. But you never bothered learning Indonesian, did you?" Elaine replied.

I didn't reply, and Elaine spoke again. "I have organised everything you asked me to. We'll board a submarine here on Banaba Island. Then, the skipper will take us to your coordinates."

"Alright, boss. Lead the way." I replied.

I GOT THE CHILLS WHEN I met the gaze of our submarine captain. It was a muscular African man, and I felt like I had met him in the past. The hostile glare he gave me strengthened my suspicion that our paths had crossed in the past.

I took Elaine to the side and spoke. "Where did you find the captain? I think I have met him in the past. I don't like his looks."

"Don't be racist, Martin. Captain Danjuma has worked for me for several years. He is loyal and discreet." Elaine replied.

"I am not a racist. I am a cynic. I hate all races equally. There is a difference." I joked.

"Very well. If you dislike all races the same, then I don't see a reason why your dislike should affect which crew I am bringing with me." Elaine stated.

"At least tell me where Captain Danjuma comes from?" I asked.

"He is from South Africa. He is a talented man whose operations went down during the South African Civil War in 2023. But enough of this. I am a busy woman and I have already taken time out of my schedule to help you with this. Don't even think of delaying me through requesting to get a new replacement crew." Elaine snapped at me.

I nodded, and we boarded the submarine without saying a word.

"HERE IS YOUR GINGER black coffee, Mister." The crew member said and handed me a cup of a very aromatic and strong black coffee.

I accepted the hot beverage, but I felt a little annoyed towards Elaine. Why did she bring extra people on the submarine, when it's better to have less people knowing about this mission?

As I drank the coffee, I reflected over the bitter and powerful taste. Didn't the coffee taste a little unusual? I waved off my suspicion that it might have been spiked. I hadn't had this wonderful beverage of Indonesian ginger black coffee for years, and I have forgotten how it tasted. I finished the cup, and I felt very sleepy. I leaned back into my chair and I fell into deep unconsciousness.

I WOKE UP FROM THE burning sensation of a hard slap hitting my cheek. I looked up, and I saw Captain Danjuma grinning menacingly. Much to my dismay, I realised that someone had tied me and Elaine to a chair, and she had passed out.

"Mr. Orchard, we meet again." Danjuma said.

"Grrr! Yeah, I thought I recognised your face. When and where did we meet before? I presume it was in South Africa, October 2023?" I fumed.

"Yes. Our meeting in South Africa was brief, but it left me with permanent marks." Danjuma said and pulled off his shirt.

I looked at Danjuma's torso. While he had a chiselled physique, he also had several deep scars on the side of his body, signs that he was once bitten and clawed by a lion.

"Playing it tough in the bedroom with your missus?" I taunted. Danjuma punched me in the face as soon as I was done mocking him. Argh, when would I ever learn to keep my old mouth shut?

"You have caused these marks on my body. I was one of the poachers that you left for dead, when you released our captured lions to let them eat us alive. The lions killed many of my peers, but some of us survived. We found your details in Chim Mwanza's office some days later." Danjuma disclosed.

"So, you were one of those pathetic poachers working tirelessly to fund SVAPO's revolution against South African government? I heard your terrorist group lost the war. I am sorry for leaving you alive, I should have made sure all of you were dead." I mocked.

Danjuma grunted angrily and punched me in the face again, harder this time. The chair toppled, and I hit the floor. The chair didn't break and I had not broken any jaws or lost any teeth, just some bleeding on my gums and a nasty bruised left eye.

Danjuma's two accomplices raised my chair up and Danjuma spoke again. "Shut your fucking mouth, white mongrel! We will kill you slowly for what you did to us."

"There is a problem with that plan, however. I have proven to be exceedingly difficult to kill." I mocked.

Danjuma pulled up his pistol and hit me with the back of it. *Ouch, fucking hell.* I needed to learn when to not be sarcastic. I decided to contact

Rangda to get me out of this pickle. "Empress Rangda. I am in a bit of a pickle. Help me outta 'ere."

"The Monocle has a defence mechanism against unauthorised users. Whoever who is not the owner of the monocle will burn when they touch the device. Offer Danjuma the monocle. Then grab his pistol and kill the two others when the monocle kills him." Rangda suggested.

"Thanks, Empress," I replied and disconnected from Rangda.

"Hey, Crazy Fucker. Who were you talking too?" Danjuma exclaimed.

"I was talking to my divine guidance. Look, you are winning in this game. I'm tied up to a chair and you have beaten me up really good. I have nothing to offer but my apology for letting you get bitten by lions. Here, you have proven yourself worthy to receive this monocle. It is a treasure that will elevate your consciousness." I replied.

"Proven yourself worthy? Fuck off! I can take it off your dead body if I want to." Danjuma taunted.

"Why don't you take it now?" I replied.

Danjuma reached for my monocle and it burnt his hand when his skin encountered the monocle's forcefield.

"Boss, let's kill this white mongrel now. He is setting a trap for us!" Danjuma's accomplices shouted.

"Silence, Jabu and Luan. With this technology at our hands, SVAPO can rise again. We will create a new future for South Africans. We will expel the white invaders once and for all. Black Powa' Foreva'!" Danjuma proclaimed.

Danjuma turned to me and spoke: "Martin, give me the monocle, and you might get out of this alive."

I tapped the top of the monocle, and it disconnected from my iris. I handed it to Danjuma, when Jabu interrupted. "You must be possessed, white devil! Your eyeball is haunting me!"

"What's the matter? Have you never seen a glowing purple iris before?" I taunted while staring at Jabu with my purple icy glare.

Danjuma didn't seem to mind, and he connected the monocle to his iris. After a few seconds, he exclaimed. "This is a miracle. My mind has changed. I feel so smart!"

"Be ready for the magnificent show! He will be burnt alive" Rangda whispered.

A few seconds later, Danjuma started screaming in pain, which distracted Jabu and Luan and caused them to panic. I tilted the chair sideways towards Danjuma, and I grabbed the knife from his holster as I was still tied up in the chair. I managed to cut the rope to let go of my hand, and I took his gun as Danjuma was being burnt alive. I shot towards Jabu and Luan. After the third shot, the pistol jammed. I managed to kill Luan, but Jabu was not mortally wounded, and he came after me with a vengeance. Jabu lunged at me with his legs shot and started strangling me while I was still bound to the chair. I panicked as I didn't have the help of the monocle. Besides, I was still tied up and unable to defend myself. My vision was flickering when a miracle saved me. The monocle had combusted and killed Danjuma, and his burning body fell towards Jabu, burning his back.

Jabu rolled away, screaming in pain. I saw an opportunity to get free. I wriggled and cut the rest of the ropes that tied me to the chair. I got up and I rushed off to Jabu and kicked him in the head. Then I picked up Luan's pistol and turned towards Jabu. "Hasta la vista, Jabu!" I said and shot him in the head just like Arnold Schwarzenegger in The Terminator.

Then I made my way to Danjuma and disconnected the perfectly unharmed and shining monocle from his burnt corpse. The monocle had drilled into his brain stem, and specks of blood covered it. *Yuck, that would need a rinse before I used it again.*

I was going to check on Elaine, but before I got to where she was lying on the floor, my adrenaline kick had worn off and my extreme exhaustion started to unravel. The combination of my injuries and the sedatives that Danjuma had drugged me with had caused me to fall on my knees, and I blacked out.

"MARTIN! MARTIN! WHAT happened here?" Elaine shouted frantically, while trying to wake me up.

I opened my eyes. Yup, I was still in the same submarine where just moments before, I had killed three African men. *At least it was in self-defence this time.* I thought to myself.

"Danjuma attacked me, and I had to defend myself," I replied.

"Unbelievable. I hired them as my bodyguards, and they turned out to be your past enemies?" Elaine retorted.

"You should have done some background checks before you hire them as your bodyguards. It is past the point of diplomacy when my enemy drugs me, ties me to a chair, and plans to kill me!" I retaliated.

Elaine took a deep breath and replied. "I'm sorry. You're right, I should have done my research beforehand. The bastards must have drugged me as well. So damn hard to find loyal employees these days!"

"Why did you hire Africans in the first place?" I asked.

"They are my Varangian guard," Elaine replied.

"Varangian guard?" I asked.

"The Byzantine emperor during medieval times hired foreigners as his personal bodyguards. The idea was that those foreigners had no local loyalties and depended on the emperor for their own success. It has worked out well for me over the last four years, getting random bodyguards." Elaine revealed.

"I see," I replied.

"Yes. May I ask why these men decided to kill you out of the blue?" Elaine asked.

I pondered over my options. I wanted to lie to Elaine and said that her bodyguards had attacked me for no reason whatsoever, but I doubted that she would believe in it, and besides, what kind of man would I be if I lied to my own closest ally? I decided to tell Elaine the truth.

"They were animal poachers hired by SVAPO terrorists. I had a deadly altercation with some of them when I visited South Africa, three years ago." I admitted.

"You're bloody hopeless. Don't just sit there. You killed the men. You better attach weights to them and flush them out via the airlock." Elaine commanded.

"But I am wounded, and they are heavy." I wringed in pain.

Elaine fetched a compression bandage, and she stopped the bleeding in my wound. The punches and cuts only caused superficial wounds, and hadn't damaged the bone, so it wasn't a life-threatening injury.

After dressing my wounds up, Elaine spoke again. "Well, at least you live to fight another day. Chop, chop. Get to work. Dispose of the bodies." Having said this, Elaine got up and left the room.

As I dragged the heavy corpses to the airlock, I had an epiphany. Being a clueless protagonist, travelling around the world looking for alien artefacts, is bloody arduous work!

"WOW, IT'S MAGNIFICENT!" Elaine said in awe as the Sunken Pyramid of Kiribati appeared in front of us. It was a magnificent sight, 100 meters below the ocean's surface.

I could only agree. The sunken pyramid was gigantic, it was covered in unimaginable amount of sea plankton, corals, seaweed and algae, and tonnes of beautiful ocean fish were swimming around the Pyramid, as if the pyramid had been untouched for centuries. The pyramid looked massive, but its exact dimensions were hard to determine from our position. After all, we were at a massive depth and the only light source was the headlights on our submarine.

"So, what do we do now? Elaine asked.

It was a valid question, and I hadn't thought about it. I planned to use radio-controlled mini-submarines to enter and investigate the pyramids. This was for several reasons. First of all, it was way too dangerous to swim into a pitch-black tunnel at a depth of over 100 metres. My second reason was that I feared that Zetan sentry squid-like drones would be lurking in the depths of the pyramid, ready to attack us, just as I had experienced before.

"We'll send in radio-controlled autonomous sea drones. They can map the pyramid for us and bring out anything we find of value." I said.

"But what about if there are any Zetan sentries guarding it?" Elaine fretted.

"Well, then we better hope those robots aren't smart enough to swim outside of the pyramid looking for us." I replied and swiftly added in. "But let's make sure to stay some distance away from the entrance of the sunken pyramid."

We sent out the mini-submarines to survey the pyramid. The Harapan Conglomerate had developed advanced miniature sea submarines.

"Make sure to film everything." I reminded Elaine as we sent in the sea drones into the underwater tunnels of the pyramid. We watched the video feeds from the sea drones. It was a disappointing view. The inside of the pyramid was dark, empty and uninteresting. It was like what you'd expect of an archaic empty building, submerged for millennia. There was nothing of value.

An hour later, the sea drones had mapped the whole pyramid. We stared at the video images and the dimensions of the pyramid. Nothing was indicating an alien presence, and there were no treasures to be found.

"Well, I guess an archaeologist, or a marine biologist, or a historian would find this place more interesting," Elaine stated.

"Yes, but that's not why we came here. We came to look for the Primordial Zeto crystal," I replied.

"So, what do we do now?" Elaine asked.

I pondered the question when I remembered that I still had the replicated Zeto Crystal that I found in Spain. After some frantic searching, I found it at the bottom of my backpack.

"We'll send this Zeto Crystal with one of the sea drones. Since the Zetans powered their structures with these things, I am hoping that it will have power to activate the pyramid's mechanism." I said.

"Okay. That makes sense, it's worth a shot." Elaine approved.

I attached the Zeto crystal to the claw of one of the autonomous sea drones and set them on the expedition. The sea drones entered the Pyramid and I watched the feed carefully. For a long time, nothing seemed to happen. But at one dead-end tunnel, the drone accidentally dropped the crystal to the pyramid floor. As the replicated Zeto Crystal hit the pyramid floor, it shattered to hundreds of pieces. As it shattered, it sent a surge of energy and a very bright spark, lighting up the entire architecture of the ancient sunken pyramid. The bright light caused the walls to shine in majestic electric blue beams and they revealed several blueprints of advanced technologies hieroglyphs and symbols, written on the walls of the ancient pyramid.

"Wow! What a marvellous find! Make sure to save the video feed and record everything that the drones are filming. These blueprints can be invaluable." I said in awe.

"Of course! Our video feeds will be stored permanently as soon as they are recorded, at the Harapan Info Data Bank. But it seems that you woke something else up as well." Elaine shuddered.

I looked at the video feeds from the submarine drones. Elaine was correct. The energy surge from the scattered Zeto Crystal had awoken The Zetan squid-like sentry robots. They progressed to attack our sea drones, and the video feeds died. How lucky that we didn't enter the pyramid ourselves!

"Let's get the hell out of here. Leave those squid-like robots where they are, we don't want to risk our lives to their ferocious metal tentacles!" I exclaimed.

"Yes. Let's get out of here!" Elaine agreed, and we steered the submarine with full speed away from the pyramid, setting it to go back up to the surface.

WE WERE SITTING IN our private suite at Tarawa Boutique Hotel in Kiribati. Elaine had decided that we shouldn't go back to her research laboratory on Banaba Island. Since our submarine bodyguards had tried to kill us, it was likely that there are others with murderous intentions among her employees on the island. I sighed. I had lost a Zeto Crystal, but I hadn't found anything that would help me with my quest, aside from the video feed of the strange hieroglyphs and symbols written on the wall.

"Well, that was a disappointment. We got nowhere and people tried to kill us." I said.

"Don't be so negative, Martin. We recorded some incredibly intelligent and mysterious alien technologies on those walls. We have teams of very smart scientists working for us at the Harapan Conglomerate. I believe that one of the hieroglyphs is a written method of making an invisibility cloaking device. It can make us billions, and it will be particularly useful for covert military operations and top-secret government activities." Elaine replied.

"Congratulations. But we are still facing the issue of getting those Zetan sentries out of the pyramid." I remarked.

"Don't worry about it, Martin. I have technology and deep pockets. I'll send some armed mini-submarines to destroy the squid-like sentries. Eventually, corrosion from acid beams and damage from my drone attacks will destroy them. I'll let you know once the coast is clear." Elaine replied.

"Thanks, Elaine," I approved.

I felt hungry, so I picked up a room service menu. There was only seafood on the menu, and they were very exotic dishes. I decided to have Fish with Pandanus fruit, mostly because I had never tried Pandanus before, and I wanted to know how it tasted.

"Hey, Elaine. I am going to order some food. Would you like something to eat?" I asked.

"No. I am heading back to Jakarta asap. My private jet will arrive to pick me up. I'll eat on my private jet." Elaine replied.

"Oh, I see. Can I come with you?" I pleaded.

"No. We've hung out for three days, and you've managed to kill my body-guards and destroyed my sea drones. It's nothing personal. But I just feel that you always attract too much trouble." Elaine pointed out.

"So, what do you suggest that I do?" I asked.

"Well you can either stay here, or you can join up with Ben Yehuda and search for the primordial Zeto Crystal in Jerusalem. I am leaving now." Elaine stated and left the hotel room.

"I guess I'll stay here," I mumbled to myself. I leaned back in my bed and fell asleep, feeling disappointed with myself for letting her go.

TWO YEARS LATER, I was still on Kiribati island. Something was pleasantly soothing about being alone at the last frontier. I had settled on an uninhabited island and I had used some of my wealth to build myself a comfortable dwelling. I didn't see much people, and in my solitude, I found peace. The world would never forgive my crimes if they knew, but the world wasn't around me much and the world didn't know. I was by myself most of the time, and I had realised that I had to forgive myself for the terrible things that I had done. It was the only way for me to survive.

I got my food and supplies delivered by a local Pacific islander named Alani Mariwati. She was raising her daughter Elenoa on her own, and I paid her a good wage to make sure that she could live a good life. At times, I thought about whether I loved Alani or not. I concluded that I couldn't know. She was the only person I knew in the island, aside from her daughter

Elenoa. Was love perhaps just a desperate need to be part of something greater in life?

I decided to give it a shot. After all, what was the point of owning all this wealth if I couldn't share my time with anyone? While I feared that Alani would hate me if I told her about my past, what exactly did I have to lose? In my solitude, I was merely counting the days to my distant death.

Having made this decision, I felt happy. I would marry Alani, tempt her with the opportunity to provide a good life for herself and her daughter. While she wouldn't necessarily love me back, she could at least accept me.

With light steps, I rushed to the quay when I heard the noise of a motorboat. Once I got there, I fell into deep despair. My visitor was James Winter, accompanied by a group of armed CIA agents.

"So, this is where you are hiding, Martin. Get on board. We got a job to do." James commanded.

I thought about refusing, but I realised that it was pointless. I would die if I chose to fight today, and even if I won the fight against James and the others, what would I achieve?

"Okay. I am coming. I just need to do something first." I sighed.

"Bah, what could you need to do? You have been living off the grid for two years!" James replied.

"I'll donate this house and my Kiribati bank account to my friend and housekeeper Alani. She needs it more than I will." I replied.

"You're right about that. Very well. Hurry up, I don't like waiting." James urged.

A while later, I was on a motorboat heading to the Tarawa International Airport. Destiny had shown itself. It was time for me to stop pursuing inner peace and continue doing what I was good at. For the better or worse for humankind!

Chapter 13: Washington, November 2028

I was sitting in the lounge room of a deluxe suite in the Jefferson Hotel in Washington DC. I sighed. Why was I dragged back into this predicament? Just when I had planned to resign from my life of villainy, destiny pulled me back into it. I speculated why James Winter had come all the way to Kiribati to drag me out of retirement. I suspected that the election of Eva Moreno as the next American president had something to do with it. Eva Moreno was an independent politician who had won an upset victory in the American presidential election, a few weeks earlier. She had defeated both the Republican and the Democrat candidate. An unprecedented occurrence.

Eva Moreno had based her campaign on exposing the corruption within the dominating political parties, corruption abetted by the CIA and its director James Winter. The American population had enough of corrupt politicians starting phony wars, and had voted for a change. This was something that would not be in James' interests.

Speaking of the devil, he entered the room carrying a file.

"Isn't having a file with a stack of documents a precarious way to deliver information?" I remarked.

"Quite the contrary. In our world with hackers and advanced digital encryption, paper copies are the safest option, particularly in the way I store them." James replied and smiled a crooked smile.

James handed me the file, and I glanced at the pages. They were full of incomprehensible gibberish.

"What is this nonsense?" I asked in bewilderment.

"Exactly the response I'm after. That's what people who are checking this folder would think. However, if you use encryption key X72 in your monocle, the truth will show." James replied.

I did as James instructed, and the text became legible. As I had expected, it was about Eva Moreno. 'Project Safe Eagle: Termination of Eva Moreno's Presidential Candidacy.' The header of the document read.

"So, are you planning to commit treason, and are you using me as a tool? How unpatriotic of you." I needled.

"I would never commit treason!" James hissed.

His remark confused me. Wasn't he about to ask me to kill the next president? I tapped the encrypted document a few times and gave him a questioning look. "Well then, what is this document?" I asked.

"Well, technically Eva Moreno is only a presidential candidate. The electoral college hasn't ratified her yet." James explained.

"What's the difference between killing her now or later?" I asked.

"It's a monumental difference. At this moment, Eva Moreno is just a regular citizen who poses a threat to national security, so she must be eliminated. It is my patriotic duty. Once the electoral college has ratified Eva, then she becomes the president. Killing her when she becomes the president would be treason." James argued.

I shook my head. I wasn't particularly interested in meddling into American politics. Besides, I couldn't see how killing Eva Moreno would prevent the apocalypse from happening in the year 2131.

"I am out. I am not going to abolish American democracy through killing president elects that you don't approve of." I snarked

"Martin. Please read the document before you make uninformed statements. I never tasked you with killing Eva Moreno." James taunted.

I grimaced at James, but I didn't say anything. I read through the document. The rest of the monocle conspiracy had convened in the Harapan Conglomerate headquarters in Jakarta. During the meeting, they had agreed to eliminate Eva Moreno. This was so to make sure that the corrupt and corporate-friendly Damien Vanderbilt would become the new president. Damien was currently ranked second among the candidates and would become president if something happened to Eva Moreno. The monocle conspiracy had not hired a shooter for the assassination. But they were aware that a Taiwanese nationalist, Tzi Tsong planned to kill Eva to cause conflict between China and the USA.

After finishing reading the document, I felt confused. What did any of this have to do with me? I decided to ask James. "Hey James, I don't understand. What am I meant to do?"

"Oh, yes. Sorry about that. We want Tzi Tsong to kill Eva, but there is a problem. The Secret service has counter snipers that will scan the rooftops for potential attackers. Someone will have to eliminate these obstacles. You are that someone." James replied.

"Why would I agree to that?" I asked.

"Because you owe us. I brought you back from the dead. Both Elaine and Pierre have also helped you on several occasions." James replied.

"What if I don't feel like repaying you?" I sneered.

"That would be unfortunate. But I am sure you will be cooperative. After all, I can cause you immeasurable pain at any moment!" James smirked.

A terrible pain gripped me, and I collapsed to the floor, shaking uncontrollably. A few seconds later, it all ended, and James looked down on me. "Do you see what I mean?" James taunted.

"How did you do that?" I asked.

"When we had you in our medical care, we filled your body with nanorobots close to your nerves. If you dissent, I can turn your own bioelectricity into terrible nerve pain." James revealed.

"I guess I have no choice but to comply. What are the specifics?" I asked.

"Excellent. Let me help you up now that we have resolved this misunderstanding." James said and lent me a helping hand to get up from the floor.

Once I got seated by the table, James spoke again. "Eva's speech will start at 1300. Your job is to swiftly take out the counter snipers at 1259 just before she comes out. I will provide you with a list detailing the positions of the counter snipers. I'll also supply you with the with a silenced sniper rifle without a scope."

"Why no scope?" I asked.

"Because the monocle gives you a lot better aim than any scope would do. You're not a trained sniper. Besides, with a silenced rifle, and no reflection from your scope, you'd be almost invisible to your enemies." James explained.

I nodded and realised that I only had one question. "Hey, James. Why don't you kill the counter snipers yourself? You'd be a great shot, and you also have a Zetan Monocle." I asked.

"I will stand next to Eva Moreno during her speech. That's the only way for me to avoid becoming a suspect. Let's hope that Tzi Tsong is a good shot!" James replied.

"I am sure, the monocle would help you to dodge the bullet if you came into the firing line," I replied.

"Yes, but it would ruin my alibi," James remarked.

James walked towards the door. "I'll see you tomorrow, Martin. Be prepared." James said and left the hotel room.

After James left, I poured myself a big drink from the minibar. I had been back to civilisation for less than 24 hours, and I was already involved in another murder conspiracy. How I missed my solitude on Kiribati.

AFTER A FEW TOO MANY drinks from the minibar, I decided to do what anyone would do. I decided to confront my estranged wife, Elaine, over the phone. Normally, I don't condone this kind of behaviour, but when your ex involves you in a murder conspiracy against your will, it's reasonable to feel upset.

As Elaine picked up the phone, I ranted. "Hey, callous bitch. Why did you agree to send me on this mission? I had withdrawn. I was trying to make amends. I was trying to start a new life for myself."

"Martin, it's not that easy. You can't disappear and expect everyone to forgive you. I have done you many favours. Now you need to stop Eva Moreno for the rest of us." Elaine replied.

"But, it's not the right thing to do. The people voted for change. They deserve change." I objected.

"The masses lead unremarkable lives and never account for much. We are not going to give up our long-term goals to please their whims and wishes. Killing Eva and blaming the assassination on China will yield the best results. Damien Vanderbilt will not do anything to impede our progress. Starting a new cold war will accelerate the space race, improving our prospects of building space colonies by 2131." Elaine explained.

I realised that there was no point in arguing. I could either complete the mission and keep the others satisfied, or I could refuse and have the entire world coming after me. "Okay boss. I'll do as you say." I sighed and hung up the phone.

THE NEXT DAY I WAS on a rooftop in Washington. It was a chilly November day, and the wind made me shiver to the bone. I had lived on a tropical island for the last two years, so I wasn't used to the cold. I entered combat mode on my monocle, and I realised that I could only spot three out of four counter snipers. What would I do? I thought of shooting Eva Moreno myself, but that wasn't an option, as I didn't have the view of her from my position.

'12:58'

Tzi Tsong would show up at any moment, and as soon as he pulled out the rifle, the Secret Service agents would kill him. I saw Tzi take his position via infrared vision. I had to move now.

I swiftly shot the three secret service snipers from my position with my silenced sniper rifle. Tzi Tsong was just about to shoot Eva when he got shot himself. Getting shot, Tzi Tsong's shot was off its target.

My perception of time froze. My monocle showed the estimated trajectory of Tzi Tsong's shot, it would miss by five metres. But, if I could shoot and nudge the bullet mid-air, that could change its trajectory to kill Eva. 'Probability of success: 1 in 1 billion' my monocle revealed. 'Oh well, I have already won the Powerball,' I thought, and I took the shot.

'Double kill!' appeared on my monocle, and I didn't understand anything at all. "Is Eva dead?" I transmitted to James via the monocle. "Yes. Get the hell out of there!" James replied.

Reading this, I disassembled the rifle and packed it into a backpack. After that, I used the 'Avoid-Confrontation' mode on my monocle and got back undetected to my hotel.

THERE IS A SCIENTIFIC theory that one could strike straight through a wall without any contact. This is due to the gaps and positioning between the atoms. I don't recommend anyone trying it, as it would take trillions of years to get it right. The replay of my double kill shot that killed Eva Moreno and the fourth counter-sniper reminded me of this theory.

Not only had I managed to hit Tzi's misaimed bullet mid-air redirecting it to a collision course with Eva's head. The collision had also changed the trajectory of my bullet, causing it to hit the fourth counter-sniper who I hadn't even seen. I reckon that if time was reset an infinite amount of times, I wouldn't be able to replicate the shot.

James entered my hotel suite, brandishing a smug grin. "Excellent shooting, Martin. You are no longer in my debt." James said.

"Did you see those shots? The last shot was a miracle!" I said in awe.

James gave me a sceptical look and replied. "I don't know what you are talking about. Your fourth shot was the easiest of the four. It's a shame you couldn't kill the counter-sniper in time, but as soon as he had revealed himself, it was an easy shot."

"But I shot Tzi's bullet mid-air. This changed the direction of both bullets, causing Tzi's to hit Eva and mine to hit the fourth sniper." I replied.

Hearing this, James studied me for a while. After a long pause, he replied. "Look, that's not how it happened. When explaining something, always go with the easiest explanation. If our jobs weren't so secret, I'd recommend you seek out a mental health professional."

I realised that there was no point arguing my case. James' explanation made a lot more sense, and what did I have to gain from proving my crazy story?

"So, what happens now?" I asked.

"Well. We have placed a dead Iranian agent at your Sniper's location. I have framed a senior Secret Service employee with giving out the Secret Service snipers locations to help the attack. Washington police found Tzi Tsong where he got shot. We will claim that this was a coordinated attack by Iran and China." James revealed.

"So, will there be war?" I asked.

"Not a proper war. This outcome delights everyone in Washington. It's business as usual as there is no more threat to your average politician and their wealthy donors. There will be retaliatory strikes, of course. But we in the

CIA will coordinate these strikes with China and Iran. That way, they can fill the attacked sites by undesirables from their own countries." James explained.

"So, you got it all figured out. What happens to me?" I asked.

"You'll re-join with the Templars and the Mossad. Ben and Szymon have been struggling to open that damn door in Jerusalem. Go give them a hand, will you?" James commanded.

"I'd rather go back to my home in Kiribati!" I objected.

"I am not stopping you, and your debt to me is repaid. But I doubt Ben, Szymon and Pierre will see it the same way." James replied.

I walked over to the couch and collapsed on it in resignation. When would this damn nightmare end? I realised that I couldn't go back to Kiribati until everyone considered my debt to be repaid. I studied the photo of Alani. Now that I was back in civilisation, I saw her for what she was, a 40-year-old plain-looking widow. Even though this itself wasn't a problem, the facts remained. The only way that I could keep Alani and Elenoa safe was to stay away until I had fulfilled my destiny.

Next stop, Jerusalem.

Chapter 14: Jerusalem, November 2028

"Welcome home, Martin!"

My previous aides, James and Michael, met me with enthusiasm as I passed customs at Tel Aviv International Airport. I experienced mixed feelings seeing them again. I hadn't seen them for almost four years. A terrorist attack in Rome had injured James and Michael. My inaction in Rome had allowed the Salafist terror attack to take place, killing hundreds of people including the Pope. I had never felt suitable for my appointment as the grandmaster for the revitalised Templar Order. But now I was back, and while I didn't feel enthusiastic about it, at least I had a purpose in life again.

"I am glad that God kept you safe, James," I said and forced a pretentious smile. I had seen James and Michael when they were in a coma after the Salafist attack. I had felt compelled to leave, to get as far away from Rome as possible. My guilt had driven me, yet if I had cared a bit, wouldn't I have visited them in the years that followed?

"I am glad that you found Jesus and came back home," James replied.

"Yes, we thought that we had lost you," Michael added in.

"Well, I am back now. Who is the leader of the Templar order these days?" I asked.

"You are!" James replied.

"I am? So, you were leaderless for over three years?" I asked.

"A body cannot live without the head. Your departure left us in a predicament." Michael replied.

"But to be fair, we were doing rehab for most of the time, and we were unable to perform active duties anyways," James admitted.

I nodded, but I didn't say anything. I was the reluctant leader for a defunct religious organisation. And I didn't even share the religious beliefs of the organisation.

"So, are we going to the Templar Tunnels to unlock that bloody door?" I scoffed.

"Yes, Grandmaster. But first, we must head to the grave of the Virgin Mary and pay our respects, as is the custom for our organisation." James replied.

"Of course. Lead the way, Brother James." I replied.

I WATCHED JAMES AND Michael as they prayed to the statue of the Virgin Mary. The worship of Virgin Mary had always fascinated me. Even if Mary were a virgin when she got pregnant with Jesus, which seems far-fetched, she did have other children later. At some point, she would have to stop being a virgin for this to happen, or god would have to keep busy, while Josef would be the saddest man in antiquity!

"Why are they praying to a dead human?" Rangda asked in the back of my head.

I walked away from the others. I didn't want to disturb their prayers by speaking to myself like a madman in front of them.

"I guess it brings them comfort, believing in something higher than themselves," I replied.

"It's nonsense. No matter how powerful they believe that Mary was during her lifetime, she is dead now. What do they hope to achieve?" Rangda objected.

"Well, are you jealous? Would you rather have them pray to you?" I taunted.

"I don't care for human worship. I only care for human obedience." Rangda replied.

"So, who should they pray to?" I asked.

"If they must pray, they can pray to the True Maker, the creator of our universe. But that would be a waste of time." Rangda replied.

"Why is that?" I asked.

"Because the True Maker never does anything. She is just watching as time flows by. How species rise and fall. That's why I will depose her. Together we will spread life to a mostly lifeless galaxy." Rangda ranted.

"Understood!" I replied

"Now, tell your subordinates to stop wasting time. You need to get to that door, open it, and retrieve my crystal." Rangda commanded.

"Understood, Empress Rangda," I said and disconnected from Rangda. After that, I urged James and Michael to hurry up.

"WE MEET AGAIN, AL-SHAM." Ben Yehuda said and twirled his moustache.

"Yes. It has been two years. Can you tell me what is delaying you from opening that damn door?" I growled.

"Relax, Al-Sham. Remember where you are." Szymon replied.

I calmed down and didn't say anything.

"So, so gentlemen. Let me show you our progress so far." Ben said.

I walked in silence behind the Yehuda Brothers, who led us to the Templar Tunnels under the Solomon Temple. It was the same tunnels I had spent months combing for clues during my last stint with the Templars. Being back here, I was curious about what the Yehuda Brothers had figured out. As we came to the end of a pathway, I noticed that a tunnel on the right had opened since my last visit. I felt a strong aura streaming from the tunnel and my heart rate increased as Ben led us onto the right-hand-path.

We reached the end of the tunnel, and it was a dead-end. Ben and Szymon stared at the wall and I felt compelled to speak. "Hey, what's this? Why did you bring me here?" I asked.

Ben took up his phone and handed it to me. "This is why!" Ben said. I looked at the phone. On the picture, the entire wall was lit up with ancient symbols.

"I assume you used a Zeto Crystal to energise the wall?" I asked.

"Yes. We have wasted several Zeto Crystals trying to open this wall. We don't know the correct sequence and the damn wall electrocutes us and shuts down the moment we put in the wrong password." Ben Yehuda revealed.

I studied the picture. I recognised some of the symbols from the tattoo that the Zetans gave me in 2019. Could my tattoo be the password?

"Hey, Ben. Do you have any more Zeto Crystals?"

"Yes, I got one. Why? Do you think you know the correct sequence?" Ben asked.

"Yes, I believe that my tattoo might contain the correct sequence," I replied.

The Yehuda Brothers walked up to me, and they checked out my tattoo. They gave each other a long look. Eventually, Ben nodded towards Szymon and Szymon handed me a replicated Zeto Crystal.

"Use it well. Don't get the sequence wrong." Szymon said.

"I won't fail," I said, and I grabbed the crystal.

"Where is the slot for this crystal?" I asked.

"There isn't any. You'll have to slam it towards the wall to discharge the energy." Ben instructed.

I thought about the proposition. It sounded wasteful, but with a priceless treasure on the other side of the wall, I had to give it a shot. I slammed the Zeto Crystal against the wall, and it sent out a burst of blue energy that lit up the wall.

I felt how my pulse rose. I was so close to the end of my journey. Once I had the Primordial Zeto Crystal, I could open the portal to the Divine Dimension and avert the oncoming apocalypse.

I worried that the Yehuda Brothers would try to use the Zeto Crystal for their own nefarious purpose. The Yehuda Brothers wanted to ethnically cleanse the Holy Land and make way for the Jewish master race. But I did have trump on hand. I assumed that the crystal would be out of charge when we found it. The only way to charge it, which I knew of, was to wrap it in Pachamama's Veil and drop it into an active volcano. So, I would let the Yehuda Brothers take the crystal for now, and then steal it back from them once they believed that it was useless.

Having planned my next move, I approached the alien symbols on the wall and entered the sequence from my tattoo.

'poof!!'

The room blackened and I felt a burning pain before everything faded to black.

"AL-SHAM, YOU WASTED our Zeto Crystal." Szymon barked.

The thing I hated the most about my life, was that every time something knocked me unconscious, I was never met with love and concern when I woke up. Instead, it was always someone whinging or arguing, making me want to fall back into unconsciousness to get away from it all. I decided to try this approach. I kept my eyes closed, pretending to not hear the Yehuda Brothers.

Unfortunately, Szymon Yehuda saw through my ruse and spoke. "Al-Sham. I have drinks and food. I can play this game all day long. Don't pretend to be unconscious."

I realised that Szymon had a compelling argument, and I opened my eyes.

"My brother isn't happy with you," Szymon said.

"Why is that, I heard you guys also stuffed up the sequence!" I replied.

"Yes. But you used up the last Zeto Crystal. Now we must find a new crystal or ask Pierre for another one."

"Not a big deal, Pierre is wealthy. He can send us a few." I replied.

"I suggest that you tell Pierre yourself. I am sending you and the other Templars to Mexico. There might be a clue for us there in the Sun Pyramid. See if you can recruit some local agents while you are at it. I hope our next meeting will be under more joyful circumstances." Szymon said and left my hospital room.

I got up from the bed. My back was very sore, but I didn't want to stay here any longer. Keeping active was my best way to find the solution, and the further away I was from the Yehuda Brothers, the better. I got up from my bed, and I contacted Michael and James.

'KEILA EISENSTEIN DOES not generate any matches.'

I was searching the internet as well as the CIA's secret files for any clues about Keila Eisenstein. The woman was a ghost, or she didn't exist. I had re-called that the Zetans tasked me with finding Keila while I got the tattoo.

The two had to be related. Ergo, finding Keila Eisenstein was the key to deciphering the tattoo and retrieving the primordial Zeto Crystal. But finding Keila seemed to be as tricky as interpreting the tattoo. But what were my options? I couldn't guess the sequence out of millions of possible solutions. Every incorrect guess would get me electrocuted and lose me a Zeto Crystal. I had to find Keila, it was my only option.

I decided to confide in Michael and James. Finding a woman in hiding was like finding a needle in a haystack. If three people were looking for the damn needle, that would reduce the time finding it.

"Michael and James. There is one thing you need to know about the mission ahead of us." I said.

"What is that, Grandmaster?" Michael asked.

"We need to keep an eye out for a woman called Keila Eisenstein," I replied.

"What do we know about this woman?" James asked.

"I know nothing about her. The name doesn't exist in any database, but I know that she is important for our success." I replied.

Michael and James studied me sceptically for a while. Eventually, Michael spoke: "Okay, Martin. I promise to keep an eye out. But let's focus on our mission in Mexico. Let's see if we can find the Royal Tomb in The Sun Pyramid."

I nodded in acknowledgement. We couldn't travel the world, looking for a random woman that could be anywhere. We had to focus on following the clues that we had on hand. Next stop, the Sun Pyramid in Mexico City.

Chapter 15: Jerusalem, December 2037

I was adding the finishing touches to my 25th novel. It was a splendid work of fiction, and I hoped that this would be my breakthrough. I have never heard about anyone having a breakthrough on their 25th novel, but I have never heard of the opposite either, so this was it.

The nine last years had been both eventful and uneventful at the same time. I had travelled the world with James and Michael, looking for alien artefacts or clues to unlock the door in the Templar Tunnels. While exploring the corners of the world, we had also tried to recruit followers.

Neither of our objectives had been successful. I lacked the religious zeal to be a credible spiritual leader, and our strained relationship with the Vatican didn't help. When it came to our search for ancient artefacts, we hadn't found anything useful. In the tunnels below, that damn door still impeded our progress, stopping us from getting to the primordial Zeto Crystal. In our desperation to get ahead, we had tried both explosives and lasers, without even denting the door. While this proved that something valuable was on the other side, it didn't get us closer to our goal.

I stopped writing, as Mossad agent Dov Dorevitch stormed into my office.

"Martin Al-Sham. I know that you are up to something bad." Dov shouted.

I was reflecting over Dov's statement. Was this a sign from the True Maker that my 25th book wouldn't be successful? Or was Dov talking about something else? 'Only one way to find out,' I thought, and I replied. "What are you talking about. I am writing a novel. What do you think I am up to?"

Dov shook his head and replied. "I don't care about your book. But you are the leader of a militant Christian faction in a contested region of the world. There are rumours about a terrorist attack taking place tomorrow."

I sighed and poured myself and Dov, a glass of red wine each from an ornamental golden carafe I had in my office.

"I am not drinking while performing my duty. Answer my question!" Dov growled.

"I didn't hear a question. I heard an unrelated statement." I argued.

"Al-Sham. You are the leader of a militant Christian order. Can you prove that your group isn't involved in the last few years' repeated attacks?" Dov insinuated.

"Proving innocence is an impossible task. That's why the justice system is about proving guilt. Can you prove that the Mossad isn't behind the rapid increase in terrorist attacks?" I smirked.

I knew that the Yehuda Brothers, together with Pierre Beaumont and the World Bank, financed Islamic terrorism. The ruling elites wanted terrorism as a distraction to their own nefarious schemes. As for the Yehuda Brothers, they hoped that Islamic terrorism would unite the Jews to drive the Muslims away from the Holy Land.

"I cannot prove that the Mossad is innocent when it comes to this. As a matter of fact, I believe that elements within the Mossad are conspiring against the Israeli people." Dov disclosed.

"That's interesting. Unfortunately, I am sold out of tin foil hats. The Knights Templar is not a militant organisation in the sense that you describe us. The things we have in common with our precursor organisation is our discipline, our religious zeal, and our chastity." I stated.

"Weren't you too busy frequenting high-end brothels in Rome, to save Pope Septimus' life?" Dov insinuated.

I decided to not answer Dov's statement. His presence both annoyed and terrified me. He was an issue that I needed to deal with, but first, he needed to leave my office. "Was there anything else?" I asked.

"Yes. As a matter of fact, there is. This girl landed at the airport a few hours ago. An 18-year-old travelling from Australia, flying with expensive Orbit Flight tickets. Highly suspicious!" Dov said and put a document on my desk.

I was about to answer when I had a quick look at the document. The content of the document stunned me. A certain Sabina Hines had landed earlier today. I looked at her picture. It was the spitting image of Ellen Hines, the woman I had a short tryst with 18 years earlier. But didn't Sabina and Ellen die in the South African Civil War in 2023?

I realised that I had never verified the deaths of Ellen and Sabina. I had been filled with guilt and terror and had not dared to face the truth. Instead, I had assumed that they were dead from seeing the dead girl on television news. If Sabina was alive and had come to Jerusalem, I had to see her. There were so many unresolved questions that I had. Among them, I needed to find out whether she was my daughter or not.

"As I thought. You know this girl, don't you? I'll be watching you, Al-Sham." Dov said, picked up the document, and left me speechless.

"DOV IS COMING AFTER us. We need to act now." I said to Ben Yehuda over the encrypted phone.

"You worry about nothing, Al-Sham. Let him believe that we involve ourselves with this Sabina Hines woman. It will direct his focus in the wrong direction. We will deal with Dov if it becomes necessary." Ben replied.

"So, what is going to happen tomorrow?" I asked.

"The bloodred sun will rise again. Hopefully, it will bring my people a better future." Ben replied. "Will there be another attack?" I asked.

"I hope so. But since I don't carry out the actual attacks, I cannot know for certain. Don't worry, Martin. Stay away from the Western Wall and focus on your books. Pierre or I will contact you about future assignments. Dismissed." Ben replied and hung up the phone.

After the phone call, I felt anxious. Ben knew that Sabina was in Jerusalem. While it was trivial knowledge to him, I would still feel more comfortable if he didn't know. I decided to arrange a meeting with James and Michael to discuss the matter further.

IT WAS CLOSE TO MIDNIGHT when my fellow templars James and Michael entered my office. They got seated by my dining table, and I poured them each a goblet of red wine. As we drank the wine, we cheered and praised the Virgin Mary. After the usual formalities, Michael spoke.

"What is going on, Grandmaster. Why are we gathering like this, in the middle of the night?" Michael asked.

"There is going to be another attack tomorrow. A Salafist attack near the Western Wall." I revealed.

"Thanks for the warning, Grandmaster. But that doesn't explain why we are meeting like this. Let the infidels kill each other, for all I care." Michael replied.

I paused, took a large sip of my wine, and I spoke again. "There is a girl we need to look for. Both Dov and Ben mentioned her today. She might be crucial for the success of our mission here."

"Who is this girl, Grandmaster?" James asked.

"Her name is Sabina Hines; we need to find her and speak to her," I replied.

"Understood. We will start searching for the girl tomorrow. God bless you, Grandmaster." Michael said.

Michael and James got up and left the room. I hesitated for a moment. I wanted to start the search for Sabina tonight, but I didn't want to reveal to them why it was so urgent for me to see her.

Fortunately, I had another contact who didn't mind working in the middle of the night. I sent a message on the darknet, and I headed to our designated meeting spot.

"DID YOU BRING THE MONEY?" Simona fretted.

I chucked a stash of shekel notes on the floor, and I studied the girl. Simona was a skinny and black-haired girl. She was younger than 20, with very boyish looks and mannerism. I knew that she was a lesbian, but that didn't stop me from feeling attracted to her. I had never acted on this attraction, as I assumed that a 52-year-old man wouldn't be that attractive to an 18-year-old lesbian. Besides, I could get sex elsewhere but finding someone with Simona's talents was worth a fortune.

Simona had been my protégé for the last two years. Her family had disowned her when they discovered that she was a lesbian. This had forced Simona to move in with her girlfriend, Leah. Unfortunately, Leah had been an activist dedicated to bringing down the Yehuda Brothers. Once Ben Yehuda had found Leah's identity, he had decided to kill her himself. Simona had witnessed the murder from a hiding spot. I didn't know why Ben had left Simona alive, and I couldn't find out without compromising her identity.

Simona finished counting the money and turned towards me. "What do you need done?" Simona asked.

"There is someone I need you to find and contact. Her name is Sabina Hines, and I suspect that she is here on a mission." I replied.

"Why do you believe that?" Simona asked.

"18-year-old backpackers don't pay USD 30,000 for a one-way-ticket flying an Orbit Flight from Sydney. Besides, it's notoriously hard to get a tourist visa to Israel these days." I replied.

Simona nodded and replied. "So, what do you want me to do?"

"I want you to find out everything you can about Sabina. If possible, try to meet her. Someone with your talents would be useful for her if she is in Jerusalem on a mission." I replied.

"And do you want me to help her?" Simona asked.

"Find out what she aims to do first, and then we can discuss the best course of action," I replied.

"And what about my payment?" Simona asked.

"You'll be well-compensated. Enough to leave this shithole and start a new life." I replied.

"Fair enough. I accept your offer." Simona said.

"Good. I expect your initial report by noontime tomorrow. Get to work, Simona" I said and left the safehouse.

KABOOM

The sound of a distant explosion woke me up. I looked at my phone. It was 1030 AM already. No early bird for me this morning, but to my defence I had been up late, hiring Simona to track down Sabina.

I got up from my bed and made my way to the coffee machine when I heard a multitude of sirens from emergency vehicles. It was apparent to me that another big terrorist attack had taken place. I didn't mind, as it didn't affect me or my plans.

But then, anxiety gripped me. What if Sabina or Simona was among the killed? Sabina could be my daughter, and Simona was my protégé and crucial for my goals. I didn't want any of them to get injured in the blast. I called Simona.

"Hello?" Simona replied with a sleepy voice.

"I am waking you up for our meeting. See you in one hour, Simona!" I replied and hung up.

While I felt relieved that Simona was okay, I still didn't know about the fate of Sabina. I was getting ready for meeting Simona when I saw something that shocked me. The television news showed the CCTV footage from the terrorist attack. In the centre of the footage, I saw Sabina. I felt terrified when the explosion went off next to her, and the camera died.

'Don't focus on things you cannot change. Focus on what you can do,' I told myself, and I hurried to the safe house where I'd meet Simona.

"THAT WAS AN INTERESTING girl you asked me to investigate. Unbelievably cute as well." Simona said and hinted a rare smile.

"I am sure that she'll be super attracted by the girl who spent the whole night hacking websites to uncover her secrets." I taunted.

"A girl got to have dreams!" Simona snapped back.

"Whatever. What did you find out?" I replied

Simona took a deep breath and then she read aloud from her tablet. "Sabina Hines is an Australian citizen, born in South Africa on 20th October 2019. Her parents are John Hines and Ellen Hines. Her father is Jewish, and that was how she got her visa to Israel. Sabina has no known affiliations with any groups."

"Hmm, not much to go on. Did you find out anything else?" I asked.

"Yes. Sabina graduated high school with the highest possible marks. She made $300,000 doing online trading for one month. Yesterday she bought SplitCoin for $150,000." Simona replied.

"Perfect. You have earnt a reward." I said and transferred some SplitCoin to Simona.

Simona checked her phone and gave me a sour look. "Only $1,000?" How am I going to start a new life on that little money?"

"You're not going to start a new life until we have completed this mission. And unlike the Mossad, I pay in gold and not in lead. Try to organise a meeting with Sabina. I'll make sure to make it worth your while." I replied.

I was walking towards the door when I felt sentimental. I walked back to Simona, hugged her, and spoke. "Simona, be careful out there. I might not show it, but I do care about you."

Simona stared at me in disbelief. After some awkward silence, I turned around and left the apartment.

I WAS IN MY OFFICE in the inconspicuous Templar Headquarters, nervously staring at the clock. It was 9 PM, and I had not received any news from Simona, and I didn't even know if Sabina had survived the terrorist attack.

Suddenly, Ben Yehuda entered my office. I thought of snapping at him, but I realised that I should hire competent security guards to prevent this from happening.

"I have some urgent news about a mutual friend," Ben stated.

Ben's statement confused me. I disliked Ben, and I couldn't recall us having any mutual friends. I realised that this remark wouldn't add to the conversation, so instead, I replied: "Tell me, Ben."

"Dov implicated Sabina Hines for the terrorist attack at the Western Wall this morning. During the interrogation, he snapped and kidnapped Sabina at gunpoint. Jakub Kluger followed them and shot Dov. Before Jakub could bring Sabina back, lightning struck him. Jakub is receiving intensive care at the hospital, and Sabina is missing." Ben revealed.

Ben's revelation relieved me. I had worried that Sabina died during the attack, but she was alive and kicking. I hid my feelings from Ben and replied. "Okay. So, what do you suggest that we do?"

"That depends. I can either send out an arrest order for Sabina, classifying her as a dangerous terrorist. Every police officer and every CCTV camera will be looking for her." Ben replied.

"And what is the second option?" I asked, hoping that it would be a better option for my goals.

"I can delete everything about Sabina in our registry and keep the files on my personal drive." Ben revealed.

I studied Ben Yehuda. Was he testing me, and what would I respond? It would seem strange if I was too keen on the second option. But I didn't want to dissuade from picking that option either. Eventually, I replied. "I see. Why do you want Sabina Hines to remain secret?"

Ben Yehuda handed me a tablet. On the tablet, there was a video from the interrogation. In the video, Dov was screaming at Sabina, until she grabbed his arm and stared into his eyes for a few seconds. After that, Dov seemed hypnotised. Dov unlocked Sabina's handcuffs and led her out from the interrogation room and the video ended. I stared at the video in disbelief. What had I witnessed?

"What was that?" I asked in confusion.

"I believe that Sabina is a touch empath," Ben replied.

"A touch empath? What is that?" I asked.

"One of the ancient forbidden Torah's is about Malka, who was a touch empath. Malka was a powerful sorceress who could influence minds through the power of touch." Ben revealed.

"So, what are you suggesting?" I asked.

"I am suggesting that we lure Sabina to the door blocking the Zeto Crystal. We have exhausted all options to open that door. Perhaps a touch empath can do better." Ben speculated.

I thought about Ben's proposal. It was a dangerous plan, and I didn't want to expose Sabina to Ben. But unfortunately, he already knew about her. I realised that it was better if only Ben knew about Sabina than if the entire country was chasing her.

"Okay, what do you suggest that we do?" I asked.

"You must find her and catch her attention. But, before she gets the chance to manipulate your mind via touch, I'll come and stage your murder. That will send her on the run and lead her straight to the Templar Tunnels and the locked door. Hopefully, she is powerful enough to unlock it for us." Ben instructed.

"And what if she fails?" I asked.

"Then we'll have another corpse, and the door remains locked. Nothing won, nothing lost." Ben replied.

I got angry at Ben's statement. Sabina was potentially my daughter, and I couldn't let Ben murder her. But I kept calm and redirected the topic. "Have you discussed this with the others?" I asked.

"Szymon is on a secret mission in Africa, and it wouldn't be suitable to contact him now. I don't see any reason to contact the others." Ben replied.

I noticed a text message notification from Simona on my smartwatch, and I decided to finish up my conversation with Ben. "Okay, let's do things like you say. I will keep an eye out for Sabina." I said.

"Are you going somewhere?" Ben remarked.

"Yes, I have a hot date. I can't let your whims and wishes destroy my sex life, can I?" I scoffed.

Ben stood silent for a second. Clearly, he wanted to object to my excuse. After a moment of silence, Ben gave in. "Very well, Al-Sham. Enjoy your godless copulation. As long as you're ready to serve on short notice. Dismissed." Ben sighed.

"Aye, Aye, Sir," I replied. Then I mock-saluted Ben Yehuda and left my office.

After leaving my office, I contacted Simona and organised a meeting.

"SABINA CONTACTED ME via the dark web. She needed to find a safe place to stay. I sent her to the safehouse at E-Zahra Street." Simona revealed.

I was experiencing a lot of emotions bubbling up to the surface. I wanted to go there at once, warn Sabina about Ben Yehuda and leave Israel as fast as possible. But I also wanted to use Sabina to open the locked passageway in the Templar Tunnels to secure the primordial Zeto Crystal. Securing the Zeto Crystal was far more important than the well-being of a girl who might or might not be my daughter.

"Is there anything bothering you?" Simona asked.

"I was thinking. We need to track Sabina and see what she is up to. Did she order any equipment or only accommodation?" I asked.

"She ordered the whole kit. Phone, Laptop, fake ID, prepaid credit card and clothes." Simona replied.

This was great news. If Sabina ordered a phone, we could track her movements by inserting a tracking chip on her phone. The only problem was that she might discover it. Someone tech-savvy, ordering new gear, paying with crypto-currency over the darknet, could detect if we tracked her. But if she was a real pro, Simona wouldn't have figured out Sabina's real identity. I decided to ask Simona to insert a tracking chip in the phone.

"Can you insert a tracking chip in the phone, the laptop and the clothes?" I asked.

"That would be against my professional code. My reputation would be irreversibly damaged if it came out that I was tracking my clients." Simona objected.

"Like I promised before, I can pay you enough to leave this city for good!" I replied.

"My code is not about money, it's about the principle!" Simona exclaimed.

I sighed. I hated dealing with political idealists. They were always so self-righteous and hard to persuade.

"But there is one thing that I want. But it's not about money." Simona revealed.

I nodded. I suspected that money would have been easier, but I wanted to hear Simona's conditions. "So, what do you want, Simona?" I asked.

"I want justice. I want to kill Ben Yehuda to avenge Leah." Simona replied.

I sighed. I wanted to kill Ben as well, but if I did, Pierre, Szymon and Vladimir would come after me. They would also send a vast array of assassins. But, If Simona killed Ben, and I could convince the others that I wasn't involved, that would kill two birds with one stone.

"Deal. Help me with this mission, and I'll get you within reach of Ben Yehuda. Killing him will be on you." I replied.

"Deal. I would better get going. I promised to deliver by midday tomorrow." Simona said.

"I'll need to inspect the products before you deliver them. I'll pay you an extra $10,000 for your troubles."

"Okay, meet me here at 1130 tomorrow!" Simona said and left the premises.

I WAS WAITING FOR SIMONA at the meeting spot. I felt exhausted. This life was too stressful for me, and I needed to get out of here. I dreamt of going back to Kiribati to enjoy the solitude on my secluded island. I dreamt even more about returning to 2018 before this whole mess began. But neither would happen, at least not the time travel option, and I needed to focus on the task at hand.

Without a word, Simona left the package on a table for me to check out the goods. I scanned the devices to make sure that Simona had inserted tracking bugs, which I could connect to. I also checked the ID.

As I checked the ID, I stared at the letters forming the name. They read 'Keila Eisenstein'. The same name that Brahma had tasked me with finding 18 years earlier. This could not be a coincidence.

"Who picked this name?" I asked in shock.

"What's the matter with the name?" Simona asked.

"There is nothing wrong with the name. But I want to know who picked it." I replied.

"Sabina asked me to create a fake ID with that name," Simona replied.

"Very well. Here is your cash, I'll send you the rest in SplitCoin. Now hurry up and deliver the package!" I said and handed Simona a wad of Shekel notes.

Simona took the money without saying a word, grabbed the package and left the building.

'WOAH, THAT WAS A CLOSE one,' I thought as the police officer who had stopped Sabina, let her go. I realised that we needed to intercept Sabina. The sooner that we could convince Sabina to help us, the sooner I could get out of Jerusalem. I thought of the fates of my fellow templars, James and Michael. If things came to worst, I would have to betray them to reach my goals. That would be a bittersweet end to my time in Jerusalem.

"She has entered a coffee shop. Prepare to move." I told the others.

"Shouldn't you fill me in, first?" I heard Ben Yehuda say.

'Oh shit!' I thought, and I turned around. Ben Yehuda, together with two police officers dressed in combat gear stood behind me.

"So, you were planning to move on the sorceress without telling me first. How disappointing!" Ben Yehuda remarked.

"We had to move fast. I did message you." I lied.

"But of course, you did! How unfortunate that the mobile network is so unreliable here." Ben mocked.

I didn't say anything, and Ben spoke again. "Al-Sham, I have ways of keeping track of you. Remember the plan. Enter the coffee shop, lock the door behind you, speak to her for a short while. Then I'll bang on the door. Make her hide and let her witness our conversation where we mention the locked door in the Templar Tunnels. Then my men will shoot you guys, and you'll play dead. Once the girl has snuck out, I will give the all-clear and we can leave."

"Understood!" I replied.

"Oh, and one more thing. Take off your monocle. It doesn't make sense that we are wearing the same monocle if we are enemies." Ben ordered.

I did as Ben instructed, and I took off my monocle, put it in my pocket and inserted a blue-tinted contact lens.

THE COFFEE SHOP WAS empty as we walked in, except for Sabina and the owner. I signalled the owner to leave the premises. The fearful owner complied without a word, and I locked the front door behind me. It was time to act. I removed my turban and approached Sabina. "Keila Eisenstein. We have been looking for you." I stated.

The girl looked at me, and I sensed that she emitted a powerful and strange aura. I heard Rangda whisper in the back of my head. *"This girl is incredibly powerful, be careful."*

"Yes, I am Keila Eisenstein. Who am I talking to?" Sabina replied.

"I am Martin Al-Sham. I have been looking for you for almost 20 years." I stated.

"How can that be? I am only 18. You must be mistaken?" Sabina replied.

"No, I am certain that you are the Chosen One. I met with Zetan deities 19 years ago. They gave me this tattoo, and they tasked me with finding Keila Eisenstein and asking her to decipher its message." I claimed.

Having said this, I rolled up my sleeve, and I showed Sabina my tattoo. Sabina looked attentively at the tattoo. She grabbed my hand and stroke the tattoo with her other hand. Feeling her touch, I experienced opposed feelings. On the one hand, I felt complete bliss and peace. But I also felt terrified. Ben was correct, Sabina must be some kind of sorceress.

"I told you to be careful. The girl is trying to access your mind. I'll try to block her powers!" Rangda whispered at the back of my head.

"I can sense that there is a message in these markings, yet I cannot decipher them," Sabina said.

"Her mind is too strong. I cannot hold her off for much longer. You need to get out of her grip." Rangda urged me.

I felt that I was losing grip of my mind. My mind wandered all over the place. I saw things that had been, things that were and some things that would be.

I woke up from my trance when there was a hard knock on the door followed by "This is the police. Open the door now."

Hearing this, Sabina released her grip of my arm, and I got back to my senses. "Hide in that ventilation shaft. We'll delay them!" I said.

Sabina nodded, took a photo of the tattoo, and hid in the ventilation shaft.

I opened the door, and Ben Yehuda accompanied by two masked police officers, entered the coffee shop. We had our scripted conversation, and we made sure to mention the Templar Tunnels. After that, Ben Yehuda shot me ten times with the blank bullets. It hurt a lot, but I shut up. After all, people that get shot ten times tend to die, not complain about bruises.

15 minutes later, Ben signalled that Sabina had left, and we got up. We walked away from the coffee shop. Once we were a few blocks away, Ben pressed a button on his phone, and I heard a loud detonation.

"What was that?" I asked.

"I didn't see any shop owner in there. I am making sure that he or she didn't survive eavesdropping on us." Ben explained.

"What now?" I asked.

"You don't look that well. Go get some sleep. I will contact you when the sorceress makes her move." Ben replied.

"LET ME IN. I NEED TO see Martin!"

I woke up to the voice of a young female arguing with James downstairs. I looked at my watch. The time was 8AM, and I had slept for over 12 hours!

I walked downstairs to see what the commotion was about. I saw Simona arguing with James.

"Simona? What are you doing here?" I asked in bewilderment.

"I needed to see you," Simona replied.

"Come with me!" I urged, and we walked upstairs to my office, far away from James' prying ears.

I made two cups of coffee, and I got seated.

"You could have organised a meeting," I stated.

"Yes, I suppose. I met Sabina 30 minutes ago. She wanted me to supply her with a new ID, phone and some cash." Simona revealed.

"I hope that you planted a tracking chip in the new phone as well?" I asked

"Yes, I'll send you the tracking code," Simona replied.

I accessed the tracking program, and I saw Sabina's current location. I smiled at Simona, and then I picked up a wad of Shekel notes from my drawer and handed them to her.

"Smart girl. You are getting paid from both sides. You'll be rich in no time." I sneered.

Simona ignored the sarcasm in my voice and spoke again. "There is one thing bothering me. I am falling in love with Sabina." Simona admitted.

"This is a complication. You are only meant to supply Sabina with equipment. You're not meant to sleep with her." I warned.

"I haven't slept with her. I haven't even spoken to her!" Simona protested.

"And yet, you love her? Foolish girl!" I mocked.

"I am not proud of it either. But Sabina's aura is unique. We had a short physical contact when I handed her the package. I have never felt anything like it." Simona admitted.

I nodded at Simona. Her story proved what Ben Yehuda had told me and what I had sensed. Sabina was unique and had unique powers. I would have reacted the same way to Sabina's touch if Rangda hadn't warned me about her abilities.

"Don't worry about it, Simona. I am sure you are still grieving Leah's death. Your mind is playing tricks on you. After this mission, I will take you out of here so you can start a new life." I replied.

"So, what should I do now?" Simona asked.

I thought about what the best option for the mission would be. I realised that Sabina was a powerful entity. But was she good or bad? The Zetans had told me to find Keila Eisenstein, and Sabina was no doubt the same person. I had stopped justifying the actions of myself and my peers in the monocle conspiracy a long time ago. It wasn't the greater good that drove our actions, but greed, selfishness, and fear. Was Sabina like us, or was she our opposite?

"Tell Sabina how you feel, the next time you meet her. Perhaps you're destined to be together. Or maybe you delude yourself. In either case, you are better off knowing." I replied.

"What do you think?" Simona asked.

"I am too old to cast judgement on teenage love affairs. Now go my protégé. Get some sleep and be ready to serve if the need arises." I said.

After saying this, I firmly put my hand on Simona's back and let her out of my office.

EIGHT HOURS LATER, Simona returned to my office. I gave her a disapproving look. If she kept visiting my office, the others would find out that she was working for me.

"It's happening tonight!" Simona exclaimed.

"What? Is Sabina going to the Templar Tunnels tonight?" I asked.

"Yes. Sabina asked me to tag along. Apparently, she is looking for the Holy Grail. Is that what this is all about? An ancient mythological treasure?" Simona asked, and gave me a very sceptical look.

I decided that there was no point in lying to Simona. She was dependent on me, and if anyone would betray me, it was James that I worried about.

"We are looking for an ancient treasure but not the Holy Grail," I replied and paused.

"We are looking for the primordial Zeto Crystal, which contains a part of god's soul. The Zeto Crystal is a potent artefact," I explained further.

"That sounds very much like the description of the Holy Grail," Simona smirked.

I realised that Simona didn't believe me and that it was better if she didn't. But her participation was problematic for the mission. I wanted to keep her alive, but I was confident that Ben Yehuda would see things differently. I came up with a solution. The only way to save Simona was to fake her death!

"Simona, your participation tonight is causing us problems. Ben Yehuda will insist on killing you to avoid leaving witnesses, but I have a solution." I started.

"Yes, we must kill Ben Yehuda. He killed Leah, and he caused terrorists to attack my people." Simona stated.

"I agree, but we cannot kill Ben Yehuda yet. Instead, I need to fake your death. Wear this body armour with attached blood bags. When the time is right, I will shoot you. The blood bags will burst and create the illusion that I killed you." I instructed.

"But, why not kill Ben Yehuda straight away?" Simona objected.

"Simona, don't question me. I am trying to get you out of this alive. I want to help you start a new life. What more can you ask for?" I replied.

Simona didn't say anything. Instead, she took off her jumper, put on the body armour with attached blood bags and then put her jumper on top. "We will be at the Templar Tunnels in two hours, send Ben Yehuda to the afterlife for me!" Simona said and left the room.

I WAS DOWN IN THE TEMPLAR Tunnels together with Ben Yehuda, James, and Michael. Ben picked up a replicated Zeto Crystal and smashed it against the wall to reveal the control panel for the door.

"The sorceress is here. Let's hide until she opens the door. After that, we move in and seize the Zeto Crystal." Ben ordered.

"How do you know she is here?" I asked.

"I put out hidden security cameras around the temple complex. I connected them to my monocle, so they are for my eyes only. Sabina knocked out the security guard with her powers, and they walked down the tunnels." Ben stated.

"They?" James asked.

"She is bringing some skinny, black-haired girl," Ben replied.

Before James had the time to answer, Ben spoke again. "Enough questions, let's get out of the way!"

I was shaking with anticipation when following the group. If everything went well, I would finally see the primordial Zeto Crystal. But the prospect of risking the life of Simona, made me feel sick.

We went to the opposite side of the complex, and the others spoke in loud Hebrew to give Sabina and Simona a false sense of security. Ben wanted to make it seem like we discussed something and wouldn't notice them.

"Now!" Ben commanded. We snuck towards the locked room, without making a noise, thanks to our Mossad issued, noise-reduction shoes.

When we reached the girls, Sabina was close to the altar with the Zeto Crystal and Simona was ten steps behind her. I grabbed Simona from behind, and we all aimed our pistols at her.

"Not so fast, or your friend will die!" Ben Yehuda commanded.

Sabina turned around and gave us a sad facial expression.

"Thank you for opening that door, Keila. We have been trying for the last decade." Ben taunted.

Sabina didn't reply, and she looked anxiously at Simona.

"You are here to steal the Zeto Crystal? Isn't that so, Keila? That is never going to happen. It is the tool I need to become the messiah for my people.

The man who cleansed this land from foul heretics and fulfilled my God-given purpose." Ben ranted.

"My name is not Keila Eisenstein. I used a fake ID." Sabina revealed.

"I care little for your real identity." Ben taunted and continued. "But I do know of your powers. Very impressive, albeit not particularly useful at gunpoint."

Sabina stared away in the distance, mumbling to herself before she gazed towards Ben and spoke with a commanding voice. "Ben Yehuda. How do you intend to achieve your goals?" Sabina asked.

"Why would I tell you?" Ben scoffed.

"Because I need to know whether I should stop you or not," Sabina stated.

"Very well. I intend to use the crystal to drive the unbelievers back into the desert. The rivers will run red with blood, but I will fulfil the Divine Plan. The master race shall be the sole inhabitants of this Holy Land." Ben stated.

Sabina sighed and replied. "It seems that I have to stop you, Ben Yehuda." Sabina turned her gaze towards Simona. "I'm sorry for failing you, Simona," Sabina whispered, turned around and dashed for the Zeto Crystal.

Acting instinctively, I shot Simona several times at the body armour with the blood bags to make it look like I killed her. Seeing Simona collapse to the ground, Ben, James, and Michael pursued Sabina to the other side of the altar, and I heard dozens of pistol shots.

Witnessing the murder of my potential daughter, was too much for me. Murderous frenzy filled my mind. I grabbed my pistol, and I ran up to the others, quickly shooting them all in their heads.

I dropped my pistol and shock took hold of my body.

"YOU SAVED ME." I HEARD Sabina say.

I looked at her in amazement. She was clinging the primordial Zeto Crystal to her chest. The dozens of bullets fired at her had only pierced her skin with the tip, with the rest of the bullets hanging out at the front.

"Michael and James were good friends, and yet I killed them," I mumbled, in shock from the whole episode.

"Why did you save me?" Sabina asked.

"I... I don't know. How did you survive all those bullets?" I replied.

"The crystal saved me," Sabina stated.

We looked at the Zeto Crystal. It was almost drained now. 'Had this been for nothing or could I recharge it with Pachamama's Veil?' I asked myself.

I noticed how Sabina rushed over to Simona and almost touched her. I signalled to Simona to stay quiet, and I dragged Sabina away from Simona's 'dead' body. "We need to hurry up. I'll patch you up at the Templar Headquarters, and then we need to leave Israel." I urged Sabina.

"I am sorry for causing your death, Simona!" Sabina said, got up and left the scene with me. I thought of closing the door behind me, but I didn't. I wasn't sure whether it was possible to open the door from the inside, and I couldn't trap Simona in there.

We ran as fast as we could, leaving the others where they lay.

WE WERE IN THE MEDICAL room of the Templar Headquarters. It was the middle of the night, and no one was in, which was a great relief. It would have been stressful to explain who Sabina was, and what had happened to James and Michael. I sent a message to Simona with instructions. "Simona, I hope that you closed the door behind you when you left? I have sent you $5 million to your SplitCoin account. Use that money to start a new life somewhere else." I wrote.

"Yes. Thank you, Martin!" Simona replied.

I put away the phone and turned towards Sabina. "Please get on the operation table, and I'll stitch you up. I must warn you. I am not a medical professional and you might need urgent medical attention." I stated.

"No. I am chased by the government and I have a priceless magical artefact in my possession. Besides, you killed four people. We need to stay under the radar." Sabina replied.

I reflected over how this young woman could sound like a seasoned professional. Sabina was wrong about one thing. She wasn't pursued by the government as Ben Yehuda had deleted her official record. Regardless it was better to stitch up her wounds here, as a hospital visit would bring up a lot of questions.

"Okay, then. Get up on the table, and I'll stitch you up." I said.

Sabina complied and got on the operation table without a word.

I put on a pair of gloves, and I pluck all the bullets that were hanging out from Sabina's torso like pins to a pinboard. After that, I used a pair of scissors to cut up her sweatshirts.

I studied Sabina's body, covered by shallow wounds. I noticed that Sabina had a very tight and luscious body. I stopped myself, and I felt appalled by myself thinking this way. Sabina was severely wounded, and she was likely to be my biological daughter. I reminded myself that I needed to save a sample of her blood so that I could do a paternity test if I got out of this mess alive.

"This will hurt a lot; do you need some morphine?" I asked.

"No. I need to keep a clear head for the challenges ahead." Sabina stated.

I nodded, and I poured disinfectant alcohol solution into Sabina's wounds before stitching her up. I could tell that Sabina was in pain from the agonised expression on her face, but she didn't say anything. I finished my task an hour later. Stitches and bandages covered Sabina's body.

"Make sure to find a discreet medical professional when you get out of here to get it properly done," I advised.

"Thank you, Martin," Sabina replied.

Sabina got seated and looked at me. She tried to grab my hand. Knowing about Sabina's powers, I pulled my hand away. Sabina didn't comment on my reluctance to her touch, and instead, she changed the topic. "So, how come you helped Ben Yehuda when you didn't like his plan for the Middle East?" Sabina asked.

I reflected on my options, and I decided to tell Sabina the truth.

"I came across some Zetan deities 19 years ago. They told me to find Keila Eisenstein. A few years later, I found out about the primordial Zeto Crystal, and that I needed to find it to stop the apocalypse." I replied.

"I'm here to look for the Holy Grail, also known as primordial Zeto crystal. So, we are both looking to achieve the same thing?" Sabina said and smiled.

"Yes. It seems that way." I replied.

"So, what do we do now?" Sabina asked.

"I am finished. The others will come after me for betraying them. We need to get you out of here and get the Zeto Crystal to safety." I urged.

"Do you have any plan for that?" Sabina asked.

"Yes, you're in luck. Ben Yehuda kept all your possessions in his private house. I can access the Mossad database from there and delete your record. After that, we can leave Israel." I replied.

"Very well, let's get going," Sabina said and got back on her feet.

Sabina's energy and determination impressed me, but I didn't say anything. I grabbed my pistol, and we headed towards Ben Yehuda's house.

"YOU'D BETTER STAY HERE," I said.

"Why is that?" Sabina asked.

"Ben's house is full of security cameras. I don't want his brother to find out about you." I replied. "Okay. I'll stay here." Sabina said.

I got into the house. Finding Sabina's possessions were the easy part. But how would I delete the computer drives if I couldn't access the computer? If Simona was here, she could have helped, but she wasn't.

I decided to blow up the place. I hoped that would be enough to destroy the drives. I set some C4 explosives, ran outside and blew up the building. After that, I hurried to Sabina. She gave me a frightened look. "What did you do?" Sabina said.

"I collected your bag and blew up the building to get rid of the evidence. Hurry up!" I exclaimed, and I handed Sabina her backpack. The moment I gave it to her, I felt a piercing pain in my back. and I heard a shot.

"Hurry up, I'll delay them." I urged. Sabina made a run for it, and I picked up my pistol to fire back at the attackers.

I didn't stand a chance. I didn't wear my monocle as I didn't want to expose my real affiliation to Sabina, and without it, I wasn't a master marksman. A few seconds later, I was panting for air on the ground, as I got hit by several bullets. The agents ran up to me and kicked away the pistol from me, and everything turned black.

Chapter 16: Switzerland & Sweden, February 2040

Blackness and nothingness surrounded me. I felt nothing, and I was nothing. Just a peaceful slumber. How long had I been in this state, and why wasn't I reflecting over it until now?

Fragmented memories appeared in front of my eyes. I re-lived my death in Israel.

"You betrayed us."

"I saw the combination to the room from the hidden cameras that Ben placed there."

"Who are those two young women that helped you?

Szymon had interrogated me for days on end. He was furious, and I understood him. His brother was dead, and with the death of Ben Yehuda, I had stopped Szymon's dream of committing genocide to reclaim the Holy Land.

I hadn't revealed Sabina's or Simona's identities. I worried most about Sabina. Simona was a professional hacker, and she had access to millions of dollars after my generous donation. She would create herself a new identity and be outside of Mossad's reach. But how would Sabina hold up?

I had realised that there was nothing I could do to help Sabina. It had come as a relief when Szymon had pulled up his pistol and killed me.

But why was I back? Why wasn't I allowed to enjoy the endless bliss that was the afterlife?

I pushed myself, and I opened my eyes. I heard voices and the dazzling light in the room blinded my eyes. Weariness took hold of me, the voices faded into the background, and I fell back into unconsciousness.

THE NEXT TIME I WOKE up, I felt a bit better. It didn't feel surreal any-more, but it felt like waking up from a long relaxing sleep. I opened my eyes and while the light still hurt my eyes, I could see the contours of the room now.

"The subject is awake, let the boss know." I heard a scientist say to another.

"Don't worry, you'll be fine." I heard a female voice say.

She held my hand while injecting me with a needle. The warmth of her hand filled me with blissfulness, and I receded into unconsciousness.

"MARTIN. WAKE UP! AND welcome back." Pierre said.

Of course. It was Pierre that brought me back from the dead. Who else would want to bring me back? But why had Pierre brought me back? That was the real question.

I opened my eyes, and I noticed that Pierre, James, and Vladimir were the only members of the Monocle Conspiracy in the room.

"Why did you bring me back to life?" I wheezed.

"Tsk, Tsk. Thank you, Pierre, for saving my life is the correct sentence." Pierre taunted.

"Okay. Thank you, Pierre." I replied in resignation.

"That's better, Martin. Much Better!" Pierre smirked.

I sighed without saying anything.

"We got a job for you. It is a crucial task that requires your co-operation." Pierre stated.

"What if I don't want to cooperate? What if I am pissed off because you disturbed my peaceful death with this bullshit?" I argued.

"Don't you dare you son of a bitch. I went through a lot of trouble find-ing those stupid crystals to revive you." Vladimir hissed.

"Are you issuing a death threat to a man who wants nothing more than to return to the afterlife?" I taunted.

Vladimir didn't reply. Instead, he grabbed a small electronic device and showed it to me.

"This, Mr Orchard, is a nerve pain amplifier. It sends out a signal convincing your nerve cells that you are in insufferable pain. It's the ultimate torture tool of the 21st century. The best part about it is that it doesn't actually kill you, so we can go on torturing you forever. Would you care for a demonstration?" Vladimir taunted.

Vladimir was not interested in my answer. Instead, he started using the device on me. It was the worst pain I have ever experienced. My entire body felt like it was on fire, and the madness didn't seem to stop. I screamed my lungs out and passed out for a second.

When I woke up, the pain was gone, and Vladimir smiled at me. "How did you enjoy the feeling of being burnt alive? The device has 50 more settings available. You can be my next test subject." Vladimir taunted.

"You guys put in a lot of effort to bring me back and torture me. Not particularly good for the finances, Pierre." I mocked.

Pierre sighed, took off his monocle, showing his purple iris, and spoke. "I didn't bring you back to torture you. I do not operate on such base desires. I brought you back because Elaine requested me to."

"Elaine? I haven't spoken to her for ages. Why did she want to resurrect me?" I asked.

"Martin, you haven't spoken to anyone for ages. You have been dead for two years." Pierre stated.

"Two years?" I asked.

"Yes, two years. As Vladimir mentioned reviving you was troublesome. We had to coax Szymon Yehuda to hand over your body, and then we struggled to find a strong enough Crystal to revive you." Pierre replied.

"But you found a way to convince Szymon?" I queried.

"Yes, reviving you is the only way we can revive his brother. The replicated Zeto Crystals only work on you. To revive Ben, we need the primordial Zeto Crystal. But you must be starving. Let's have dinner upstairs and I fill you in on your mission!" Pierre said and gave me a helping hand to get up from the hospital bed.

SOMETIME LATER, I HAD showered and dressed up for the luxurious dining venue upstairs. We were sitting in an exclusive member's only club overlooking the beautiful Geneva Lake. It felt surreal to have this exclusive dining room on top of a secret research lab, but here I was.

"Wow, this place is splendid," I said in amazement.

"Yes, it cost us a fortune to run, but it pays itself back a hundredfold. Here we invite world leaders to socialise and indulge in all the vices you can think of. This creates priceless bonds between the bank and the politicians that we control." Pierre revealed.

"I guess one can have a pretty good time here?" I replied.

"Indeed. I will let you use our services for free as a signup bonus." Pierre tempted.

"Sure, but let's talk about what exactly you want me to do?" I replied.

Pierre took a deep sniff of the red wine he was drinking, tasted a sip and smiled.

"Ah, Penfolds Grange Hermitage. They got some good wines in your former home country." Pierre said.

"I wouldn't know, I tended to drink the ones from the cask!" I replied.

"Not a man of great taste, I see," Pierre remarked.

"Just tell me the mission, and I will be on my way," I replied.

While I wasn't keen on carrying out the mission, I was even less keen on socialising with Pierre, Vladimir, and James. They had brought me back to life and tortured me, to make me work for them.

"Your mission is to find the primordial Zeto Crystal, charge it, and bring it to Pierre." James stated.

"Ah, so not to the CIA?" I taunted.

"The CIA is less secure. The government can shut us down. No-one shuts the World Bank down, as Mexico will soon find out." James replied.

"There is a problem with your plan. I don't know where the Zeto Crystal is, and I don't know how to recharge it." I said.

Pierre sighed, walked away for a moment, and then came back with a folder. "You should read this," Pierre stated.

I checked the document. It was from the paternity test I had planned to do with Sabina's blood but never got around to do as a few bullets stopped me dead in my tracks. It was a positive, the test confirmed that Sabina was my biological daughter.

"Your daughter, Sabina Hines, is a 21-year-old woman who has made a fortune from online trading. She spends her days making money for her charity, 'Building a Better World Pty Ltd'." Pierre stated.

"Why are you telling me this?" I asked.

"Because Martin, I am giving you a choice. If you convince Sabina to surrender the Zeto Crystal, then I will allow her to live a happy life focusing on her charity work." Pierre stated.

"And if I fail?" I asked.

"Then you'll both die! After your deaths, I will resurrect the two of you, so that Vladimir have test subjects for his torture methods. How is that for spending quality time with your daughter? Experiencing endless torment together." Pierre taunted

"You're very convincing, Pierre. I'll do you bidding. Now please let me distract my mind through enjoying this steak. After that, I'd love to enjoy some of the sign-up bonus upstairs." I replied.

Hearing this, Vladimir cut a portion of his rare steak and showed it to me. "Enjoy your food and sex, Mr Orchard. Because if you fail on your mission, you'll be spending a lot of time with me, and you won't enjoy that."

"One of my life goals is to spend as little time with you as possible Vladimir!" I said and took the lift to the courtesans upstairs.

A FEW DAYS LATER, I was in my Swedish hometown, Helsingborg. I wasn't there to visit relatives. My parents were long gone, and I doubted that being dead for two years had brought me closer to my siblings.

I studied the address that Simona had given me via an encrypted email. I had assumed that $ 5 million would get her a better house than this, but perhaps she preferred to keep a low profile?

A beautiful blonde girl met me at the door. "Hi, Martin. It's so nice to see you again."

This confused me. While I am always happy when a smiling, beautiful woman greets me, I had no idea who she was.

"I am looking for Simona Fischbein," I said.

"Ja, men det är ju jag. Fast jag kallar mig Sara Nilsson nuförtiden." Simona replied.

"Simona? You speak Swedish these days." I asked in amazement.

"Yes, it's been over two years. I speak better Swedish than you speak English." Simona smirked.

"Not a particularly great achievement!" I winked.

"Come on in. I'll show you my place." Simona said.

I followed her in. Simona's place contained a vast array of electronic gadgets lying around. We got inside, and she served me filter coffee and the Swedish pastry, punsch-roll.

"So, how did you do it? Learning Swedish? Getting a new identity?" I asked.

"You forgot my background. I hacked the Swedish registry and I took the identity of a woman reported as missing. I made a fake passport, and I bought this house in her name. I learnt Swedish from watching videos and using computer-assisted vocal training for my pronunciation." Simona revealed.

I nodded in acknowledgement. Simona was an extraordinary character.

"What about you, Martin? I thought you were dead." Simona replied.

"So did I, yet here I am. With another mission on my hand." I sighed.

"Don't be like that old man. Being on a mission is good for the spirit. It beats sitting here suffering from unrequited love." Simona sighed.

Hearing this surprised me, and I also felt a bit guilty. If I had told Simona what Sabina was back then, she would have an easier time getting over her infatuation. I decided that it was time for Simona to know the truth.

"There is something you should know about Sabina." I started.

"I found out two things about her in the last few years." I hinted.

"Share with me!" Simona said.

"Sabina is my biological daughter. And she is a touch empath." I revealed.

Simona looked at me for a while. Eventually, she spoke with an afterthought. "I am not surprised that she is your daughter, considering how you acted in Jerusalem. But what the heck is a touch empath?" Simona asked.

"A touch empath is someone who can access and alter someone's mind through establishing physical contact with that person. It's an obscure theological subject discussed in the Torah of Malka. No scientific evidence exists." I replied.

Simona stared at me in disbelief. After a long silence, she spoke. "So, you believe that Sabina is some kind of sorceress who cast a love spell on me?"

"It sounds dumb, but something like that," I replied.

"That's ridiculous. Sabina revealed that she is straight, and she married a man, Alex, last year." Simona replied.

"So, have you been talking to her?" I asked.

"No, I haven't. I have just been sitting here, studying her from the other side of the world. How sad is that?" Simona asked.

I didn't answer Simona's statement and instead I changed the topic. "Hmm, perhaps she was trying to influence you into helping her, and her magic had unexpected consequences?" I speculated.

"Yes, that might be. In either case, I want to meet Sabina and confront her for what she did to me." Simona said.

"Don't get carried away. I don't think Sabina intended to hurt you." I replied.

Simona slammed her coffee cup against the wall, with coffee dripping along the wall. Then she took off and locked herself into her bedroom. I could hear her crying from the inside of the room. I was hesitant about what to do. I worried about Simona, but I didn't have the right to force myself into her bedroom.

"I'll wait in the lounge room if you want to talk," I shouted through the door.

"Go away! I hate you!" Simona shouted back.

Realising that I hadn't made a new friend today, I decided to sit in the loungeroom, hoping for Simona to calm down.

I HAD FALLEN ASLEEP on the couch when Simona woke me up. I could tell from her eyes that she had cried a lot.

"Don't you have any other place to go?" Simona asked.

"Not really," I replied.

Simona smiled a sad smile and replied. "I guess that makes it two of us."

I nodded without saying anything.

"Why did you come here, Martin?" Simona said.

"I need help. Pierre brought me back from the dead to work for him. He wants me to convince Sabina to give up the Zeto Crystal to him. Otherwise, he'll catch us both, and expose us to endless torture." I revealed.

"Wow, is all your friends complete assholes?" Simona exclaimed.

"I guess my charming personality attracts certain characters!" I joked.

"No doubt!" Simona replied.

I hesitated for a while before replying. "So, are you willing to help me?"

"Depends. What do you need?" Simona replied.

"I need your talents to determine Sabina's true motives. I am considering joining up with Sabina against the others." I replied.

"I am not a psychic." Simona objected.

"Correct. But you're a damn good computer hacker. Come with me to Sydney. Let's find out what Sabina is up to before I make my move." I urged.

Simona left the room for a moment, and then she came back with her passport. "Alright old man, it's time for Sara Nilsson to visit Sydney," Simona exclaimed and gave me a friendly push.

I nodded. It was time to learn about Sabina's real motives. If Sabina's motives were benign to the world, I could help her. That way, I would redeem myself for a lifetime of villainy, and stop Pierre once and for all.

Chapter 17: Sydney, March 2040

I experienced mixed feelings when my Orbit Flight from Copenhagen landed in Sydney. Australia was my second home country, and on this day the sky was blue, and the Sydney Harbour was stunning. Simona seemed to be mesmerised by the view. Australia on a sunny day was better than a wintery Sweden or a war-torn Israel.

"So, this is what Australia looks like." Simona chirped.

"Yes. I promise to take you around once we have finished researching Sabina." I replied.

"I can't wait!" Simona replied.

I realised that Simona was in dire need of friends. She was keeping too much to herself and should be hanging out with people her own age. Instead an older man like me dragged her around the world. Oh well, it was none of my business, and I needed her help.

"So, how do you intend to research on Sabina?" Simona said.

"I need your talents to figure out how she makes and spends her money. We also need to find people that have things to tell us about her. Finally, we need to access her home security cameras to spy on her." I instructed.

"Hmm. How do you suggest that we contact Sabina's old friends and classmates? That would seem suspicious to most people." Simona asked.

"We claim to come from Time Magazine. With the massive amounts that Sabina has raised for charity, it makes sense to write an article about her. You're researching her childhood to find suitable anecdotes."

"Alright. This will be fun. Let's get to our hotel. I am dying to have a shower and get to sleep." Simona said.

"Bah, like an old woman. At 21 you should want to stay at a hostel and get on the piss!" I jeered.

"Go to sleep, old man. You don't know what you're talking about!" Simona chuckled.

After some more banter, we took a cab to a nearby 5-star hotel.

I WAS WALKING ALONG the Maroubra to Coogee Ocean Walk. I enjoyed the breeze from the ocean and the majestic coastal cliffs. How strange it felt to be back. Could I resettle in Australia after all these years? I knew that there was work that I had to do, and before I had achieved my objectives, I couldn't focus on my future. I knew one thing though; I did not intend to end up in Vladimir's torture chamber.

I thought of calling Simona to get a progress report. I felt silly for dragging her to Sydney so that she could do my work. What stopped me from seeking out Ellen Hines or Sabina myself for instance?

With Sabina, the answer was fear. I knew of her powers, but I didn't know about her intentions. But what about seeking out Ellen? I brushed the thought aside. I doubted that she would reveal Sabina's secrets to me, even if she agreed to speak to me. Speaking to Ellen would also alert Sabina of my presence.

So, no matter how I felt, walking along the ocean by myself, I realised that inaction was my best course of action.

As my eyes followed the flight of a sea eagle, my monocle started flashing. 'Proximity alert: Sabina Hines is approaching.'

I reflected on the information conveyed. Of course, the predictive capabilities of the Zetan monocle could figure out that Sabina Hines was an important person. But what would I do? Why was I even walking on the coastal walk close to Sabina's house in the first place?

I hid under an overhanging cliff edge hoping for Sabina to pass by. But she didn't. Instead, she got seated together with someone with her feet hanging over the edge. From her idle conversation, I realised that she was talking to her husband, Alex.

But what would I do? Would I walk out and say. 'Hi, Sabina. Funny story. I didn't die in Jerusalem. Besides, you're my daughter and I need your magical crystal. Otherwise, an evil conspiracy will capture me and torture me!'

"Beep beep!"

My monocle displayed: 'unsuitable approach!' regarding that thought. 'Oh well, I guess I'll stay here and eavesdrop like a creep.' I thought, and so I did.

Sabina and Alex kept on talking forever. During their lengthy conversation, Sabina didn't reveal her plans or what she intended to do with primordial Zeto Crystal. Instead, they discussed various movies they had seen or holidays they wanted to go on. This went on for hours, and eventually, I could not hold my bladder anymore, so I peed behind the rocks.

"Hmm, let's go. It smells bad here." Alex said.

"Yes, it does. Uggh! Let's go home." Sabina replied.

As they left, I could finally get away from my hiding spot. I planned to take a self-driving AutoCar Deluxe back to my hotel. But as the taxi arrived, the doors wouldn't open. I checked my phone and it revealed the following message: 'Our sensors detected an unsanitary smell from you. AutoCar PTY Ltd requires all customers to fulfil basic hygiene requirements before ordering a cab. Please have a shower and try again later.' I thought about arguing with the bot, but I realised that was a losing battle. Soiled and embarrassed, I walked the seven kilometres back to my hotel!

"SO, HOW DID YOU GO today?" Simona asked when we had dinner at the hotel restaurant.

"Oh, it went great. I accidentally eavesdropped on Sabina for hours today." I replied.

"How do you accidentally eavesdrop on someone?" Simona asked.

"I was out walking on my own, reflecting over life when my alien monocle told me to hide from my sorceress daughter who thinks I am dead!" I replied.

"You do realise how absurd that sounds?" Simona heckled.

"I can imagine. At least now I know that Sabina likes eating crispy cauliflower bites and that she reckons South Sydney Rabbitohs won't win the NRL this year either." I replied.

"Was that the most important parts you found out from eavesdropping for hours?" Simona taunted

"More or less," I replied hesitantly.

Simona smiled at me and pulled up her tablet.

"How lucky that you brought me along. I found out a lot more about Sabina." Simona stated.

"Shoot!" I replied.

"Sabina's husband Alex, donated $10 million to 'Escuelas para los pobres Fundación.'" Simona revealed.

"Why is that important? Donating to the poor in Mexico seems like a legit cause for any charity." I replied.

Simona handed me her tablet and spoke. "Look who is also donating large sums to the same charity. I also found out who is behind the charity."

I looked at the tablet. Pierre had also donated a lot of money to the Mexican foundation. The tablet also revealed that Jesus Ortega, an alleged Mexican drug lord, controlled the foundation.

"So, do you reckon Sabina is involving herself in the upcoming Civil War in Mexico?" I asked.

"Doesn't look better, does it?" Simona contemplated.

I pondered Simona's statement. Why were Sabina and the World Bank supporting the same Mexican drug lord? Could Alex's donation be a mistake? I decided that this question shouldn't sidestep me, so I changed the topic.

"Did you find out anything else?" I asked.

"Yes. One of Sabina's former classmates, Joshua Harkins, turned insane and tried to rape her on his 18th-year party. Instead of achieving his vile objective, he turned to self-harm. Joshua chopped off his own testicles with a shard of glass and was institutionalised." Simona revealed.

"What? That's insane!" I exclaimed.

"The work of a sorceress?" I asked.

"Only one way to find out. Let's visit Joshua at the mental hospital and ask him ourselves." Simona stated.

Having finished our work-related conversation, we carried on enjoying the food from the restaurant. After a few glasses of wine, I felt how I was struggling. I was too aroused by my young lesbian assistant to behave in my usual cold and distant manner. I excused myself and ran up to my room where I had a long cold shower.

THE FOLLOWING DAY, we visited Joshua at the mental hospital. The high standard of the facility surprised me. I had expected psychiatric hospitals to be gloomy places, but this was a beautiful private facility with large rooms and ocean views. Perfect for myself if I finally snapped!

Joshua agreed to meet us. He seemed happy to have visitors. Joshua's parents, who paid the exorbitant fees for this facility, didn't seem interested in socialising with him.

"Hi, who are you guys? I don't get visitors often." Joshua stated.

"We are journalists for Time Magazine," Simona stated.

"Are you here to dig up dirt on my dad? It's not his fault that I am here." Joshua croaked.

"No. Malcolm Harkins is of no interest to us. We are more interested in your relationship with Sabina Hines." Simona replied.

Hearing Sabina's name, Joshua had an outburst and threw the plastic coffee cup with lukewarm tea into the wall.

"Don't mention that name. The bitch destroyed my life!" Joshua roared and then fell into rage-filled crying.

"Tell us what happened?" Simona replied.

"What's the point? You'll just call me crazy anyway." Joshua complained.

"Well, throwing coffee cups into the wall doesn't disprove your craziness. At least I know why they serve the drinks lukewarm in plastic cups at this facility." I taunted.

Joshua gave me a dark look, and Simona held me back.

"I apologise for my colleague. He is a dickhead. Tell us with your words, what happened." Simona encouraged.

"I had a mental breakdown, tried to rape a girl, and ended up injuring myself." Joshua sighed.

"That's what other people have told you about the incident. I want to hear it with your words. You were a good-looking bloke. Why would you rape Sabina?" Simona asked.

Joshua sighed. His eyes kept moving between Simona and the door. Eventually, he got up and started walking towards the door.

"Wait, don't go. I know that Sabina manipulated you!" Simona shouted.

Joshua turned around and looked at Simona attentively.

"Why would you say that?" Joshua asked.

"Because she did the same thing to me. She cast a spell on me. To make me love her and then she rejected me." Simona replied.

"You're not really journalists, are you?" Joshua asked.

"Smart boy!" I taunted.

Joshua sighed and walked back to our table with his head bowed.

"I used to be so popular among girls. I was the athletic and good-looking Joshua Harkins, son of the property magnate Malcolm Harkins. Everything changed when Sabina came into my life." Joshua revealed.

"And when was that exactly. You were classmates, right?" Simona asked.

"Yes. But I never thought much about Sabina. Sure, she was a good sort, but pretty girls are a dime a dozen to me." Joshua replied.

"So, what changed?" Simona asked.

"Well. We were close to graduating, so I thought that I would find out more about this mysterious girl who didn't socialise much. So, I invited her to my 18-year-old celebration. But she wanted to bring her stupid friend Eric, whom I hated." Joshua recalled.

"Eric? Is that Eric Orchard that works for Sabina at Building a Better World Pty Ltd?" Simona asked.

Joshua clenched his jaw in anger and replied. "Yes. When I said no, Sabina held my hand and looked into my eyes, asking me to let him come. At that moment something changed inside my head. I couldn't say no anymore. I had to oblige and I wanted to own her."

"That seems like an attempt from a pretty girl to use her looks to her advantage. What did Sabina do differently?" I asked.

"You don't understand. When Sabina held my hand and looked into my eyes, she stared into my soul. That's not how it feels when a pretty girl flirt with me." Joshua shouted.

"What happened after that?" Simona asked.

"After that, Sabina filled my mind. I couldn't sleep, I couldn't think of anything but how I wanted her. When she came to the party, I tried to impress her, but she rejected me. Later I lured her to my room. I lost control of myself and was about to force myself on her when she spoke. I will never forget those words." Joshua shivered.

Simona cast a quick glance at me. I nodded, and she spoke again. "Can you tell us the words, Joshua?"

Joshua nodded and replied. "Sabina's words were: 'Joshua Harkins. By the power bestowed upon me by the True Maker, I command you to let go of evil, and repent for your sins.'"

Having recited this phrase, Joshua collapsed to the floor crying uncontrollably.

Joshua's reaction amazed me. This was an event that took place years ago. I pressed the alarm button, and a few nurses came in with sedatives.

Simona and I left the mental hospital. We had got what we came for, but we were not any wiser. Joshua's story proved Sabina's immense powers, but we still didn't know what her motives were. Joshua was a deranged lunatic, and from Sabina's perspective, she had only defended herself. Unless she had arranged the whole scenario to happen, in which case she was devious and dangerous.

I WAS HAVING DINNER with Simona at a Japanese restaurant. I was sitting silent, avoiding alcoholic drinks to calm my desires.

Between pieces of sushi, Simona broke the silence. "What are you thinking about, Martin?"

I realised that 'your naked body' would be an inappropriate answer, so instead I replied. "I don't know what to do about Sabina. She survived explosions and dozens of bullets. I need to get the Zeto Crystal otherwise Pierre and his many hired assassins will come after me. But I stand no chance against someone of Sabina's calibre.

Simona passed me her phone and replied. "Yes, you seemed stuck. Sabina thought that I died in Solomon Temple. She had been keeping my phone as a memory of me. That's why I sent her this message via the darknet."

I looked at the phone. The message that was sent to Simona's old phone read, 'Simona, I am worried about you. I have found out who is funding the conspiracy within the Mossad. It's funded by Pierre Beaumont from the World Bank. Please contact me. /Joanne.'

I handed the phone back to Simona and gave her a puzzled look. "I don't understand this message. Who is Joanne, and why would Sabina care?"

"Joanne is a fake name. I faked this name to fool Sabina into meeting up with Pierre Beaumont. I wanted to make Sabina think that there was a connection between the Mossad and the World Bank. If she is in league with him, she will contact him and warn him." Simona replied.

"And why would Joanne message Sabina?" I asked.

"She didn't. She messaged me on my old phone that Sabina owns and checks. I changed the date stamp on the message to make it look two years old. This will work." Simona revealed.

I thought of Simona's plan. It was a dangerous plan, particularly for Sabina. If Pierre came after her, she'd be dead. But I understood where Simona was coming from. Unrequited love was a tricky thing.

I sighed.

"Yes, I guess I'll find out. Pierre will attend the World Economic Forum in Sydney next week. Let's keep track of them and see if Pierre and Sabina meet." I said.

"So, what will we do until then?" Simona asked.

"I'd suggest that you do some sightseeing. I will lock myself into my hotel room and focus on finishing my 25th book." I replied.

"Are you still working on that book? You were almost finished with it back in 2037." Simona teased.

"Well, being dead for two years set me behind schedule!" I replied.

Simona smiled, got up from the table and walked away. After a few steps, she turned around and walked back to me. "Martin, are you avoiding me because you are in love with me, but you feel ashamed because I am 35 years younger and a lesbian?" Simona asked

"Yes," I replied.

"Well, at least you know how I feel for Sabina. I'll see you when you are ready to continue on the mission." Simona said and walked off.

'If I only knew what to do.' I thought and sighed.

Chapter 18: Sydney, April 2040

"Veuve Clicquot. Cheap, but drinkable." Pierre said with a smug smile and raised the champagne glass.

"Well, cheers I guess" I replied and took a sip from my glass.

We were at Randwick Racecourse, spending some time gambling. Pierre was in a great mood.

"The politicians. They crawl at my feet. They all fear and respect the wealth that I hold." Pierre stated.

"How is it going with Mexico?" I asked.

"I am visiting Mexico next week to discuss my ownership request for the Prensa de la Muerte dam. Jesus Ortega and his army stand ready. If President Santander refuses my request, she'll have a Civil War on her hands." Pierre revealed.

The PA system announced that the next race was on, and a few minutes later, horse number 8 'Happy Slapper', had won the race.

"I told you that Happy Slapper was a certain win!" Pierre exclaimed.

"Easy to say when you rigged the race." I sniped.

Pierre wasn't affected by my claims of cheating. Instead, he replied. "I play to win. You should learn from me."

"I don't care enough about horse racing to rig the races," I claimed.

"Very well. When people lose, they always claim to not care. But we both know that isn't true." Pierre mocked.

I didn't reply. Instead, I skolled my champagne and I picked up another glass from a nearby waiter's tray.

"I met with your lovechild Sabina, yesterday," Pierre said.

I already knew about this since Simona, and I kept Sabina under supervision. But I didn't want to reveal this knowledge, so I replied. "Oh, really? What was the occasion?"

"Sabina booked one of the VIP 'Meet and Greet packages with World Economic Forum. I had to give her ten minutes of my time for a neat $250,000." Pierre replied.

"I doubt you need the money," I said.

"I don't. But charging a premium for meetings is the best way to keep unworthy people away from me." Pierre replied.

I nodded, had another sip of my champagne, and replied. "So, what did Sabina want?"

"Well, she pretended to seek my help with her ocean clean-up project," Pierre replied.

"What do you think she wanted?" I asked.

"Well, it's evident that she wanted to use some of her famed 'empath' abilities on me. She tried to hug me. What a joke." Pierre scoffed.

I thought about Pierre's statement. It was unlikely that Sabina was an ally of Pierre since he told me about their meeting. So, most likely, her sponsorship of Jesus Ortega was a mistake. But why hadn't Sabina's empath abilities worked on Pierre? Could the monocle be the key to blocking her abilities? I decided to find out. "Pierre. Did you wear the monocle during your meeting with Sabina?"

Pierre gave me a disapproving look and replied. "Bah. What kind of question is that? Of course, I did. I rarely take it off."

I decided to change the subject. "So, who is winning the next race?" I asked.

Pierre shook his head and replied. "I don't know. But I know that 'Sphinx' will win race number 8. And like I said. I only play to win."

I picked up my phone and placed a large bet on Sphinx. There was nothing wrong with winning free money on rigged races, after all.

Pierre tapped on my shoulder and gave me a serious look. "Martin. You're running out of time. Szymon Yehuda is coming on Wednesday. Either you have the primordial Zeto Crystal by then, or I'll authorise Szymon to take it by force. Do we have an understanding?" Pierre threatened.

I nodded without saying anything.

"Excellent. I bid you a momentous day at the races. I have many other dignitaries to meet with today. Farewell and good luck with your quest." Pierre said and walked off.

I realised that I needed to act, so I called Simona, and I headed over to the computer lab, which I had hired for her.

SIMONA WAS BLASTING techno on her headphones and didn't notice me when I approached her. I walked up to her and lifted off her headphones to catch her attention.

"Hey, don't kill my rhythm," Simona shouted.

"Hey, you are lucky I am not planning to kill something else. You need to pay attention!" I urged.

"Bah, if you were someone else, I'd be long gone. I saw you on the video feed." Simona replied.

I sighed. Dealing with the rebellious 21-year-old Simona was a daunting task, but she was damn good at her job, so it was worth it.

"Simona, we need to make a move. Have you managed to figure out the passcode to Sabina's safe from your video feed?" I asked.

"Yes. I am fairly certain that the code is 22-03-2850." Simona replied.

"I need full certainty. I can't break into Sabina's house to get stuck at the safe." I scoffed.

"Well, the video doesn't show the display, but I made an educated guess. Look at the video and see for yourself."

Simona turned on the video, and I followed Sabina's finger movements when she entered the code. It looked like 22-03-2850.

I consulted my monocle, and I realised what a fool I had been. 'Estimated passkey 22-03-2850. Be advised, Sabina might be using a key panel where digits swap places.'

"Do you have a second video of Sabina opening the safe?" I asked.

"Why?" Simona asked.

"Because it might be a display where the digits swap places between uses," I replied.

"That's the only video I have. We'll have to wait until the next time Sabina opens the safe to confirm." Simona replied.

"I can't fucking wait. I am in deep shit and I need to get in there now!" I shouted.

Simona gave me a puzzled look and replied. "What's wrong, old man?"

I took a deep breath and replied. "Pierre has run out of patience. He told me that Szymon Yehuda will come and use violence if we haven't got the Ze-to Crystal by Tuesday.

"Thanks for telling me. I am booking my flights for Monday night." Simona replied.

"Very helpful!" I whinged.

"Okay, I guess we'll break in once Sabina leaves. I can't hack the biometric lock to the house, but I have an idea." Simona said.

"What's your suggestion?" I asked.

"I have computer-generated a 3D model of Sabina's eyeball. The model should have an exact copy of her iris. This replica will trick the eye scanner at the door. If we 3D print a copy, that should do the trick." Simona explained.

"Excellent. Things like this are the reason I brought you along. Finish the glass eyeball and I am good to go." I replied, leaned back into the chair, and fell asleep.

"HEY LOOK WHAT I'VE got!"

I woke up a few hours later, as Simona held a very lifelike 3D glass eyeball next to my face.

"Sobered up now?" Simona teased.

I thought of objecting to Simona's statement, but I realised that I stunk of alcohol.

"Yes. Any news?" I asked.

"No. Sabina seems completely absorbed by whatever she is doing. She hasn't left that chair for many hours, not even drinking water or going to the bathroom."

"Okay. Anything else?" I said.

"I checked the videos. It seems that Sabina had an argument with Alex yesterday. He took off and flew to Brisbane." Simona replied.

"That makes the house more accessible. See if you can find a drone via the darknet. We need to verify that Sabina is in the room. She might have found a way to outsmart you, Simona." I speculated.

Simona made an angry grimace towards me. Clearly, she didn't like my suggestion that there existed smarter people than her in the world.

"Okay boss, I have ordered the drone now. We'll have it first thing in the morning." Simona said.

"Excellent. Let's eat and then get some sleep. Not much use sitting at a computer staring at someone sitting by a computer." I replied.

"Okay. I'll set my phone to alert me if anything changes in the room." Simona replied and we left the computer lab for a well-needed rest.

IT WAS MONDAY MORNING, and noontime was approaching. Sabina had been sitting there for over 72 hours straight and I had no idea what she was doing. We had used the drones to confirm her presence in the room, but we couldn't figure out what she was doing or how she did it.

I was dozing off looking at Sabina through the spycam video feed when I noticed a change. Sabina had collapsed to the floor. As Alex, still wasn't in the house, this was the opportunity to get in and grab the crystal.

"It is time to move. Turn off the cameras in the house before we go in." I instructed Simona, and we got to our car. We parked close to Sabina's South Coogee mansion and I used Simona's replica eyeball to get into the house. We hurried upstairs where I found Sabina cold and unconscious. I walked over to the safe and much to my relief, I entered the correct passcode.

"Once you have the primordial Zeto crystal, use the Pachamama's Veil and wrap the Crystal with the Veil, and throw it into an active volcano in Kiribati", Rangda's words kept circling in my head.

I took out the primordial Zeto Crystal from Sabina's safe. This was it. Now I needed to go to Indonesia, pick up Pachamama's Veil from Elaine, and then wrap the Crystal in the Veil and throw it into an active volcano. That should charge the primordial Zeto Crystal. Possessing such a powerful arte-fact, I could deal with Pierre, James and Vladimir.

But then what? What would I do with the Zeto Crystal? How would I stop the apocalypse? I held the crystal in my hand, and I looked at Sabina. 'Sabina is dead.' My monocle displayed, and I had no reason to question it.

"We can't do anything for her now. Let's go!" Simona urged.

I froze for a second, and then I had an epiphany. I had to save Sabina. She was the future. She was the Chosen One and the only one who could save us.

"No, I need to save Sabina," I said, and I rubbed the Zeto Crystal along Sabina's cheek.

The power from the Zeto Crystal revived Sabina, and I could hear her breathing.

I walked over to the safe and put the Crystal back. Then I kneeled next to Sabina and whispered. "You're dying Sabina. The Crystal will revive you. Once it has revived you, make sure to drink plenty of water and head straight to bed."

Then I got up, and I left the room. Simona ran after me. "What are you doing, Martin? Have you lost your mind?" Simona protested.

"I am helping Sabina save the future. It's going to get messy. I recommend that you leave Australia and hide for a while." I stated.

"You are fucking insane. What was the point of all this then?" Simona argued.

"It helped me figuring out what I needed to do!" I stated.

Simona shook her head and hurried out, before she left, I shouted. "Simona!"

Simona turned around and looked at me.

"Thank you for all the help. I hope we'll still be friends when this is over." I replied.

Simona didn't reply. I could hear movement from upstairs, and I rushed to leave the house before Sabina saw me.

"YOUR TIME IS UP. SZYMON has landed in Sydney, and his group will deal with Sabina and recover the Crystal." Pierre said over the hologram phone.

"Fuck you, Pierre!" I screamed back.

"Vladimir will have a lot of fun with you. Not even death will save you!" Pierre roared and hung up the phone.

'I could have handled that better,' I thought, and I contacted Sabina. I didn't know how she would react to hearing from me, but this forced my hand. A legion of cold-blooded killers wanted to kill us and then resurrect us to torture us. Under such circumstances, one can only fight, and getting Sabina to join me was the only way to go.

'Okay, I'll see you at Barangaroo Wharf in one hour.' Sabina responded via encrypted messaging app.

I holstered my pistols, and I put on a bulletproof vest under my suit. I took off my monocle and hid it in my pocket. I needed to win Sabina's trust before revealing what I was. Only then would we stand a chance to save the future from the apocalypse.

I SAW SABINA AS SHE was waiting for me at Barangaroo Wharf. I felt worried, but I hoped that the location would deter Szymon and his operatives from attacking us.

I walked up to Sabina and spoke. "Thank you for seeing me, Sabina!"

"It's the least I could do. You saved my life, and you helped me escape Israel. I thought you were dead. What happened?"

"I survived. The gunshot wounds were not life-threatening, and I faced only minor charges. I suppose they never found the bodies." I replied.

Having said this, I bit myself in the tongue. Why had I lied to Sabina? She if anyone would believe in my true story.

Sabina gave me a sceptical look and spoke. "So, why have you waited until now to visit me?"

"I saw you in a dream. You were dying, and the Zeto Crystal saved you. I knew that I had to come to Sydney and see you." I replied.

More lies. Goddammit, why was it so hard to speak the truth. What exactly hindered me? I was sweating profusely and the fear of my death and subsequent torture haunted me and prevented me from thinking straight.

"Okay. My mother, Ellen, would like to thank you for saving my life in Jerusalem. She is sitting over there." Sabina said.

Fuck. Why was Ellen here as well? Would Ellen recognise me from 21 years ago? Probably not, but it was still a complication, and I didn't want her to come into harm's way.

"Is that blonde woman in the red jacket your mother?" I slurred.

"Yes, have the two of you met before?" Sabina asked.

'You could put it that way,' I thought, but I didn't have the time to say it, as there was an interruption.

"WE FINALLY MEET, MISS Hines. Or should I say, Miss Keila Eisenstein?"

I turned around. It was Szymon Yehuda with a group of Mossad agents.

"Ben Yehuda, is that you?" Sabina asked in amazement.

"No, I am Szymon Yehuda. Ben is dead. Martin Al-Sham betrayed us and murdered my dear brother." Szymon replied.

"Wow. Exactly the man I have been waiting to meet!" Sabina taunted.

"Of that, I am certain!" Szymon mocked.

After a few seconds of tense silence, Szymon spoke again. "I am not here to avenge my brother. I am here to take back the crystal that you stole from us. Give me the crystal, and you might get out of this alive." Szymon taunted.

"Do you mean this crystal?" Sabina asked.

"Yes, give it to me, Sabina!" Szymon said with his eyes glowing with greed and bloodlust.

"Not unless you tell me how you intend to use it." Sabina teased.

Szymon couldn't resist the urge to brag about his genocidal 'divine plan'. Sabina listened attentively, and when Szymon dropped his guard, she slammed him in the face with the Zeto Crystal. Then she backflipped into the water, while the other Mossad agents shot after her.

I knew that I needed to act. I jumped backwards, and I landed with my back on the ground. I ignored the pain, and I swiftly inserted the monocle with my left hand while pulling out my pistol with my right hand. I activated combat mode, and I headshotted the Mossad agents. I got up and walked over to Szymon who was still fazed from Sabina's mighty blow. "Fuck you, Szymon!" I said and fired off my remaining bullets into his ugly face.

I turned my monocle to avoid confrontation mode. 'Option not available.' I sighed. I could hear multiple police sirens in the background. I entered combat mode, and I was about to fight my way out when something knocked me unconscious.

Chapter 19: Jakarta, April 2040.

I woke up in a luxurious bedroom, with smooth Egyptian cotton sheets and a superb view. It wasn't bad at all, much better than waking up in Vladimir's torture chamber! I looked out through the window. The view was magnificent, but where was I? The door opened, and Elaine entered the room.

"How do you like my new penthouse?" Elaine asked.

"It's amazing. What happened?" I asked

"Do you refer to my good looks, or how I got you out of the mess you created in Sydney?" Elaine smirked.

I looked at Elaine. She looked amazing; it was like she was young again. I decided to flatter her looks before I moved on to more relevant topics.

"You look amazing, Elaine. How did you do it?" I asked.

"I was looking for the fountain of youth and I found it. My chemists found a way to replicate the chemical composition of a type of mud, found in a temple on Kalaotoa Island." Elaine revealed.

"Amazing, you can make a fortune from beauty products, you look like you are in your 20's" I replied.

"No. I'll save the best for myself. That's how I saved your life." Elaine replied.

I nodded. I guess it was time to find out there more important question. How did Elaine save my life?

"So, how did you save me in Sydney?" I asked.

"Do you remember the invisibility suits that we found schematics for in the Sunken Pyramid of Kiribati?" Elaine stated.

"Yes, of course, I do," I replied.

"I have kept the technology secret. Only a handful of my most loyal followers know about it. When I heard about your trip to Sydney, I sent my agents Budi and Rexi to follow you around." Elaine revealed.

"I didn't notice anything?" I asked.

"You can't see what you are not looking for. My agents weren't a threat, so your monocle didn't perceive them as such." Elaine replied.

I nodded. The invisibility armour was a marvellous invention, albeit easy to detect for someone actively looking for it.

"How did your agents get me out of there?" I asked.

"After the shootout, I realised that my agents needed to intervene. I ordered Budi and Rexi to knock you out and cover you in a blanket that made you invisible. After that, they carried you to one of my safe houses, where they sedated you. After nightfall, they drove you to the airport and flew you here." Elaine revealed.

"Thank you, Elaine," I replied.

"Don't worry about it. I have been thinking of going after Pierre Beaumont for a long time. It might be time for us to strike back against that bastard." Elaine replied.

"Agreed. Any news about Sabina." I asked.

Hearing Sabina's name, Elaine's gaze darkened. "I don't want to talk about that spawn of your infidelity!" Elaine shouted.

"So, you would rather be angry about things happening 20 years ago than doing what is right for our future?" I pleaded.

Elaine calmed down and said, "Okay, I'll ask my associates to keep an eye out for her. Have a rest, Martin. You have serious wounds, and I got a business to run."

Elaine left the room, and I got into the bubble bath in the bathroom. I calmed down. I had saved Sabina's life, but there was nothing more I could do now. Leaving the relative safety of Elaine penthouse in Jakarta was a terrible idea as that would put a target on my back. No matter what I did, I couldn't help Sabina anymore. I lay back in the hot water, and I hoped that Sabina really was the destined saviour of humankind.

I WAS SITTING IN THE private dining room of the Harapan Conglomerate building. I hadn't seen much of Elaine since I spoke to her three days earlier. It was just as well; I did not know what we would talk about in any case.

I was enjoying some chicken skewers with Indonesian Gado-Gado salad when Elaine approached me.

"Pierre and Sandra are dead. They both died in the Mexican Civil War." Elaine said with a shocked voice.

"Pierre's death should be a cause for celebration. So, why the long face?" I replied.

Elaine got seated opposite me at the dining table. "I am not sad about Pierre's death. It's just..." Elaine said.

"Just what?" I asked.

"The monocles gave us all so much intelligence. Such great opportunities to shape the world to the better. And look what happened to us. Ben and Szymon obsessed about a religious genocide and you killed them. Pierre started wars to make more money and did nothing to improve humankind, despite owning more than he could ever spend. You travelled the world looking for magical artefacts leaving a trail of corpses and destruction wherever you went..." Elaine sighed.

"What about you? Jakarta looks like the perfect city. You did something good for humanity." I replied.

"There are mass graves found all over Indonesia. I used my control over the media to silence the news. When I ordered a clean-up of our capital, I looked the other way when corrupt officials butchered the poor and disabled. While I didn't order their deaths, I am still complicit." Elaine revealed.

I pondered Elaine's statement. She was correct when she blamed her actions. But I didn't want to criticise my host and guardian angel, so I replied. "At least you didn't order their deaths. But there is still one person who can change this world for the better."

"Sabina?" Elaine asked.

"Yes!" I replied.

"You have too high hopes on that girl. She'll also become a tyrant if the world allows it." Elaine sighed

"One must hope for a better future, otherwise there is no point in living," I stated.

"Okay, I'll see what I can do," Elaine replied.

Elaine got up from the table and was about to leave when one of her agents came in.

"Kami telah menemukan gadis itu. Dia ada di Hawaii." The agent said.

I had studied enough Indonesian during the past few days to know what that meant. Sabina was in Hawaii!

"ELAINE, I NEED TO BORROW a private jet, some clothes and a suitcase," I said.

"Of course. Hold on, I will conjure these objects like a genie." Elaine scoffed.

I sighed. This wasn't going to be an easy conversation.

"Elaine. Sabina is in Hawaii. I need to bring her Pachamama's Veil so that she can recharge the Zeto Crystal." I pleaded.

"What are you going to do after that? Having some father-daughter time and kill people? You are on your own." Elaine taunted.

I heard the voice of Rangda in the back of my head. *"Tell Elaine that you are bringing Sabina to the Sunken Pyramid of Kiribati. Tell her that Sabina is the only one who can open the portal inside the pyramid and stop the apocalypse."*

I reiterated what Rangda told me to Elaine and she gave me a cold stare. "Is that your words or Rangda's words?" Elaine mocked.

"Rangda's", I sighed.

Elaine sat down and seemed to think for a while. Eventually, she spoke. "I am helping you on one condition."

"What's your condition?" I asked.

"That you approach Sabina as her captor and not as her ally!" Elaine stated.

"Her captor? How do you suggest that I capture a supernatural sorceress aided by an ancient deity?" I scoffed.

"We kidnap Alex. Alex is Sabina's weakness, and he is not protected. We'll force her to follow our commands using him as a hostage." Elaine suggested.

"Why? That seems unnecessary. I am sure she'll come by her own will if I explain things to her." I replied.

"That's beside the point. You're sending this girl to face Rangda, and Rangda wants you to send her. Sabina doesn't have a chance. You shouldn't pretend to be the friend of Sabina and then send her to her doom. I am sick of your duplicitousness." Elaine ranted.

I didn't like Elaine's suggestion, but I agreed to it. There was most likely an international arrest warrant after me so I couldn't travel with regular flights.

"Okay, Elaine. Let's do things your way. Get your men ready and we'll pay Mr Alexander O'Neill a visit in Hawaii.

Chapter 20: Hawaii, April 2040

I watched in anticipation as our private jet prepared to land on the beautiful Hawaiian Islands. It had been many years since Elaine, and I had been travelling together. For a moment, I could almost imagine that none of the dreadful things had happened.

Then I opened my eyes, and I saw Elaine's rough-looking agents Budi and Rexi, which reminded me of why we were going to Hawaii. We weren't going for a holiday; we were going to continue our lifetime of villainy.

"So, you gave up your idea about having a Varangian Guard?" I asked.

"Yes, the incident in Kiribati proved the foolishness in surrounding myself with criminals from the other end of the world." Elaine replied.

"So, how are you recruiting your inner circle now?" I asked.

"I recruit them from the orphanages that I operate. Budi and Rexi are like my foster children. They and my other agents respect my vision and follow my commands." Elaine replied.

"Well, at least they haven't tried to kill me yet," I smirked.

We got out of the plane. The weather was perfect, warm, and sunny, with a cooling breeze from the ocean. The mountains in the background seemed ideal for a hike.

"Hey. How about we go on a hike tomorrow. I'd love to explore the Mountains. The Manoa Falls trail should be beautiful." I beamed.

Elaine gave me a sceptical look and replied. "Really? You want to go hiking? We came here on a mission, remember?"

I shrugged my shoulders and replied. "If Budi and Rexi could get me out of Sydney when everyone was looking for me, I am sure that they'll face no problem kidnapping Alex. I have rented a cabin off the beaten track," I replied.

Elaine studied me for a while and replied. "I guess you're right. A cabin in the wilderness is an excellent place to keep Alex while you 'persuade' Sabina to face Rangda."

"Great! We'll have a marvellous time. Let's go!" I replied.

We got in the rental car, and Budi drove us to the Cabin.

AFTER SOME MORNING rain, the sun glimmered through an opening in the cloud cover. I went out from the cabin, and I watched Budi and Rexi driving away, to kidnap Alex. I went over to Elaine who was intensely focused on her laptop.

"What are you doing, my beautiful queen?" I teased.

"I am running my business empire," Elaine replied.

"Running? You are very stationary?" I teased.

Elaine gave me an annoyed gaze.

"Come join me for a swim in the lake," I said.

"But I am busy." Elaine objected.

"Honestly. What do you think you'll regret more on your deathbed? Not swimming in this beautiful lake, or not spending more time tapping on your laptop?" I asked.

"You're right. A swim would be nice." Elaine sighed and closed her laptop.

We walked over to the jetty.

"I don't have any clothes." Elaine objected.

"You don't need any!" I teased and took off all my clothes.

Elaine studied my naked body for a while and exclaimed. "Martin, you have so many scars."

"Well I haven't aged like a fine wine; more like a piece of stale meat. But I am still the same person." I teased.

"You are not that bad," Elaine replied and undressed.

I stared at her body. The Kalaotoa Island mud, combined with some other plastic surgeries, had made her sexier than ever.

"Don't just stand there. Get in!" Elaine exclaimed, and she jumped into the water.

I followed suit, and I swam to her. Our gaze met and we kissed. There and then I felt that a heavy burden had fallen off my chest and I felt hopeful for the future.

I SPENT THE DAY CATCHING up on bedroom activities with Elaine. In the afternoon, Budi and Rexi returned with Alex bound and gagged.

I walked up to Alex, removed his blindfold and gag.

"Who are you? Is this revenge for what happened in Mexico?" the terrified Alex asked.

"Calm down, Mr O'Neill. We are happy that Pierre is dead. But we need you as a bargaining chip against Sabina." I replied.

"Sabina? What do you want from her?" Alex asked.

"I want her to fulfil her destiny. I want her to travel through the portal in the Sunken Pyramid of Kiribati and kill Rangda." I replied.

"Sabina would want that too. So why did you kidnap me?" Alex whined.

"Well, as you should have realised by now, Sabina is not entirely human. She can control the minds of others, and she survived dozens of shots in Jerusalem." I revealed.

Alex looked away for a while, sighed and replied. "Yes. I was blind for years, but I recently realised that she is different. She brought me back from the dead in Mexico." Alex admitted.

"Very well, then you realise why I need collateral?" I asked.

Alex didn't reply, and I took a photo of Alex where he sat, tied to a chair.

I was walking out of the room when Alex shouted. "Wait. Who are you, and why are you doing this? "I am Martin Al-Sham, and I am doing this because I must," I replied and left the room.

I WAS OUTSIDE ROOM 853 at the luxurious Halekulani resort, where Sabina and Alex were staying. I used Alex's key card and I opened the door.

I saw Sabina sitting on the couch overlooking the park and beach below.

"Alex, is that you?" Sabina asked and turned around.

Sabina shook her head when she spotted me. "Hmm, I reckoned that you would show up eventually." Sabina sneered.

"Did Benjamin Cook tell you to come here?" Sabina asked.

"I don't know who that is, I have other ways of finding you. Hurry up! We got a job to do!" I replied.

Sabina got up from the couch and walked up to me.

"You have no right to tell me what to do. Besides are you part of the same conspiracy as Pierre? It didn't end well for Pierre." Sabina taunted.

"I know. And that's why I have taken precautions." I replied and handed Sabina a picture of Alex.

Seeing that I had Alex in captivity, Sabina sunk down on the couch and covered her face. "Oh no! What do you want?" She cried.

"I want you to fulfil your destiny. Travel to Kiribati with me and activate the portal in the Sunken Pyramid." I commanded.

"I can't. The Zeto Crystal is out of energy." Sabina objected and showed me the dull crystal.

I looked at the crystal. There was no way to visually distinguish it from a large sapphire when it wasn't charged. I thought of touching the crystal to feel it, but I pushed that notion aside. After all, I didn't know the extent of Sabina's magical powers, so I had to be careful.

"That's not a problem. I know how to charge it." I replied.

"How?" Sabina asked.

"You'll see once we reach Kiribati. But we better hurry. My associates don't like waiting." I urged.

"And what if I refuse to come with you?" Sabina argued.

"Then I'll let you go. I am not stupid enough to threaten a woman under divine protection. But Alex doesn't have the same protection, does he?" I taunted.

Sabina sat silent and sobbed. I felt terrible for treating her this way, and I wanted to hold her and comfort her. But Elaine was right. I couldn't be friendly and pretend to care about Sabina and at the same time sent her to kill Rangda. I couldn't be kind to someone and then sacrifice her for the greater good.

Sabina wiped off her tears and spoke. "Okay. I'll come with you. We share the same goal, after all."

I nodded. "Excellent. I have a plane waiting at the airport. We are leaving at once." I commanded.

Sabina nodded, packed a few things in a small bag and followed me as I left the hotel.

Chapter 21: Kiribati, April 2040

I was studying Sabina as we sat on a private jet, heading from Hawaii to Kiribati. It felt strange. For the first time, I had the opportunity to speak with Sabina in private for an extended period of time. Yet, I did not know what to say, and things were evidently not friendly between us.

Sabina fascinated me. She was my daughter with supernatural powers destined to save the world. I believed that Elaine was wrong in her assessment. I didn't sacrifice Sabina. I sent her to save us. If anyone could save us from the apocalypse and Rangda's evil influence, it was Sabina. Rangda, in her arrogance, thought that Sabina didn't stand a chance against her. But it was such wicked arrogance that would lead to Rangda's downfall.

I woke up from my daydreaming when Sabina grabbed my arm and looked into my eyes. I could sense what she was trying to do. I couldn't blame her. We had kidnapped her husband, so of course, she would try using her powers against me.

"I wouldn't try that. The monocle protects me against your empath abilities." I scoffed.

Sabina let go of my arm and got seated in the armchair opposite me.

"So, I take it you were part of the Mossad conspiracy all along?" Sabina taunted.

Sabina's tone pissed me off. Hadn't I killed the Yehuda Brothers and put myself into harm's way to save her sorry ass? "I am not part of any conspiracy. I have been trying to help Keila Eisenstein to stop the apocalypse for the last two decades. You should thank me!" I yelled.

"Thank you? You kidnapped my husband to force me to come with you. You wouldn't live if he wasn't in your custody." Sabina roared, and her eyes were glowing with fury.

I didn't respond. Sabina had a good reason to be upset with me, and there was no need to escalate the argument.

After a few seconds, Sabina's eye colour reversed to normal, and she calmed down. "So, how do you afford this if you are not part of a conspiracy? Travelling the world, hiring planes, and kidnapping people aren't exactly cheap." Sabina asked.

I considered my options. I did not want to rat out Elaine and her company. If Sabina took out her fury on me, I wanted her trail to go cold. I feared what the powerful sorceress could achieve if she put her powers towards vengeance. I took up my wallet and handed Sabina a photo of Elaine and I winning the Powerball jackpot back in 2020.

"This is how I can afford all of this!" I stated.

"Wow! Who is this woman, and why do you look so unhappy in the photo?" Sabina asked.

"Hmm, that's very perceptive of you. I guess I can't fake a smile with my eyes?" I reflected.

Sabina didn't reply, and I spoke again. "The woman's name is Elaine, and we were unhappy because our win came at a cost," I revealed.

"Where is Elaine now?" Sabina asked.

"That's none of your business, Sabina!" I lashed out, and Sabina answered me with silence.

I moved over to another seat in the plane. Even though I wanted to speak to Sabina, and try to set everything right, it was better if we didn't speak at all, as she didn't know that I was her biological father.

"O LE A OU LE ALU I le Banaba Island. E le o toe mamao le mauga. E matautia tele." Captain Ahohako said.

Having spent a few years on Kiribati, I had some understanding of the language, and I replied "Zuo matautia. Afai asiasi ia te oe i le po nei."

After that, I opened my jacket, which concealed my pistol, to emphasise my message.

"Okay, Mr. $10,000 is fine. I'll take you to Banaba Island." Ahohako sighed.

"Cool. I'll leave the money in the boatshed. Call your wife and tell her to pick them up. And don't try any tricks." I stated.

I left the cash under a bucket in the boatshed, and I got on the boat. "Hurry up, Sabina. We are heading to Banaba Island." I shouted.

Sabina got on the boat and replied. "He didn't seem very keen to do the job despite the big payment. What's up with that?"

"He won't have much use for his money if he is dead. People expect Banaba Island to have a massive volcanic eruption at any time." I revealed.

"So, what about us?" Sabina asked.

"We'll be alright. Only a lunatic or a visionary would visit an island moments before a volcanic eruption!" I smirked.

"And you consider yourself a visionary?" Sabina heckled.

"I know that I am. The thermal energy from the erupting volcano is just what we need to recharge the primordial Zeto Crystal. Now hurry up, we don't have all day!" I said.

Sabina didn't reply. I don't know if she believed me or if she simply resigned to her fate.

Time passed, and we got closer to the Island. As Ahohako saw the giant smoke pillar and could smell sulphur from the volcano, he became agitated.

"I can't go on. We are all going to die." Ahohako whined.

I knew that if I convinced Ahohako to drop us off at the island, he would ditch us as soon as we got off the boat. That was a terrible scenario. If my plan didn't work, we would need immediate evacuation.

I looked at my pistol. If I shot Ahohako, I could anchor the boat at the island, and it would still be there when we needed to leave. I hesitated. I didn't want to kill Ahohako as I knew him since my time as a hermit on the islands. Furthermore, I did not want to kill someone in cold blood in front of Sabina. Oh yes, Sabina. She was my solution. I walked up to her and spoke:

"Sabina. I need you to use your powers. Convince Captain Ahohako to take us to the island and wait for us there, or I'll need to kill him." I said.

Sabina gave me a disapproving look, and she stared at my pistol for a long time. I felt terrified, if she were to attack me, I would perish, and the future of humankind would be at risk. Eventually, Sabina walked over to Ahohako and used her empath powers to make him cooperate.

I sighed of relief. This had been a close call.

Under Sabina's influence, Ahohako took us to the island without objecting. 10 minutes later, we got off the boat. Thick smoke covered the island and worried that the gasmasks that I had brought wouldn't be enough to save us. I took a few steps, and Sabina gave me another reason to worry as she called out to Ahohako. "Go back to your family Ahohako. Ailana needs her kidney transplant."

Screaming this, Sabina released Ahohako from her spell, and he hurried to steer the boat away from the island. I thought of shooting him to stop his escape, but it wouldn't help, and I put down my pistol.

"What's wrong with you? Why did you send the Captain away?" I asked.

"Captain Ahohako is a good man; I can't risk the life of an innocent," Sabina replied.

"But what about us, you lunatic?" I asked.

"I have divine protection under The True Maker, and I wouldn't hesitate to throw you under the bus," Sabina scoffed.

Her reply made me furious. I wanted to punch that smug, holier-than-thou smile off her face. We were screwed, and there was no way I could find someone stupid enough to evacuate me now.

I calmed down. All I needed to focus on was getting that Zeto Crystal to the volcano's crater, wrap it into Pachamama's veil, chant the verse, throw it in and hope for the best.

Thinking about the absurdity of my plan, I started laughing at it, and I replied to Sabina: "Good to know that we are on the same page. Put on this gasmask. You'll need it for the hike ahead of us."

Having said this, I put on my gas mask, and Sabina followed suit, walking behind me towards the crater.

IN THE TRADITIONAL Christian view of hell, it is a place full of fire and sulphuric vapours. From that point of view, our hike to the top of Banaba Island was a hike in hell. I usually enjoy walking in the mountains, but this was the exception to the rule.

The hot sulphuric gas burnt on my skin and coloured me yellow. I hadn't brought proper equipment to be close to an erupting volcano. All I wanted was to run down the slope and jump into the cooling water. But that wasn't an option. Once the volcano erupted, it would create a powerful tsunami that would kill everything in the vicinity of the island. Besides, we were here on a mission, and I could not give up when I was this close.

As we got close to the volcano, I pulled off my gas mask and exclaimed. "Give me the Zeto Crystal!"

To my great relief, Sabina didn't argue, and she handed me the crystal.

I wrapped the crystal in Pachamama's Veil. The hot sulphuric vapours burned into my lungs when I tried to recite the chant. "Gikan sa kalalim sa Yuta. Bag-o ang gahum nga nagdala kinabuhi." (From the depth of the Earth. Renew the power that brings life.) After that, I chucked the Zeto Crystal, wrapped in Pachamama's Veil, into the crater.

I collapsed to the ground. My lungs were burning, and I was coughing up yellowish sulphuric blood. 'I need to put on the gasmask' was my last thought before everything turned black.

"TELL ELAINE, THAT YOU are fine" Sabina urged me, as I woke up. The smoke had cleared, and Sabina held the primordial Zeto Crystal, which shone brightly in her one hand, and my satellite phone in her other hand.

I nodded, and I grabbed the phone.

"I am fine, Elaine. Everything is going according to plan. Proceed as planned, and I'll call you with further updates." I said and hung up the phone.

"So, did you plan to leave me here to die?" I asked.

"I never promised to keep you safe. You are a cold-blooded murderer, and you kidnapped my husband Alex." Sabina replied.

"I am the reason you are still alive. But lucky for Alex that you decided to help me." I taunted.

Sabina stopped herself from responding, and a few seconds later, she had changed to a friendlier approach. "Thank you, Martin, for helping me recharge the Zeto Crystal," Sabina said, forced a smile and help me up on my feet.

"Thank you, Sabina. There are some things that you should know. But I fear what telling you would mean for the task ahead of us." I said.

"What things? I doubt many truths come from your lying lips." Sabina scoffed.

I sighed and looked away. This was not the time to repair our broken relationship. There would probably never be a time for that, but regardless we needed to focus on the mission ahead of us. I picked up my satellite phone, and I called Elaine and asked her to send a helicopter. Then I took off my clothes and relaxed in one of the newly emerged thermal springs on the island.

1.5 HOURS LATER, WE were in the helicopter, hovering over the Sunken Pyramid of Kiribati. I didn't know how we would reach the pyramid since it was at over 100 metres depth. *"Send the girl to swim down. The Zeto Crystal will keep her safe."* Rangda instructed.

I decided to follow Rangda's instructions.

"This is it, Sabina. We are hovering straight on top of the Sunken Pyramid of Kiribati." I proclaimed.

"Are you sure? How comes there is nothing about this Pyramid on the Internet?" Sabina objected.

"Simple. The oceans are vast, and my associates and I decided to not tell the world about it." I stated.

Sabina looked at the surface below. She seemed hesitant. Eventually, she spoke. "So, what do you want me to do?"

"I want you to swim down there and activate the portal," I replied.

"Are you insane? I can't swim that deep. I will die!" Sabina objected.

"Aren't you the Chosen One? Anyone else would die. You have a fully charged Zeto Crystal and divine protection. You'll be fine" I taunted.

Sabina stared at the water below. Eventually, she spoke. "I'll dive down there on one condition."

"I am listening," I replied.

"I need you to release Alex first," Sabina demanded.

Sabina's demand terrified me. If I released Alex, I had no bargaining chip against her, and I knew that she was incredibly powerful.

"I can't agree with that. You'd attack me the moment you know that Alex is safe." I stated.

"What if I swear by the True Maker, to fulfil my mission and leave you unharmed?" Sabina suggested.

This was a tricky suggestion. I didn't know what attitude the True Maker had towards oaths. If I swore by Rangda to not kill anyone, that would make no difference, as Rangda didn't care about promises. But, on the other hand, I couldn't force Sabina, and she held a magical artefact in her hand.

"Okay. I accept your suggestion." I said, and I called Elaine.

"Are you okay, Martin?" Elaine asked.

"Release Alex and give him a phone. Sabina wants to talk to him once he is safe." I stated.

"Are you insane? If I release him while I am still in Hawaii, he'll call the cops on me, and you have no bargaining chip against Sabina." Elaine objected.

"She promised to not hurt us, and I trust her." I sighed.

"Very well. I'll do as you say. I am getting out of here." Elaine said and hung up the phone.

"All set, Sabina. You should receive a phone call from Alex in a couple of minutes." I stated.

Sabina nodded but didn't reply.

A few minutes later, Alex called and had a melodramatic conversation with Sabina over the phone. Paranoia struck me, and I feared that Sabina would back down on her promise. When she hung up the phone, I aimed my pistol at her.

"Don't back out on your promise, Sabina!" I threatened.

"I'm not. You have released Alex, and now I will help you." Sabina thundered.

"If you are the Chosen One, you'll swim down there, active the portal and fulfil your destiny. If not, the True Maker will not protect you anymore." I exclaimed.

Sabina stared at her Zeto Crystal and mumbled something inaudible. Eventually, she spoke. "After this, I hope to never see you again."

Before I had the time to reply, she got to the side of the helicopter and dove into the water, disappearing below the surface.

"You didn't see that. I have powerful and dangerous friends." I warned the helicopter pilot.

"Why do I always get the worst customers?" The pilot asked.

I didn't reply to the pilot's self-reflection, and instead, I ordered. "Take me back to the airport!"

The pilot sighed and changed the direction towards the airport when a blue pulse flashed in front of my eyes. I looked up, and I saw that the Sunken Pyramid had ascended from the depths and had sent a massive tsunami in the direction of the Ambo village. I had an epiphany. Ambo was close to my Kiribati mansion and the home of my former housekeeper Alani and her daughter Elenoa, who I both cared for.

"New orders. Fly to Ambo!" I shouted to the pilot while I desperately tried to call Elenoa to tell her to seek shelter.

WE ARRIVED AT AMBO ten minutes later. We were too late. The tsunami had struck and destroyed the village. There were dead and wounded people lying everywhere. "Land over there!" I commanded and pointed at Alani's house. As soon as I got out of the helicopter, the pilot flew off. 'So damn hard to find loyal employees these days,' I mumbled, even though the pilot had good reasons to stay clear from the gun-toting lunatic that I was.

I dug through Alani's house and found her lifeless. 'Another one bites the dust' I cried. I pulled myself together. Alani was gone, but I could still save Elenoa. I rummaged through the wreckage, and I shouted in relief as I found Elenoa alive. I gave her CPR, and she opened her eyes.

"Martin!" Elenoa exclaimed in surprise.

"Don't worry, Elenoa. Everything will be alright." I said and held her tight.

Chapter 22: Bidadari Island (Indonesia), May 2040

I was recovering at Bidadari Island in Indonesia. Elaine had built a large private residence there, far away from the hustle and bustle in Jakarta. We had returned to Indonesia after spending a few weeks in Kiribati working with disaster relief. I had convinced Elaine to assist in the relief effort of the affected islands, and it was good for the reputation of her company as well. Although we had been contributing to the relief effort, I still felt guilty. I was the reason that the pyramid had risen from the depths and caused the tsunami in the first place.

I pondered the fate of Sabina. We hadn't found her body when we moved in to secure the pyramid. Elaine had bribed the Kiribatian government to give her company exclusive access to the pyramid. However, we knew that others wanted and were willing to fight to get the same thing.

Elaine approached me by the pool. While the pool and its surroundings seemed paradise-like, we both felt very tense. We were sure that Vladimir would come after us, trying to avenge the Yehuda Brothers' and Pierre's death. Elaine had her own groups looking for Vladimir seeking to eliminate him. However, killing an accomplished killer, aided by alien technology, was easier said than done.

"I spoke to James Winter. He promised us CIA assistance in finding and bringing down Vladimir Kravchenko." Elaine said.

"And do you believe him?" I asked

"Yes. Vladimir is of no value to the CIA. He is a deranged lunatic and mass-murderer with no goals except for death and destruction." Elaine stated.

"Well, I hope that you are right," I replied.

"Of course, I am," Elaine replied.

I took a sip from my mango coconut smoothie and exhaled. Elaine was correct. As soon as we had dealt with Vladimir, I could enjoy retirement and focus on charity work to redeem myself.

"I'll go inside to do some work. Just relax and write a bit of your book." Elaine said, kissed me and walked away. I opened my laptop, but I felt sleepy, so I put it under my sunbed. I closed my eyes, and I fell asleep in the blissful shade under the pool umbrella.

I WAS EXPERIENCING vivid dreams when I felt a shock as if someone punched me. I opened my eyes, and I saw the battle between Rangda and Sabina, from Rangda's perspective. But why could I see things from Rangda's point of view? Had the fight between Rangda and Sabina, damaged Rangda's bionic microchips? Perhaps, a magical blast had caused the microchips to malfunction and share Rangda's vision with me.

I saw how Rangda was furiously blasting Sabina with bolts of dark energy. Sabina was struggling, and it was clear that she wouldn't stand a chance. I felt guilty for sending her to Rangda, but I couldn't stop watching, I had to see what would happen next.

Sabina collapsed after Rangda's barrage. She raised her hand and screamed, "Stop!"

"Are you ready to say your last words." Rangda taunted.

"You were right all along. I want to join you. Together we can build a better universe where only the strongest survive." Sabina replied.

"But why would I let you live since you're weak?" Rangda scoffed.

"Because turning the woman sent by the True Maker to stop you, would be your biggest triumph. Far greater than killing me." Sabina replied.

Rangda paused for a few seconds. The events shocked me. Would the sanctimonious Sabina surrender to Rangda like I had 20 years earlier? What an unexpected turn of events.

"Very well. Give me the Terran Zeto Crystal, and I'll let you serve me." Rangda mocked.

Sabina threw the crystal to Rangda, who stared at it in pure delight. A few seconds later, Sabina uttered a command and set Rangda alight with a bright holy flame.

'Wow this is amazing' I thought and got up from my chair. I couldn't wait to tell Elaine what I had seen. The next thing I saw terrified me. Sabina walked up to the dying Rangda and squeezed Rangda's cranium to access her mind. I could tell that Sabina, tried to access the Monocle control panel. 'Kill all connected users,' came up as a command. I ran towards the house and screamed. "Elaine take off your monocle now!"

I could feel that the monocle was trying to kill me. I attempted to take it off, but the system had locked down and instead, I burnt my hand. I realised that I had to remove the monocle; otherwise, it would kill me.

I grabbed a towel, put it over the monocle and pulled it with all my might. It was useless. The monocle was stuck to my face, and I couldn't get it off. I ran to a wall, and I managed to get the monocle attached to the wall. I climbed up a few steps and kicked away with my legs, allowing gravity to work. I felt excruciating pain when the monocle ripped through the bones in my eye socket, and I landed on my back.

"Ratu Sudah Mati (The Queen is dead)" I heard Elaine's agitated body-guards scream before I passed out from the pain.

THE NEXT DAY, I WOKE up in a Harapan Conglomerate medical facility. Bandages covered my head and I looked like a mummy. I screamed in terror.

Elaine's private doctor, Dr Suwardi, came rushing in.

"Mr Orchard, you're alive!" Dr Suwardi exclaimed.

"Why wouldn't I be?" I asked.

More medical staff rushed in, and I realised from the terror on their faces that my survival was a miracle.

"What happened? Why is my face covered in bandages?" I asked.

"Mr Orchard. You need to calm down." Dr Suwardi replied.

"I am not going to calm down. I command you to unwrap my face so that I can see my injuries." I commanded.

"Very well. Suit yourself." Suwardi replied, and he asked a nurse to unwrap my bandages.

When I stared in terror at my damages in the mirror, I realised why the doctors had wrapped up my face. My right eye was gone, and there were stitches all the way from my eyes socket to my mouth. It was as if someone had slammed my face with an axe.

"Please wrap up my face again," I asked, and a moment later I was back in my hospital bed.

"How did it go for Elaine?" I asked.

"She died. She wasn't as lucky as you were." Suwardi revealed.

'What luck?' I pondered. 'Elaine was the lucky one!' I meant to say, but I refrained from doing so and fell asleep instead.

"WE FOUND THIS WOMAN unconscious in the pyramid. We passed her over to her husband, who took her to a private hospital." Budi said and handed me a tablet.

It was a photograph of Sabina. Harapan Conglomerate medical staff had proclaimed Sabina braindead, and Alex had taken her with him to a private hospital in Kiribati.

I studied the picture, and I felt intense sorrow. Sabina had stopped Rangda, but she had perished herself. There was no way back from the brain damages that Sabina had. Nothing less than a miracle could save her. But why would the True Maker wait to bring her back if that was the case?

When I looked at Sabina, I felt sorrow, hate and love at the same time. Sorrow because both Sabina and Rangda had died. Thus, nothing could protect us from the Gamma-Ray blast in 2131. I felt love because Sabina was my daughter, and she had freed me from Rangda's demonic influence. I felt hate because Sabina had murdered Elaine and disfigured me despite pledging an oath to not hurt us.

I gave the tablet back to Budi and replied. "Very well. Thank you for telling me, Budi. Was there anything else?"

"Yes, the board members are arguing on how to split Elaine's inheritance. They don't want a white person in control of the company." Budi replied.

"Do you know what I want?" I asked.

"I do not," Budi replied.

"I want you and Rexi to run the company. You were loyal to Elaine, and you love your country. I can't think of anyone more suitable to run it." I replied.

"It would be an honour to continue Elaine's legacy," Budi replied.

I sighed. Budi was an orphan due to Elaine's legacy. But there was no reason to bring up this painful fact if Budi could utilise her enthusiasm for a useful purpose.

"Don't follow her legacy. Create your own legacy. One that is beneficial for your country, the environment and its people." I said.

"Yes, Master Orchard," Budi said, bowed and left my office.

After Budi had left, I thought of Sabina. She destroyed my spirit when she broke her promise and tried to kill me. I vowed to get my revenge if she ever were to wake up!

Chapter 23: Kiribati and New York, September 2041

I was sitting back in my chair, and I was doing my daily writing. I had returned to my hermit lifestyle and I lived in my mansion on a desolate island in Kiribati. It was just as well. The monocle had disfigured my face, and my interactions with the rest of humanity tended to lead to bloodshed.

I heard a motorboat approaching, and I assumed that Elenoa had come to deliver my groceries. I had helped her through her injuries and paid for her hospital bills. Elenoa repaid me by doing occasional errands and visiting me to help against my loneliness.

I walked out to greet her when I saw that I had an unexpected visitor. Simona had joined Elenoa on her boat ride to my island.

"Simona. What are you doing here?" I asked in bewilderment.

"I am checking out the neighbourhood. I heard that the Phantom of the Opera has moved to Kiribati." Simona teased.

"I am not wearing a mask, though." I objected.

"But you should!" Simona replied and handed me a mask.

I tried the mask on. It didn't fit well with the Hawaii shirt, shorts, and sandals that I wore.

I took off the mask and smirked. "You forgot to bring black clothes and a cape, Simona," I said.

"No, I didn't. They are in my suitcase in my hotel room. I will give them to you when we reach New York." Simona replied.

"Why are we going to New York?" I asked. I felt confused but at the same time a bit excited. "Because Sabina is going to give a speech at the United Nations Environment Ceremony in New York next week. We should confront her there and expose her hypocrisy to the world." Simona yapped.

This came as a shock to me. The first few months after Sabina had tried to kill me, I had obsessed about revenge. But Sabina never seemed to wake up from her coma, so eventually, I had blocked her from my mind to preserve my fragments of sanity. Hearing that Sabina was alive and well, filled me with an urge for revenge!

"Did you find out anything else?" I asked.

"You know that I did," Simona said and handed me a tablet.

I read the files. Apparently, Sabina gave birth to a daughter seven months earlier. She had named the daughter Keila. According to documents that Simona had found, Alex wasn't the father of the child. I counted backwards. Sabina would have been in the divine dimension when she conceived. Could this have anything to do with Rangda's magic?

I made up my mind. I wouldn't use violence against Sabina, but I would make her life difficult. If I could convince Sabina that Rangda made her conceive an evil daughter, that would be a lifetime of punishment towards Sabina. This would be worse than killing her as death was fast and didn't bring any lasting pain.

"I am coming with you to New York, Simona." I stated.

"Excellent. Let's go at once." Simona replied.

Elenoa, who hadn't spoken so far, decided to speak up. "What is going on? Why are you guys going to New York?"

I turned towards Elenoa and spoke. "Sabina Hines, the woman who caused the pyramid to ascend and destroyed your home village, is receiving a prize in New York. We intend to expose her crimes to the world and destroy her reputation."

"So, it was her actions that caused the pyramid to rise?" Elenoa asked sceptically.

"Yes," I replied.

Elenoa hesitated for a moment. Understandably, she doubted my explanation. Eventually, she spoke. "If this is true, she killed my mother. I am coming with you to New York."

"Why? What does this have to do with you?" Simona asked.

"The tsunami that Sabina caused killed my mother, my cousins and my grandparents. I want to see her reaction when I am calling her out!" Elenoa stated.

I thought about Elenoa's proposition. It was a great idea, better than if Simona or I would call her out. Simona was a computer hacker with a tattered record, and my list of crimes was enough to fill a whole novel. Elenoa, on the other hand, was innocent and would get more sympathy from the world.

"Very well, Elenoa. Pack your bags. You're coming with us to New York." I stated.

Simona looked like she was going to object to my idea, but she held her tongue.

"Great, I am excited to see the Big Apple," Elenoa stated.

"Then it's settled. Ladies, please return to your hotel rooms, while I organise our visas and flights to New York." I stated.

My young proteges left the island, and I was yet again to go on a mission, leaving the solitude of my empty island behind me. I hated to admit it, but the prospect of another mission made me excited.

"WOW, THIS IS SO AMAZING. I can't even see the ground!" Elenoa exclaimed happily.

We were visiting the America Supreme Mile building, which was the tallest building in the world, measuring over a mile in height. While it was impractical and expensive to build this high, America was the greatest nation in the world again. At least they had the world's most colossal phallic symbol.

I corrected my black cape and mask. While I felt like a full-on idiot dressing up like the phantom of the opera, I enjoyed it. I hadn't blended in when I wore my templar uniform either. In a way, the real me became invisible behind this stupid outfit and it was a relief. At least now I could pretend to be someone else, albeit my opera singing was a bit lacking.

"Let's go to Central Park. I have always wanted to go there because of all the movies." Elenoa chirped.

I looked at Elenoa and smiled. She was ugly, which made things easier for me. Simona's beauty had strained our relationship, but with Elenoa, this was not a problem and I could treat her like the stepdaughter I perceived her to be.

"Yes. Let's go to Central Park, and then we'll head back to the hotel. I need to brief you about tonight and tell you what you need to ask at the press conference." I stated, and we entered the lift down to the ground.

I WAS WATCHING THE United Nations press conference on TV. Sabina and her lackeys were receiving a prize for their environmental efforts. I couldn't complain about the jury's motivation, as Sabina's charity had done a lot for the environment. But I felt sickened by Sabina's sanctimonious attitude. This was a woman who manipulated people and drove them insane with her magical powers for her own gain. More importantly, she had murdered Elaine and tried to kill me, despite her oath to leave us unharmed.

Simona came up to me and spoke. "Has Elenoa asked her question yet?"

"Not yet. The Q&A is at the end of the presentation." I replied.

"So, what do you think about this?" Simona asked.

"I think that the automated ocean clean-up project is a great idea. But that's beyond the point. My conflict is on a personal level." I replied.

Simona walked over to the minibar and grabbed a beer for us each.

"Cheers!" she said.

"Cheers!" I replied, and I drank a few sips of my beer.

"Hey Simona, why are you doing this? Why do you seek revenge against Sabina?" I asked.

"Asks the man who is willing to throw his biological daughter under the bus." Simona taunted.

"Well, biological daughter is the keyword. We don't have a relationship and she doesn't even know that I am her father. My motivation is simple. Sabina killed my wife and disfigured me, despite swearing to leave us unharmed. I can't let something like that pass unpunished. Your motivation seems incoherent?"

Simona burst out into tears and left me flabbergasted. Why was she reacting like this to a simple question? Simona had always been cool and composed under pressure for all the years that I had known her.

"Have you ever experienced rape?" Simona cried.

"Well, I have experienced death and torture several times, but rape, no. Why?" I asked

"Well, I have never told anyone this before. My father didn't expel me from my home for being a lesbian. It was far worse!" Simona revealed.

"What happened?" I asked.

"When my father found out about Leah and I, he told me that he would make sure that I gave him a grandson, one way or the other. I was 16 when he raped me. I ran to Leah's place. But I didn't seek sympathy. Instead, I hacked a military drone, and I used it to kill my father. That's why Dov came after Leah, he thought that she had hacked the drone, and he wanted to stop the news from coming out." Simona revealed.

Ouch. How would I respond to this revelation? Not being an expert at dealing with people's traumas, I replied "Well, at least I know how you became the way you are. But what does this have to with Sabina?"

Simona put away the beer bottle and grabbed herself a glass of whiskey, clearly this wasn't an easy topic for her. After skolling her whiskey, she spoke. "My father was a bad man who violated me. Yet it is Sabina that destroyed my life." Simona stated.

"Because you had a crush on her?" I asked.

"No. Because Sabina used her God-given powers to manipulate my mind to love her, because she needed me. My father violated my body. But Sabina violated my soul." Simona stated.

I held back my desire to protect Sabina against Simona's judgement. While I had my own reason to seek revenge, I thought that Simona's reason was utter bollocks. She was beautiful and could find another hook-up to get over Sabina's rejection. This wasn't the right time to share this piece of timeless wisdom, so instead, I replied.

"Elenoa is also a lesbian, and she has faced a lot of traumas on her own. You can support each other?" I suggested

"Well, except that she is ugly!" Simona objected.

I wouldn't argue against this statement, so instead, I replied. "You and Sabina are both beautiful, but you killed your father with a drone, and Sabina tried to kill me with alien technology. Get down from your high horses and appreciate Elenoa for her inner beauty."

"Is that why you wanted to fuck me, while you hardly even look at Elenoa," Simona smirked.

"Don't do what I do. Do what I say!" I laughed, realising that my life story wouldn't serve as an example of good moral for the younger generations.

The Q&A section of the press conference began, and I felt satisfied when Elenoa pressured Sabina with her accusations. To everyone else in the room, the allegations would seem absurd, but they would terrify Sabina. Because Sabina would realise that I was still alive, and that I was after revenge. Because, how else could Elenoa know about her secret?

Chapter 24: Jakarta and Sydney, September 2047

"Mr Orchard. It's so nice to see you again after all this time." Budi said.

I hoped that the cordial reception was genuine, but it didn't matter. I wasn't visiting the Harapan Conglomerate headquarters as a social visit, but because I had another mission. One last mission to bring me peace before I died.

I was 62 and I could have many years ahead of me, and yet I missed the peace that lay in death. More than everything I missed vengeance. I had hoped that revealing myself to Sabina would be enough. That the looming threat of my revenge would be enough to make her miserable. But I was wrong. Reports that I received from Australia, indicated that Sabina led a happy worry-free existence.

"Nice to see you too, Budi," I replied, and I forced a smile.

Budi smiled back and pointed towards the private dining room. "This way, Martin. I have ordered the chefs to bring our greatest most expensive dishes."

I nodded, but I didn't reply, and I followed Budi to the dining hall, where our table was set with an array of expensive Indonesian foods and beverages. I was anxious to get on with the mission, but it would be rude to not accept the invitation, and I wasn't in any form of a hurry. I calmed down, and I enjoyed the assortment of delicacies while engaging in idle chatter with Budi and Rexi.

A WHILE LATER, I WAS in a top-secret research lab owned by the Harapan Conglomerate. The lab was in the basement of the headquarters, many levels below ground. Budi and Rexi accompanied me, together with a few other nameless scientists.

"Is the technology ready?" I asked.

"Yes. We have a prototype ready for you. But please tell me, Martin, what is the point of this gadget?" Rexi replied.

"The usefulness of hiding nanotechnology cameras in contact lenses should be obvious!" I scoffed.

"Yes, but the eye colour changing capability? It makes the lenses very costly and difficult to make." Rexi remarked.

"You don't need to have that feature on the final model. But I do need it on the prototype for a mission ahead of me." I replied.

Rexi stopped herself from objecting, and she replied. "Very well, please come this way."

We walked into an optics lab, and Rexi handed me a small box with contact lenses.

"Is this it? They don't look anything special?" I asked sceptically.

"Correct. The lenses wouldn't be as useful if they stood out, as yours and mistress Elaine's monocles did, before the, um, malfunction." Budi replied.

"Very well, let me try it," I stated.

I put on the contact lenses. They stung a bit, but I adapted after a while. The user interface was primitive, and the functionality limited. The scientists hadn't been able to accurately replicate the Zetan technology that we found in the Sunken Pyramid of Kiribati. But it didn't matter. All that I needed was to make sure that the lenses were fit for my purpose.

I connected the lenses to my phone, and I could tell that they were operational. I tried the camera and it worked okay. Although the cameras didn't transmit clear images, it was still a massive technological breakthrough. I tested the 'change eye colour' feature of the lenses and I smiled at my reflection. With the help of my mobile app, I could change my eye colour at the press of a button, including giving myself purple irises.

"Excellent. This is what I am after. Make sure to make a few pairs for a six-year-old child as well." I commanded.

"Yes, sir. Is there anything else that you need?" Budi asked.

"Yes. Have you hacked the Australian government websites to make sure that there is no arrest warrants and criminal charges against me?" I asked.

"Yes, I have already done this," Rexi replied.

"And have you appointed some helpers for my mission?" I asked.

"Yes, my men have already organised everything that you need." Rexi replied.

"Excellent. I am leaving at once." I stated.

I was walking towards the lift when Budi caught up with me. "Mr Orchard. Why are you spending so much on your revenge? We could just send our men to kill the family." Budi suggested.

"Killing them won't solve my issues. Causing them to suffer for a lifetime is the only way for me to avenge Elaine and get justice for Sabina's betrayal." I stated as I entered the lift.

I WAS NERVOUS AS I walked past the electronic border checkpoint at Kingsford Smith Airport. I hadn't visited Australia since 2040 for good reasons. On my last visit to Australia, I killed Szymon Yehuda and his Mossad operatives in the middle of Darling Harbour in front of hundreds of people. Budi and Rexi had intercepted me before the cops did and had smuggled me out of the country. I could only imagine the effort it had taken to clear my records after that incident.

I sighed of relief as I passed the border without incident. The Harapan agents Jaime Sanchez and Miguel Rodrigo met me at the airport. "Take me to the house that I rented for us at Seaside Parade." I ordered and we got into a car taking us to the perfect spot for stalking Sabina and continue with the plan.

I WAS SITTING IN A room on the top floor of the villa that we had hired at the top of the street. From my location, I had picturesque ocean views, and had a clear view of Sabina's house. I needed to spend time with Keila alone so

I could put the colour shifting lenses in her eyes. That was the only way for me to convince Sabina that Keila was under Rangda's influence.

Jaime Sanchez entered the room and spoke. "I have discovered something, boss."

"Good. Please share with me, Jaime" I replied.

"Sabina hires a local teenager, Eliza Shaw, to babysit Keila. Perhaps we can pay this girl to give us access to Keila." Jaime suggested.

I thought about the suggestion. It would seem suspicious to Eliza if we appeared and requested to spend time with one of the children she was looking after. But if we gave her some money, and I had a credible backstory, it could work. If it didn't, we'd have to break into Sabina's place and kidnap Keila at gunpoint.

"Let's try to convince this girl to help us, do you have her address?" I asked.

"Even better, I asked Simona to hack and track Eliza's phone. She is having coffee at the coffee shop on Malabar road." Jaime revealed.

"Very well. Let's go there and see if we can make Eliza cooperate." I said, and I picked up a wad of dollar bills. While I didn't have Sabina's supernatural empath abilities, I had another useful trick in my repertoire. I could make people choose between gold and lead!

WE WALKED INTO THE coffee shop a few minutes later. Eliza was sitting by a table gossiping with her friends. I instructed Jaime and Miguel to order coffees while I approached Eliza.

"Eliza Shaw?" I addressed her.

Eliza turned around and stared at me in terror. This was an expected reaction. My appearance and the fact that I addressed a stranger by their full name was intimidating for the feeble-hearted.

"Yes. Who are you?" Eliza stuttered.

"I am Martin Al-Sham. My friends will join us shortly, but I would appreciate if we could talk in private." I said, and I pointed in Jaime's direction.

Eliza's friend took the hint, and she left the table. Eliza was shaking in terror and spoke. "What do you want?"

"You're baby-sitting my granddaughter, Keila Hines. I would like your help in spending more time with her." I stated.

"No way. This is too strange. Fix your relationship with Keila's parents if you wish to spend time with your granddaughter." Eliza objected.

Jaime got seated next to me. He opened his jacket, to show the pistol he had holstered. After that, I took up an envelope with money, and I passed it over the table to Eliza.

"I only need to see Keila once, and nothing bad will happen. I'd prefer if you choose gold over lead." I stated.

Eliza looked terrified, and she was crying. "Okay. I will babysit Keila on Friday. Please don't hurt us." Eliza cried.

"Good. I will call you on Friday. Make sure to answer the phone, so we don't have any misunderstandings." I warned.

Eliza got up from the table and was ready to leave.

"Eliza, please don't forget the money that I paid you. I don't want to be in debt to you. Get something nice for yourself and your friend." I warned.

Eliza seemed hesitant, but eventually, she picked up the money and left the coffee shop.

I MET UP WITH ELIZA at Grant Reserve on a Friday afternoon. The sun was shining, and the ocean breeze made this a comfortable spring day. I noticed that she had brought two other children with her, and I disapproved of this.

"What's going on. Why did you bring the other two children?"

"Because I always babysit these three children together on Fridays and their mothers know each other. It would look suspicious if I insisted on only taking Keila." Eliza replied.

"Very well. But don't try my patience." I replied.

Eliza seemed agitated and spoke: "What do you intend to do with her? Remember that there are cameras and many witnesses in this park."

I shrugged my shoulders and replied: "I do not intend to do anything inappropriate or illegal. I just want to spend some time with my granddaughter. That is what I intend to do. Stay in the background and don't intervene, Eliza."

I walked up to Keila and looked at her. She was a beautiful child, even prettier than her mother. I kneeled next to her and spoke. "Hi, Keila. We meet at last."

Keila gave me a bewildered look and spoke. "Do I know you?"

"My name is Martin. I am Sabina's real dad and your grandpa." I replied.

"No. John is Sabina's dad. My grandpa." Keila replied while looking confused.

"No, Grandma Ellen is a bad woman. She told John that he was Sabina's father so that he would buy food for her and Sabina." I replied.

"Oh!" Keila replied.

"Yes. And Alex isn't your real father. Your mummy lied to you too." I revealed.

Keila started crying and replied. "Why are you saying these mean things?"

"I am telling you the truth. But don't be sad, Keila. Because your real father is a god and you're immensely powerful. As a matter of fact, I brought you a gift." I stated.

Hearing this, caught Keila's intention and she looked at me with big, fascinated eyes. "My dad is a god? You mean like Jesus?" Keila said.

"Exactly. And I am like the three wise men bringing you a gift." I replied.

"Cool. Let me see the gift." Keila replied.

I took out the box with the advanced contact lenses and showed them to Keila. "But I don't need contacts. You can give them to Jasmine, so she doesn't need to wear glasses." Keila objected.

"These are special lenses that I made for you. They can do cool things like changing your eye colour and showing you text messages from me. Do you know how to read?" I asked

"Yes, I love to read. I have been reading since I was three." Keila revealed.

"Great. You'll love these contact lenses. Do you want to try them on?" I asked with an encouraging voice.

"Yes!" Keila exclaimed happily.

I took out the contact lenses from the box, and I helped Keila put them in her eyes.

"Ouch, they are itchy!" Keila complained.

"You'll get used to them. Can you read the text in front of your eyes?" I asked.

I took up my phone, and I sent a short text for Keila's lenses to display.

"My name is Keila. And I love my grandpa, Martin." Keila read aloud.

"That's silly. I don't know you." Keila chuckled.

"I just needed to hear you say it!" I said and smiled.

"Do you want to test another eye colour now?" I asked.

"Yes. Make my eyes brown like Jasmine's eyes." Keila said.

I did as Keila requested, and she got excited when I showed her reflection in the mirror.

"Wow! Jasmine come here and look at my eyes!" Keila called to her friend.

"No, I don't want to. Eliza told me to leave you guys alone." Jasmine replied.

"Oh!" Keila replied in disappointment.

"Don't worry about Jasmine, Keila. You can play with her tomorrow. Grandpa Martin is only here today." I said.

"Okay, so what game do you want to play?" Keila asked.

"I want to show you auntie Rangda's eye colour and tell you about Rangda, the Xenos and the Zetans!" I said, and I changed Keila's eye colour via my mobile app.

Keila looked at her new purple irises and exclaimed: "Wow. This is so cool. Please tell me everything, Grandpa Martin!"

I sat down with Keila and told her everything that I knew about Rangda, the Xenos and the Zetans. At the end of my story, Keila exclaimed. "Wow. That's so cool. I never knew that mummy killed an evil alien."

"Yes, but she also killed my wife and tried to kill me" I sighed.

"Is that why you want me to threaten to kill my cat to get back at her?" Keila asked.

"Yes, we need to make mummy realise that she has been mean so that she will apologise and become nice," I replied.

"Can I see you without the mask, Grandpa Martin?" Keila asked.

I hesitated for a bit, the righthand side of my face was terrifying to most people, particularly to a child. But Keila seemed very mature and intelligent for her age, and her curiosity was a good thing. I took off the mask and Keila gasped in shock.

"Your face. Did mummy do this to you?" Keila asked.

"Yes, that's why I am angry with her," I replied.

"Wow. Now I know why you are angry with mummy. I'll pretend to kill Luna. After that, I'll give her the note and tell her where to meet you?" Keila said.

"Yes. See you tonight, Keila." I said. I put my mask back on, and I smiled.

After finishing my conversation with Keila, I walked up to Eliza and spoke. "Here is some money for your troubles. Don't mention this to anyone and our paths won't cross again."

"Understood. I will keep quiet." Eliza said and looked away.

Since there was no reason to trouble Eliza further, I left the park without a word.

I WAS LOOKING THROUGH the cameras in Keila's lenses, and I had an epiphany. My far-fetched plan shouldn't have worked, yet it seemed to work. Was I doing Sabina a favour by exposing Keila's demonic possession? I had planned to convince Sabina about Keila's demonic possession to make her life miserable, but what if something did possess Keila? It seemed strange that any child would stay and listen to a masked madman, but that was precisely what Keila had done, and she had appeared to enjoy it as well.

I saw Sabina take the knife away from Keila and lecture her about being kind to animals. I sent a message for Keila to read aloud. 'Mummy you said we shall love Luna. But I saw Luna kill a mouse the other day. Isn't that the natural order of things? The cat killed the mouse because she is stronger. Likewise, I should kill the cat to prove my strength.'

As Keila read out the message, I changed her eye colour to purple to fool Sabina that the late Rangda's spirit possessed Keila.

Keila's message terrified Sabina, and Keila handed her the note that I had given her. Much to my dismay, Sabina took out a pistol to bring to the meeting point. This was a dangerous complication.

"Bring your tranquiliser rifle and be ready to fire!" I told Jaime as we headed to the meeting spot.

I WAS OVERLOOKING THE dark ocean, and a cold, windy rain chilled me to the bone. The park was empty, and my heart was racing. I had waited several years for this moment, the moment that I would get my revenge. Yet I felt terrified. Sabina had brought her pistol and she was likely to use it. I wasn't going to kill her, there was no point in that, but what if she was going to try to kill me? She had tried before, leading to my disfigurement, and there was no reason for her to not try again.

"She is coming!" Jaime said over the radio inside my earplug, and I turned around. I saw that Sabina and Keila were approaching me.

I studied Sabina, her face showed signs of rage, and her hand was close to her pistol.

"Sabina, we meet again. How unfortunate for us!" I stated

"What do you want with my daughter?" Sabina roared.

"Justice," I replied, and I took off my mask revealing my disfigured face.

"Justice? You tell my daughter to kill my cat? What's wrong with you." Sabina shouted.

"What did you think would happen? You promised to not hurt us, yet you murdered my wife, and you tried to kill me." I shouted back.

Sabina didn't reply. Instead, Sabina gave me a death stare. Her stare made me worried. I worried that the sedative in the tranquiliser dart wouldn't be powerful enough to knock her out before she shot me.

"Did you notice Keila's eyes? Beautiful, aren't they? They are shining purple, exactly like Rangda's" I taunted.

"What did you do to Keila's eyes, you monster?" Sabina roared.

"I didn't do anything. I merely invoked the spirit of Rangda that lies dormant within her." I replied.

"Bullshit!" Sabina shouted.

"Tell me, Sabina, who do you think is your father?" I asked.

Sabina gave me a dirty look. "John Hines. Haven't you done your research?" Sabina taunted.

"Sabina, we both know that is a lie." I scoffed.

"Okay. My father was Marvin Orchard, who died many years ago. He was also the father of my best friend, Eric. This made my teenage years difficult." Sabina sighed.

"Yes, it must have been difficult rejecting the visions that told you to engage in incest, wasn't it?" I mocked.

"My visions weren't that prevalent, and I found Alex in the end," Sabina admitted.

"But Alex was sterile, so you ended up fucking a Zetan in the Divine Dimension, didn't you?" I mocked.

Sabina lost her temper and pulled up her pistol. "Don't spread lies about me in front of my daughter. Keila is young, but she is perceptive for her age." Sabina shouted.

"Perceptive, indeed. Unlike Ellen who fucked up your entire life." I taunted, and I took out a document from my jacket.

I walked up to Sabina, and I handed her the document. She skimmed through it and replied. "Is this a bad joke? You could have falsified this paternity test?" Sabina objected.

"I could have, but I did not. Ellen mixed up Martin Orchard from Sydney, with Marvin Orchard from Sydney. Mistakes happen when you are overseas fucking everyone behind your husband's back." I taunted.

Sabina reflected over my statement for a few seconds and then she replied. "It doesn't matter who my biological father is. John is the one who raised me. I doubt that you or I will ever celebrate the holidays together." Sabina scoffed.

"But it changes everything. You never followed your pre-destined attraction for Eric because you believed he was your half-brother. Because of this, you settled for the sterile Alex and ended up fucking a Zetan so you could give birth to your destined daughter. Doing so, you allowed Rangda to be reborn as Keila. Keila is still young, she'll get worse. Much worse." I stated.

Hearing this, Sabina got heartbroken, and she collapsed to the ground crying.

"Why! Why are you doing this to me?" Sabina wailed.

I pointed towards my disfigured face and replied. "Revenge. And I just got it. You'll have to make an impossible choice. You must choose between killing your own daughter or allowing Rangda to rise." I mocked.

I studied Sabina as she was crying and shaking on the floor. I had avenged Elaine, and I could return to my solitude and die a peaceful death when it was time.

Sabina got up and aimed her pistol at me. "I won't let you live to rejoice in my misery! Prepare to die, Martin!" Sabina shouted.

"Fire now!" I said over the radio, and Jaime shot Sabina in the neck with a tranquiliser dart. The dart distracted Sabina and I ran up to her and kicked the pistol out of her hand. After that, I chased after Keila, grabbed her, and injected her with a sedative. As Keila fell unconscious, I removed the contact lenses from her eyes. As I didn't want Sabina to find out about my deception.

I ran up to Jaime, and I spoke. "Let's get to the airport. I don't want to be in Australia when they wake up."

Jaime nodded, and we hurried to the private jet that would take us away from Australia.

Chapter 25: Andorra, March 2057

It was my 72nd birthday, and I celebrated it, watching the beautiful sight of the valley below, from my cliffside house. I had grown tired of the heat in Kiribati and I had decided to move to the small nation of Andorra, located in the Pyrenees between Spain and France.

I sighed, and bittersweet feelings filled my mind. The world was so beautiful, and I wanted to stay in it forever, yet it was time for me to go. I had received the news of my terminal brain cancer a few weeks earlier. My initial reaction had been to go on another treasure hunt. I had hoped to find another replicated Zeto Crystal that would heal my wounds and make me healthy again.

But then I had stopped myself. I was too weak and too weary to go on a dangerous expedition on my own. My poor vision due to my one-eyedness didn't make things easier. I had thought of asking Elenoa and Simona for help. But I had stopped myself. They were bringing up a family together and why should I risk their lives to extend my own? If something happened to either of them, and I survived the ordeal, that would be a worse punishment than death.

I thought of Simona, Elenoa and their son David. Bringing them together was one of the lasting achievements in life that I could be proud of. I had convinced Simona back in 2041 to let go of her obsession with Sabina and give Elenoa a chance to love her. Simona had followed my advice, forgotten about Sabina, and fallen in love with Elenoa. I wished that I had followed my own advice and had forgotten about Sabina there and then. That way I wouldn't have sought my vengeance against Sabina that would ruin her life, Keila's life, and my life.

I wrote my confession in a letter to Sabina, and I attached the advanced eye colour changing lenses as evidence of my claims. I would have loved to admit my lies while I was still alive, but I couldn't bring myself to it. At least this way, Sabina and Keila wouldn't need to suffer, believing that Rangda possessed Keila, after my death. The doorbell rang, and I tried to walk over and open it. I didn't get far. My cancer caused a severe migraine attack and I collapsed to the floor.

'Please give me enough strength to say farewell to everyone.' I prayed to the True Maker. My migraine disappeared, and I felt light-headed and at peace. I got up and opened the door. My adopted daughters and their son greeted me.

"CAN YOU PASS ME THE wine?" I said to Elenoa, and she passed me the wine. As I poured us glasses of wine, Elenoa made a rejective gesture.

"Are you not drinking today, Elenoa?" I asked.

Elenoa smiled and replied, "I am pregnant again, papa."

"I wish I could be there when the child is born." I sighed.

"You can. You're only 72. Don't be so gloomy, Martin." Simona replied.

I shook my head, and I handed over my medical report. Simona read it and replied. "This is not the end. I won't let it be. There must be something we can do?"

"There isn't. The replicated Zeto Crystals stopped working on me many years ago. I guess I have fulfilled my purpose." I sighed.

"We'll stand by your side until the end. I'll pray to the True Maker for a miracle." Elenoa stated.

I nodded. "You are by my side until the end. I came into this world precisely 72 turns around the sun ago. It's fitting that the day of my birth is also the day of my death." I stated.

"You can't be serious. Suicide is a terrible sin. I worry for your soul in the afterlife." Elenoa stated.

"No. Fearing death is the greatest sin. Nothing else brings more suffering to humanity." I stated. "Martin is right. Let him choose the time and place for the last step of his journey." Simona said.

Simona took Elenoa's hand and whispered softly to her. Elenoa's face changed, and she accepted the inevitable. "Okay, Martin. We'll stay with you to the end."

"Thank you, Elenoa. Deliver this letter to Sabina and ask for her forgiveness. I am sorry that my spirit is too weak to ask for forgiveness during my lifetime." I coughed.

We went out to the balcony and watched how the sun was setting behind the snow-covered mountains. It was beautiful scenery encompassing all the colours of the rainbow.

I took the syringe with a lethal dose of heroin that I had prepared and injected myself.

"What is happening, grandpa." I heard David say.

"He is moving on to the afterlife, dear. It's nothing to fear," Simona explained.

I grabbed their hands, and I felt complete bliss as my body turned comfortably numb. The scenery faded into black.

I OPENED MY EYES, AND I was in an eerie but peaceful place. Elaine was looking at me. It was not Elaine from my life but a more beautiful version, the perfect version that never exists in the real world.

"Elaine?" I asked.

Elaine shook her head and replied. "No, I am the True Maker. I took the form of the human that you love the most." The True Maker stated.

"Is this the afterlife?" I asked.

The True Maker smiled at me. "There is no afterlife. You already know this. All life consists of different states of energy, and when you die, the universe absorbs this energy." The True Maker revealed.

"So, what is this then?" I asked

"I stopped time for you, moments before the universe absorbs your energy. I wanted to thank you for fulfilling your purpose." The True Maker revealed.

"I don't understand," I said.

"You made Sabina face Rangda. This encounter stopped the future apocalypse." The True Maker revealed.

"What about the gamma-ray-burst meant to strike the earth in 2131?

"The gamma-ray-burst would have destroyed Sydney. However, your intervention caused Keila to focus on controlling her inner demons and maintain a positive outlook. Sabina and Keila will die together, absorbing the blast and saving the city." The True Maker revealed.

"So, everything turns out fine in the end?" I asked.

"Good and bad are human constructs. The life force will keep flowing on Earth for many millions of years to come. That is a positive outlook in my world." The True Maker replied.

"Thank you!" I replied.

"You're welcome, human. Is there anything else you need to know before you pass on?"

"No, I am ready," I replied.

Time resumed, and I experienced a bright white light before my consciousness became one with the universe!

The End!

Don't miss out!

Visit the website below and you can sign up to receive emails whenever Martin Lundqvist publishes a new book. There's no charge and no obligation.

https://books2read.com/r/B-A-QIOG-CCUEB

BOOKS 2 READ

Connecting independent readers to independent writers.

Did you love *The Fall of Martin Orchard*? Then you should read *Sabina Saves the Future: Complete Trilogy*[1] by Martin Lundqvist!

Being reborn in the 21st century, Sabina must stop the apocalypse from happening in the 29th century. Sabina Saves the Future is a trilogy of novellas, following the adventurous and supernaturally gifted Sabina Hines, as she travels the world and uncovers various nefarious conspiracies.

Sabina's Pursuit of the Holy Grail Sabina is a gifted 18-year-old girl living in Sydney, in the year 2037. She carries a unique secret. Sabina used to be the Chosen One, but she failed to stop the apocalypse from occurring in the year 2887. As she died, she asked The True Maker to let her be reborn in 2019 and to keep her powers.

After narrowly escaping being raped by the spoiled brat Joshua Harkins, Sabina has an epiphany: That it is time for her to set out on her mission to find the Primordial Zeto Crystal, also known as the Holy Grail. Sabina's quest takes her to Jerusalem where evil men are after the Holy Grail for their

---

1. https://books2read.com/u/mVr0NA

2. https://books2read.com/u/mVr0NA

own nefarious purposes. Facing the conspirators, Sabina sets out on a dangerous quest to find and purify the magical artefact, and to stop it from falling into the wrong hands.But stopping evil is not an easy task, and what sacrifices must Sabina make to reach her goal. Will Sabina be able to retain her innocence throughout the ordeal?

Sabina's Quest to Open the Portal

*Having secured the Zeto Crystal, Sabina must choose between love and duty.*Sabina's Quest to Open the Portal takes place straight after the ending of Sabina's Pursuit of the Holy Grail. Mentally and physically scarred from her ordeal in Israel, Sabina finds solace in the handsome and empathetic Alexander O'Neill, and she experiences romantic love for the first time.

With the Zeto Crystal de-energised Sabina focuses on her relationship with Alex and raising funds for charity.

Life is good for Sabina until one day when a new enemy emerges, which forces her to go to Mexico on the brink of civil war and face the difficult choice between love and duty.

Sabina's Expedition to Stop the Apocalypse

After many ordeals, Sabina faces her nemesis, Rangda. But will Sabina overcome the evil that she tries to stop?

Having survived the civil war in Mexico, and having stopped Pierre Beaumont's evil scheme, Sabina and Alex are recuperating in Hawaii.

Peace doesn't last for long though, as the mysterious Martin Al-Sham re-emerges. His associates kidnap Alex, to force Sabina to help Martin with a dangerous expedition.Martin reveals that he has found a way to re-energise the Zeto Crystal, and that he needs Sabina to fulfil her destiny.

Together they travel to Kiribati. First, they must scale an active volcano, before Sabina can swim down to the Sunken Pyramid of Kiribati, where the portal to the Divine Dimension is located.

Eventually, Sabina reaches Rangda, but will she be able to carry out her mission, or will she become the very evil that she tried to stop?

Read more at martinlundqvist.com.

www.ingramcontent.com/pod-product-compliance
Lightning Source LLC
Chambersburg PA
CBHW070013120726
47909CB00003B/904